DEADLY WATERS

A DETECTIVE JANE PHILLIPS NOVEL

OMJ RYAN

D1341107

INKUBATOR
BOOKS

1

DCI Phillips killed the engine of the unmarked police car and Paul McCartney's 'Wonderful Christmas Time' faded away as the radio switched off. The dashboard clock reminded her the time was just after 8 a.m.

As she sat in silence for a moment, the windows soon steamed up against the bitter December wind gusting across the barren concrete. The spot where she had chosen to park had once been a factory floor; the walls of the old building were long since demolished.

She pulled on her gloves and scarf, and stepped out into the dilapidated industrial landscape of Miles Platting, a former manufacturing hub just north of Manchester city centre. She picked her way across the treacherous ground and descended the frozen, mossy steps that lead to a now-desolate stretch of the Rochdale Canal. The canal had once been a bustling transport route for merchants moving goods to and from the North West of England. Up ahead, two uniformed officers huddled together, tense. Detective Sergeant Jones stood a few feet in front of them, head bowed, looking towards the water's edge. A couple of paramedics and a fire crew busied themselves with harnesses and safety equipment.

As she approached, her DS nodded. 'Guv.'

'So, what brings us to the glamorous world of Miles Platting this early on a Thursday morning, Jonesy?'

Jones pointed towards the ice-covered dark green water and the body being pulled out by two firemen in full fire-fighting kit. 'Looks like a young girl drowned, Guv.'

Phillips could feel her face screw up. 'A drowning. Then why are we here?'

'An enthusiastic young rookie called us in directly. He thought it could be the work of the infamous "Pusher".'

Phillips scoffed. 'What? The so-called serial killer of the Manchester canals?'

'The same, Guv.'

'I thought that fairy story was long since dead.'

Jones nodded towards the young rookie, who was now deep in what looked like an uncomfortable conference with a much older officer. 'Yeah, and so does his sergeant. From what I've heard so far, his guvnor's not best pleased the lad called us in without speaking to him first. He's been barking at him for the last twenty minutes. The poor sod.'

Phillips turned her attention back to the water's edge. She watched as the fire crew carefully laid the body of a black girl on the wet stones at the side of the canal before the paramedics moved in to complete the formalities and confirm life extinct.

Phillips and Jones were now free to examine the body – albeit limited in scope at this stage – before deciding whether or not a forensic team would be required. Moving closer, Phillips removed her leather gloves and exchanged them for a latex pair. She knelt next to the dead girl, who lay face upwards. She was dressed as if ready for a night on the town in a skimpy black skirt, red crop top and matching stilettos. It appeared odd, given the season, that she was without a coat or jacket.

'Did her coat come off in the water?' said Phillips.

'Not sure, Guv. I'll get uniform to have a look for it in a minute. In the meantime, I want to show you this.' Jones knelt down next to her, his hands also gloved, and tilted the dead girl's head to the side. He pulled the wet, matted hair out of the way so Phillips could see what he was looking at. 'I spotted something on the back of her neck, Guv, when she was face down in the water. A large, perfectly circular bruise. I thought it worth a closer look.'

Phillips stared at the mark for a long moment and rubbed it gently with her gloved index finger. 'Looks very unusual. Can't recall seeing anything like that before.'

'Me neither, but is it enough for Major Crimes to take on the case? Should we just leave it to uniform?'

Phillips let out a deep sigh. She knew Chief Superintendent Fox would be royally pissed off if she added another investigation to the team's already significant caseload; especially with the Major Crimes Unit running way over budget. She could almost hear the lecture about department stats and KPIs she'd be subjected to once she got back to Ashton House.

Looking at the petite young girl, soaking wet and frozen stiff, the striking, pretty face with dead eyes that stared into the abyss, she shook her head. It was never easy to lose a loved one, but how would her family feel, just three weeks before Christmas? The world could be a cruel place. She took another long look at the bruise. Sod the lectures, budgets and bullshit. This young girl was her responsibility now. 'Do it, Jonesy, before I change my mind. Let's stick around. See what Evans and the SOCO team have to say. Maybe then, we can find out what really happened to this poor creature.'

Jones smiled. 'Good on yer, Guv.'

Less than an hour later, Senior CSI Andy Evans and his team of investigators had replaced the fire crew at the canal side. The paramedics and uniformed officers remained in situ for now, most of them nursing steaming hot drinks and stepping from foot to foot in their efforts to keep warm.

The Scene of the Crime Operation team were quick to erect their tent over the body. Evans and his team set to work photographing the scene and removing her personal effects. They passed a thick, but cheap-looking, Bejazzled purse to Phillips. She located the driving license and inspected it. 'Chantelle Webster, twenty-four, from Stretford.' She handed the license to Jones and inspected the rest of the purse. 'Just over a hundred quid in cash and a couple of bank cards.'

Jones pulled out his iPhone. 'I'll call Entwistle and see if she's been reported missing.' He punched in the number and stepped outside of the tent.

'So what do you think, Andy?' asked Phillips

Evans produced a half smile. 'Well, I'd say it's good news, Jane. Looks like a straightforward drowning to me, so there's probably no need for a full investigation.'

Phillips pointed to the girl's neck. 'What about that bruise?'

Evans knelt next to the dead girl and inspected the bruise for a long moment, gently pulling the hair away to expose the mottled skin. 'I must admit, it does look a bit odd. I've never seen a bruise so perfectly circular before, but I'm not sure it's got anything to do with the cause of death. From where I'm standing, she drowned in this stretch of water sometime in the early hours of last night.'

'Can you be more specific about the exact time, Andy?'

'Difficult to tell. The rigor mortis is acute, but that's because of the water temperature; it was minus five last night, so I'm guessing she broke the ice when she went in. If she was conscious at that moment – and with no obvious head trauma, I'd say she was – she most likely suffered cold water shock and drowned pretty quickly.'

'Cold water shock? Is that a real thing?'

Evans nodded sagely. 'It can be deadly. In fact, there have

been many cases of people drowning from cold water shock on blistering hot summer's days. Happens all the time when kids jump into reservoirs and canals to cool off. You see, the body – once immersed in very cold water – goes into shock, causing the victim to panic and hyperventilate, often gasping for breath. They open their mouths wide and start swallowing water. Before they can regulate their heart rate and breathing, they've already used up so much energy they struggle to keep their heads above water, so begin to drown. If there's no-one around to pull them out, chances are they could be dead in a matter of minutes.'

'And you think that's what happened here?'

Evans looked the body up and down for a moment before nodding. 'Based on the lack of evidence to suggest a struggle or head trauma, I'd say so, yes. However, Chakrabortty will know for sure when she conducts the post mortem tomorrow.'

Phillips stood and patted Evans on the shoulder. 'Thanks Andy.' Stepping out of the tent, the arctic wind caught her off guard for a moment, and she was reminded of how cold the water must have been overnight. The poor girl hadn't stood a chance.

She glanced down the towpath and spotted Jones heading towards her, his collar turned up against the wind. 'No missing person report according to Entwistle, but he's given me her parents' address. They live just around the corner from her property in Stretford.'

Phillips nodded and turned back towards the SOCO tent. 'Evans reckons she drowned after suffering cold water shock.'

'And what about you, Guv?'

Phillips pushed her glasses upwards over the bridge of her nose. 'The way he describes it happening makes sense. God knows it was bloody freezing overnight, but I want to know more about how she got that bruise on her neck. It might be nothing, Jonesy, but as we both know, when a case looks so obviously open and shut, it rarely is.'

'So what you wanna do?'

Phillips removed her latex gloves and replaced them with the leather pair. 'Well, for starters, let's get out of this bloody wind. As much as I hate to do it, I think we should break the news to the girl's parents. They may be able to shed some light on how she ended up in the canal last night.'

'We can leave that to uniform can't we, Guv?'

'Call it a hunch, Jonesy.' Phillips nodded over Jones's shoulder. 'I'm not sure our young rookie is up to it yet. Are you?'

He followed her line of sight and could see the young officer standing at the side of the canal, looking forlorn and pretty sorry for himself, now his boss had finished with him. Phillips smiled. 'He'll get over it. The first bollocking is always the worst.'

2

Chantelle Webster's parents' home was situated on a large housing estate in Stretford, a densely populated town to the south-east of Manchester, not far from the world-famous Old Trafford Stadium, home to Manchester United.

The red-brick houses in the estate were a mixture of privately owned and council-lets. Like so many former local authority residents, the majority of those living here had opted to purchase their council houses for a fraction of the resale value in the eighties and nineties. Once they had all looked identical, but each now had a character of its own, made even more apparent with the approach of the Christmas holidays. Thousands of twinkling lights glowed against the dark grey clouds that hung low in the sky. Despite it being early afternoon, total darkness didn't feel far away.

Jones pulled up to the address he had punched into the squad car's Sat Nav and switched off the engine. Phillips scanned the street, noting the assortment of decorations, flashing lights, inflatable Santas and snowmen, as well as the glistening reindeer and assorted woodland creatures that grazed on the other side of the low red-brick walls surrounding the small front gardens of each house. She felt sick to her stomach, knowing what lay ahead at the Websters. 'I hate doing this. It's heart-breaking. Especially when the victims are so young.'

'It's not too late to give it back to uniform, Guv.'

Phillips took a deep breath before releasing it. 'No no, Jonesy. It's the right thing to do. And besides, I'd like to know more about her movements last night.'

A minute later, Phillips led the way and pushed open the metal garden gate, the hinge protesting the movement. They made their way up the path that ran through the middle of the well-maintained garden, and Phillips noted the winter pot plants filled with pansies in full bloom. Someone cared a lot about this place. An instant later, a small dog jumped up and began barking at the spotless double-glazed front window. The brightly decorated Christmas tree with lights flashing in a sequence of different patterns attracted her attention for a moment. As she pressed the bell, it sounded inside and she took another deep breath to steady herself.

The door opened to reveal an imposing black man in his fifties. He was tall and muscular, with grey flecks at the temples to match his salt and pepper goatee. Dark shadows under his eyes and deep creases in his forehead gave him a haunted look.

'Richard Webster?' asked Phillips.

He nodded without saying anything.

They both produced their credentials. 'I'm Detective Chief Inspector Phillips and this is Detective Sergeant Jones. May we come in?'

Webster's eyes widened. 'Is this about Chantelle? She didn't come home last night.'

'Yes, it is,' said Phillips, keeping her voice soft.

At that moment a small boy appeared and wrapped his tiny arms around the man's thick right leg. He couldn't be more than two years old, and was shooed away by Webster before he opened the door wider and invited them inside. The dog was still barking, frantic, in the next room, but was on the other side of a door.

The warmth of the house was a stark contrast to the bitter cold. Webster pushed a large wooden door open. 'Please come into the lounge. My wife will need to hear this.'

The room beyond was covered in a mass of decorations; lights and tinsel adorned every available surface, and greetings cards were hooked through a ribbon hung across the fireplace. Sitting facing them on a large red leather couch was a woman of similar age to Richard, cuddling the little boy, who now stood between her legs. A young girl, probably in her late teens, stood behind them in the dining area, her eyes fixed on the iPhone in her right hand.

Richard Webster stared at his wife. 'Anya, these people are from the police. They want to talk to us about Chantelle.'

Anya Webster opened her mouth to speak, but it was evident she was struggling. Her hand flashed to her lips a moment later as fear filled her wide, tear-stained eyes.

Webster turned his attention to the young girl. When he spoke, his tone was matter of fact. 'Lisa, take your nephew up to your room, will you?'

The young girl looked up from her phone, nodded and walked towards the young boy, holding out her hand for him. Reluctant to move, he shook his head in defiance.

Webster raised his voice a notch and pointed up the stairs. 'Ajay, do as you're told and go with Auntie Lisa upstairs.'

The boy hesitated, his eyes darting between Richard and Anya Webster.

'Do as you are told, Ajay. Now!' Webster's voice was a borderline shout.

This time the boy moved, running to the girl's outstretched hand.

As they left the room, Webster's eyes followed them both

until the door closed and the thud of footsteps on the stairs faded upwards. Apparently satisfied they were out of earshot, he turned his attention back to Phillips and Jones. 'Where is my daughter, Inspector?' he said abruptly.

Phillips could feel her anxiety rising. 'May we sit down, Mr Webster?'

He nodded but remained standing by the fireplace. His gaze never left them.

'I'm sorry to inform you that a young girl was found dead this morning in the Rochdale Canal in Miles Platting. Based on the personal effects found in her possession, we believe her to be your daughter, Chantelle Webster.'

A guttural wail erupted from Anya as she dropped her head into her hands and her body began shaking. Richard Webster remained silent as he stared at the floor. Phillips and Jones said nothing for a moment, allowing the couple to process what they'd just heard. After an uncomfortable silence, Webster eventually looked up. 'Are you sure it's Chantelle, Inspector?'

Phillips nodded. 'We found her driving licence in her purse, which confirmed her name and address as 34 Finchale Road, Stretford. Is that Chantelle's home address?'

Webster took a seat next to his wife and wrapped a big arm around her as she turned her face into his chest and sobbed. 'Yes, that's where Shanny lives with Ajay. We just look after him overnight when she's working.'

Phillips sat forwards on the chair. 'Were you looking after him last night?'

Webster nodded. 'Yes. Shanny was at work.'

Jones glanced at Phillips, his brow furrowed.

'Chantelle was working last night?' asked Phillips.

'Yes, at the McVitie's factory in Stockport. She does nights, Sunday to Thursday, in the packing team.'

'And what time did she leave for work last night?' said Phillips as Jones took out his notepad.

Webster didn't hesitate. 'Same as always, eight o'clock for a 9 p.m. start. She came here at seven forty-five, dropped off Ajay, then left to catch the bus.'

'Can I ask what she was wearing last night?'

It was Webster's turn to looked confused. 'Her normal work clothes – jeans and a T-shirt.'

'And was she wearing a coat?'

Webster stared back at Phillips, his expression incredulous. 'Of course she was. It was bloody freezing last night. Why is that important?'

Phillips dodged his question for the time being; this discrepancy was significant. 'And did she take a change of clothes with her?'

'No. Work provides overalls and hairnets. She had her purse and that was it. Why are you asking about what she was wearing? What do her clothes have to do with anything?'

Phillips wrestled with telling Webster how his daughter had been found wearing a revealing clubbing outfit, but as Anya continued to sob into his chest, she decided it was information neither of them needed to hear right now.

Jones changed the subject. 'Did she have any reason to be in Miles Platting last night?'

Webster shook his head. 'None. To be honest, she wouldn't even know where it is. She rarely strayed far from Stretford. Shanny was a real home girl.'

Jones made a note and Phillips took the lead again. 'How was she fixed for money?'

The strain was starting to show on Webster's face. 'A black single parent earning a basic wage. Hardly a recipe for financial success is it?' he said, his voice curt.

'And how was she in herself of late? Was she showing any signs of stress, or low mood?'

'She wasn't very well. The last few months she seemed to have a constant cold and a wicked cough. I kept telling her to go to the doctors to get it sorted, but whenever I did, she'd blow up at me, telling me to leave her alone.'

'And was that normal, her blowing up like that?'

'Recently, yes...'

Anya continued to sob, and Webster appeared close to breaking down himself, biting his lip as his chest heaved. 'But she wasn't always like that.'

Phillips nodded.

'How did she die, Inspector?' Webster asked, regaining his composure.

'I'm afraid we won't know until the post mortem, but at this stage it looks like she drowned. I'm so sorry, Mr Webster. I really am.'

'How am I going to tell Ajay his mummy is dead?' he mumbled.

Phillips had been in this situation enough times to know when to quit. The Websters needed to be left in peace to come to terms with what they had just heard, and to grieve for their daughter. She glanced at Jones, who nodded back. He always seemed to know what she was thinking.

'Mr Webster, we will need someone to identify Chantelle in the next few days. It's not something any parent should have to do, but the sooner we can make the official ID, the sooner this will all be over.' She passed him her card. 'Call that number when you're ready, and I'll make the arrangements for you to see her in the Chapel of Rest at the MRI.'

Phillips and Jones stood up and took their leave. As they pulled open the lounge door, Phillips glanced back and saw tears streaming down Richard Webster's cheeks. Her heart went out to him.

His eyes locked on hers. 'Did she suffer, Inspector?' His voice was low, barely audible.

'At this stage we can't say for sure, but I hope not, Mr Webster. I really do.'

3

T he child – Fletch, as it is known – covers its ears and cowers behind the small threadbare sofa, trying to hide from the violence and block out the shouts. But it's no use. The mother falls hard, face first on the floor, directly in front of the child, and lets out a guttural moan. The man is immediately upon the mother, grabbing her dirty matted hair in his large fingers, which are covered in golden rings. He pulls her up from the floor. Blood pours from her nose. 'Bitch, whore, slut!' is the soundtrack to the attack. Yet another vicious attack.

The man is not Fletch's father, of course. He's just one in a succession of violent, brutal men who believe Fletch's mother is an object to be owned and sold as they see fit. She's a hooker with a drug addiction so advanced, she's long since lost any sense of love or care for anything in the world aside from heroin. The shouts and screams continue as furniture is displaced and broken across the tiny bedsit. A door slams, and silence descends.

It's not over. Fletch knows this is just the beginning.

The same way as all the other times, the mother begins to sob, and Fletch braces for what's to come. The mother clambers to her feet and pulls the leather belt from her disgusting, piss-stained jeans.

'This is all your fault, you little shit!' screams the mother as she wraps the belt around her hand, the heavy buckle swinging in the air as she walks forwards. 'He did this because of you.'

Fletch's eyes close in silent prayer; please let it to be over quickly.

The beating begins.

4

The door to the morgue buzzed open and Phillips and Jones stepped inside the cool, clinical space. After signing in at reception, Jones took a chair but Phillips remained standing, glancing through various social media apps on her phone – more out of habit than design – as they waited for the chief pathologist.

Doctor Tan Chakrabortty appeared in full scrubs a few minutes later. 'Guys, sorry to keep you. It's been a very busy morning.'

Phillips looked up from her phone before placing it in her coat pocket. 'Wow, you're looking well,' she said, scanning the doctor up and down. 'You've lost weight.'

Chakrabortty blushed. 'Running the New York Marathon can do that to you.'

Jones had a soft spot for the doctor, and Phillips smiled to herself as he took the opportunity to trace his eyes over her long Indian limbs encased in green scrubs. 'How did you do?' he asked eventually.

'A PB of three hours, so pretty pleased with myself. I had

hoped to go sub-three, but the conditions weren't great and my right hip started to play up over the last couple of miles. Still, I'm hoping to break three hours in the London Marathon in April.'

Jones chuckled harder than was necessary. 'I struggle to run a bath, never mind twenty-six miles.'

Chakrabortty produced a polite smile and Phillips rolled her eyes. It was a good job Jones was married.

'Shall we go through and take a look at your canal body?' said Chakrabortty.

'Good idea,' said Phillips, signalling for Jones to follow the doctor down the corridor.

Inside the examination room, Chantelle Webster lay on a large metal table. Her body was covered in a light green surgical sheet, her shoulders, head and feet visible. As ever, the room was spotless, housing a collection of sparkling metal tools laid out on rolling tables. The strong aroma of cleaning agents and embalming fluids filled the air, causing a small wave of nausea to pass through Phillips. As much as she loved Tan, she hated this place and what she had seen here over the last fifteen years.

Chakrabortty walked round to the far side of the table and pulled on first a pair of latex gloves, then a surgeon's mask. She pulled back the green sheet to expose Webster's large breasts and bloated torso. Next, she picked up a large scalpel and pressed it against Webster's chest, ready to make an incision. Her large brown eyes fixed on them both for a moment. 'I'd better warn you. We can assume she swallowed a lot of canal water and, as you can see from her bulging gut, there are a lot of gases inside her stomach. It's fair to say, this one is going to smell.'

Phillips swallowed hard and Jones nodded.

They waited for the inevitable as she made the incision.

Chakrabortty hadn't lied. The stench was ungodly. A sudden wave of nausea washed over Phillips and for a moment she thought she would vomit. Taking a deep breath, she closed her eyes and fought back the bile rising in her throat. She exhaled and swallowed hard, and it began to subside. Next to her, though, rocking back and forth from his heels to his toes, Jones was doing his best to appear stoic. However, his milky white complexion appeared a shade greener than usual. Chakrabortty of course seemed unfazed.

The post mortem took just an hour and a half. As Chakrabortty moved through the various stages of the examination, she was careful to point out anything of interest.

The reality was, there was little evidence to suggest anything other than a drowning. Webster's head was free from abrasions or any sign of trauma, which indicated she was conscious when she went into the water. Her fingernails were painted and intact – if not quite up to the standard of a professional manicure.

Plus, there were no marks on her knees, wrists or elbows, meaning it was unlikely she had tried to climb out. As expected, her lungs were full of dirty canal water, indicating she had drowned. She had traces of a spermicidal lubricant in her vagina, likely from a condom used in the twenty-four hours prior to her death, but with no bruising or trauma in the pelvic area, there was no suggestion of sexual assault. She also had large traces of heroin in her bloodstream.

As Chakrabortty wrapped up, Phillips summed up the exam. 'So, it looks like she was conscious when she went in, but made no effort to get out?'

Chakrabortty nodded and pulled down her surgical mask to reveal her handsome face. 'Her shoes are unmarked around the toes too. The walls of those canals are vertical and slippery. If she had tried to climb out, they'd be scuffed and covered in moss, mud and grime at the front. Instead, there are marks around the sides and instep, with traces of water reeds and metal from a shopping trolley submerged where she was found. All consistent with treading water.'

'So, what are we saying? It's suicide?'

Chakrabortty said nothing for a moment, pursing her lips. 'Everything points to it, but that's down to the coroner and her team, not me.'

'What about the bruise on the neck?'

'I agree it's unusual, particularly as its almost a perfect circle, but there's nothing to connect it to her being in the water or her drowning.'

Jones looked puzzled. 'But who gets dressed up to kill themselves? And why not just take a shit-load of heroin if you want to be dead. That's got to be easier than travelling across the city on a bus – in one of the coldest Decembers in history – before walking down to the water and throwing yourself in?'

'He makes a good point, Tan,' said Phillips.

Chakrabortty shrugged her shoulders. 'I don't know what else to tell you both. I can only present the evidence as I find it. From what I've seen, she was conscious when she went into the water and made no effort to get out – not that that would have made much of a difference. In those temperatures, once her body was submerged, there was little chance she could survive the onset of cold water shock.'

'Evans mentioned that when we fished her out,' Phillips said. 'Is it true it can kill someone in minutes?'

'I'm afraid so. And it can affect even the strongest of swimmers.'

Phillips ran her hand through her hair. 'It doesn't make sense to me at all.'

'Or me,' added Jones.

'And you're sure the bruise had nothing to do with her death?'

'As sure as I can be, Jane. Sorry guys, but in my professional opinion, Chantelle Webster drowned.' Chakrabortty began to pull off her latex gloves. 'And like I said, whether it was suicide, accidental or death by misadventure, well, that's down to the Coroner. My work here is done.'

5

The McVitie's biscuit factory had been a significant employer in Manchester since the Stockport production facility first opened in 1914. Established to cope with the demand of supplying the troops fighting in Europe during the First World War, the site was now a mixture of architectural styles and four times the size of the flagship redbrick building.

Bovalino pulled the squad car across Wellington Road North and up to the red and white barrier, where a smart uniformed security officer greeted Jones and him with a smile in spite of the freezing temperatures. Following his directions, they parked up in the visitors' bay and headed inside to the reception, both eager to get out of the cold.

The middle-aged receptionist's smile matched that of the security guard. She chatted happily as she signed them in, explaining it would take ten minutes for Jon Springwood, Chantelle Webster's boss, to walk across from the factory floor. She organised hot tea whilst they took a seat in the reception area, along with a plate filled with chocolate hobnobs, one of

McVitie's' signature biscuits and a staple in the squad room at Ashton House.

Jones dunked his thick biscuit into his steaming cup. 'It's not often we're made to feel so welcome.'

'I could get used to this,' agreed Bovalino through a mouthful of biscuit. He leaned forwards and grabbed another, as if scared someone might whisk them away.

They continued eating in silence for a moment and finished their tea.

A door marked 'Staff Only' opened and a man in a blue overall and white hat stepped through. He spoke briefly to the receptionist, who pointed in their direction. He crossed the reception area towards them, rubbed his chin and frowned. 'Are you gents from the police?' His accent was thick Mancunian.

Jones stood, followed by Bovalino, his mouth still full of his fourth biscuit. 'Detective Sergeant Jones and Detective Constable Bovalino, Manchester's Major Crimes Unit,' Jones said. They produced their credentials. 'Are you Jon Springwood?'

The man nodded. 'What's this about?'

'We'd like to speak to you about Chantelle Webster,' said Jones.

'Jesus. That lunatic. What's she done now?'

'She's dead,' said Bovalino.

Springwood looked shocked and blushed. 'Oh God, I'm sorry to hear that. Did she finally OD then?'

Looking over Springwood's shoulder, Jones noted the receptionist was listening with avid attention. 'Is there somewhere we could speak in private, Mr Springwood?'

'Of course, and please call me Jon. We can go through to one of the offices; just give me a second to find out which ones are free.' He turned and walked back to speak to the receptionist.

Returning a moment later, he ushered them through a door

off the reception area marked 'Administration Team' and guided them along a narrow corridor towards a room marked 'Conference One'. He led the way into the semi-darkened room with small frosted windows. As he flicked a sequence of switches, the room flooded with artificial light. Despite the fluorescent glow from the overhead bulbs, it felt cold and damp as if unused for some time. Springwood pointed towards the large conference table and, as Jones and Bovalino took seats together, pulled out a chair opposite them before removing his hat and placing it on the table in front of him.

Bovalino pulled out his notepad, ready to make notes, as Jones started the interview. 'You asked if she had OD'd. Why would you say that?'

Embarrassment flashed across Springwood's now-forlorn face. 'Look. I don't want to speak ill of the dead, but she was a junkie, wasn't she?'

'And do you know that for certain or are you just speculating?' asked Jones.

'One hundred per cent certain.' Springwood appeared more confident now. 'I caught her smoking heroin in one of the empty wagons out the back. That's why she got the sack.'

'When was that?'

Springwood took a moment to answer. 'Must have been about October, I reckon. I'm sure it was around the time the clocks change.'

'And why does that stick in your memory?'

'Because she was an hour late one Sunday and blamed it on the clocks going back. I pulled her into the office for that, and she was fired not long afterwards.'

'And was she late a lot?' asked Jones.

'Not at first, but since the end of the summer it had become a frequent issue. I was in the middle of a disciplinary process with her. I had just implemented a performance review programme.

The HR team made us go through it with the troublesome staff so we could exit them through the proper legal channels. So I was monitoring her activity when one day I spotted she'd gone missing from the factory floor outside of a scheduled break. When I went looking for her, I found her huddled in the back of one of the lorries. She was smoking heroin from a piece of foil. I sacked her on the spot, and I've not seen her since.'

Jones took a moment to process the information. 'You mentioned her timekeeping wasn't always an issue. What do you think changed?'

'She did, Sergeant. Not sure why. She used to be one of my best workers, and then she started to drift – if you know what I mean? At one point I even had her earmarked for promotion. When I found out I was moving to the day shift, I put her forward to succeed me as overnight supervisor.'

'And what happened?'

'She started turning up late night after night, and she looked like shit. Sometimes she smelt that way too. One night I had to send her home because she smelt like she'd run a marathon and hadn't bothered to shower. We can't have bad hygiene around food.'

Jones nodded. 'What was her role at the factory?'

'She was a packer. Like I said, a good worker until a few months back, but then she went downhill pretty rapid. I suspected it might have something to do with drugs, based on her deteriorating appearance and demeanour. When she first started, she was fresh-faced and the life and soul of the team. Always cracking jokes and singing. She had a wonderful voice and would sing along to the radio all night. But by the end of her time with us, she was all washed out and her skin was full of acne. Her eyes were always bloodshot, and her singing had long since become silence. It was all I could do to get her to speak some nights.'

Jones changed tack now. 'Was Chantelle close to anyone at the factory?'

'Not anymore. She kept herself to herself and, to be honest, no one wanted much to do with her in the end either.'

'And before that? When she was singing and enjoying work, anyone then?'

Springwood nodded. 'There was one girl, Kerry Baldwin.'

'And could we speak to her?'

'Sure, but she'll not be in until nine tonight. You're better off catching her at home.' Springwood checked his watch. 'Give her a couple of hours and she'll probably be awake. Most night workers get up and start their day around 3 p.m.'

'Could we have her contact details?' said Bovalino.

'Of course.' Springwood pulled out his phone. He took a moment to locate Baldwin's contact details, then dictated the number. Bovalino scribbled it down on his pad.

Jones pushed his chair back and stood. 'Well, you've been most helpful.'

'Glad I could be of use.'

Bovalino stood and slipped his notepad into his overcoat pocket.

'Was it drugs that killed her?' asked Springwood.

Jones shook his head. 'No. She drowned in the Rochdale Canal.'

Shock spread across Springwood's face. 'Bloody hell! How did that happen?'

Jones looked him dead in the eye. 'That's what we intend to find out, Mr Springwood.'

After signing out, they made their way back to the squad car. The weather had taken a turn for the worse and the rain was coming at them sideways.

Jumping into the car, they brushed the surface water from their overcoats as Bovalino started the engine. The heat of their bodies soon caused the windscreen and windows to steam up, and they waited for the air-conditioning to clear the fog.

'Well, his description of her as a junkie matches the post mortem results,' said Bovalino.

Jones nodded. 'Indeed it does. But, let's check in with Kerry Baldwin this afternoon and see what she has to say about it all. The guv has arranged to meet with Richard Webster tomorrow at the MRI. He's agreed to do the formal ID for Chantelle. She'll want all the information we can gather before then.'

'Jesus. What a shitty thing for any parent to have to do.'

'I know. As a parent myself, I can't imagine. And so close to Christmas as well.'

6

Despite the intense volume of the dilapidated television booming in the corner of the bedsit, Fletch can still hear strange noises coming through the open door. Moving carefully across the room, Fletch peers out onto the stairwell. The large, sweating man from the flat below comes into view. He's stood on the concrete landing halfway between the floors, his back to the breeze block wall. His face is contorted, his eyes half closed. He's grunting and moaning as if in pain. His hands are out of view, but his right arm is visible, moving up and down to a steady rhythm. Fletch wants to look away, to close the door and block out the view of what's below, but an overriding curiosity draws Fletch closer. Fletch's mother is on her knees in the stairwell. As usual, she's half dressed, the mottled, spotty skin of her back a stark contrast to her thick red bra. Her face is in the man's crotch. His trousers are pulled open and down around his thighs. His fingers are interlocked in the mother's greasy red hair.

The man opens his eyes for a moment and stares up at Fletch, whose instinct is to run, to get away from this living hell. But there is no-one, and nowhere, to run to.

'Looks like we have company,' the man mumbles to the mother.

She stops and looks up at him, then follows his line of sight. When she turns to face Fletch, her eyes are glazed over as if half asleep. 'I'm working. Go back inside, for fuck's sake.' Her shout echoes up the stairwell and her speech is slurred,

The mother doesn't bother to wait for a response or a reaction. Instead, she turns back and continues, as if what she's doing is the most normal thing in the world: performing oral sex in a communal stairwell.

The man smiles and closes his eyes once more. His moaning returns.

Fletch does as instructed and returns to the grubby bedsit and the solace of the TV, turning it up and up, desperate to drown out the sound of 'mother at work'.

7

The multi-storey car park at the MRI was packed to the rafters and Phillips's stress levels began to climb. She feared she would be late to meet Richard Webster at the Chapel of Rest.

Jones had called last night. Both Chantelle's former boss and a Kerry Baldwin, a former colleague, had confirmed she had a problem with heroin. She dreaded breaking the news to Webster.

With each floor that passed with no available spaces, her anxiety rose. On the top floor, which was exposed to the elements, she eventually spotted a set of white reversing lights and a smoking exhaust. She came to a stop, switched on her indicator, and waited. She watched, drumming her fingers on the steering wheel with impatience, as an elderly man attempted to navigate his escape from the space. After what felt like an age, the car crawled past her at a snail's pace, the old man's head just about visible above the steering wheel. His hands appeared to be gripping it like the safety barrier of a white-knuckle ride.

At last she swung her car into the space and leaped out. She pulled her collar up against the torrential downpour and rushed towards the stairwell. The Chapel of Rest was just a few minutes away on foot.

Slipping inside, she shook the rain from her hair and headed towards the facilities to dry off. She needed a few minutes to prepare herself to watch a heartbroken father identify his dead child. Having wiped her rain-speckled glasses dry with toilet paper, she used the upturned hand-dryer to dry her face and what hair she could before checking herself in the mirror. 'It'll all be over in a few minutes,' she said out loud to the empty toilets.

As Phillips stepped out into the reception area, she spotted Richard Webster sitting on one of the plastic chairs with his back to her. He stared into space, his shoulders hanging low under the weight of his grief.

'Mr Webster.' She kept her voice soft as she approached.

He turned to face her. Pain was etched across his features, his eyes red and puffy. 'Inspector.'

Phillips could just about hear him. She smiled. 'Are you ready?'

Webster nodded. He stepped up from the chair and followed her towards the door marked 'Relatives'. The room beyond was small. The wall opposite the door was filled by a large window, beyond which hung a closed purple curtain. Webster moved towards it and took a deep breath.

Phillips did the same. 'In a moment, I'll open the curtains and you'll be able to see Chantelle. There's nothing for you to worry about. She's been well looked after and will appear to be sleeping.'

Webster stared at his reflection in the glass.

'Are you ok for me to proceed?'

Webster nodded, fists clenched by his side.

Phillips pressed the button. As the curtains parted, Chantelle appeared.

The big man took a slight step backwards and his shoulders sagged. 'My baby,' he whispered, before reaching into his pocket and pulling out a large white handkerchief. 'She looks so small.'

'Would you like a moment alone?'

Webster nodded, his gaze fixed on his daughter. 'Please.'

'I'll wait outside. Take all the time you need.'

As Phillips stepped out into the waiting room, it took all her strength to push down the pain surging through her chest. Far from getting easier every time, it was harder. It was as if the protective barriers she had built over the years were eroding. She took a seat in the waiting area and stared at the floor, her mind a complete blank. She could feel her jaw clenching as her teeth ground against each other.

A few minutes passed and, filled with overwhelming unease, she felt a compulsion to get up from the chair and pace. Therapy had helped her come to terms with and manage her PTSD, but it had chipped away at the protective mask she had built against the horrors of the job. The loss and pain of victims' families was starting to get to her.

Webster emerged from the door behind her and broke her train of thought. She turned to face him. 'I'm so sorry for your loss, Mr Webster.'

The big man said nothing. Normally so physically imposing, as he walked towards her he was stooped, and appeared an inch shorter; as if carrying his grief on his shoulders.

Phillips found herself battling between her desire to protect him from any further pain and her duty to find out the truth of how his daughter had died. For a long moment, she debated whether to share the autopsy results – or even Jones and Bovalino's findings about her drug use – with him. Was it necessary for him to know his daughter was a heroin addict? Phillips already knew the answer to that question, but it didn't make what she was about to do any easier. 'Would you mind if I ask you a few questions, Mr Webster?'

Webster nodded and took a seat.

Phillips perched on the edge of the seat opposite him. 'My officers spoke to Chantelle's boss, and one of her ex-McVitie's' colleagues yesterday. Both confirmed she was a regular heroin user. Were you aware of that?'

Webster's eyes, brimming with tears, locked on hers. 'That's a lie.'

Phillips nodded and felt genuine sympathy for his pain. 'I know it must be hard to hear, Mr Webster, but the post mortem also confirmed the presence of heroin in her system the day she died.'

Webster dropped his face into his hands and began to sob.

Phillips touched his shoulder but remained silent. After a couple of minutes, Webster wiped his face with his hanky and sat upright.

'We understand too that Chantelle was sacked from her job in late October for using heroin.'

Webster shook his head. His mouth fell open for a long moment before he finally spoke. 'But I don't understand. She'd been going to work every night, right up until she died.'

'Could she have found another job and just not told you?'

Webster snorted. 'How should I know, Inspector? Until a couple of days ago, I'd have said there was no chance of Chantelle lying to me and her mother. Now, after what you've said, who knows what was going on with her?'

'She was found with a hundred pounds in cash in her purse. When we spoke the other day, you mentioned she was struggling with her finances?'

'Yes, she was – or at least we *thought* she was.'

'Could she have been dealing heroin, perhaps?'

Webster screwed his eyes tight and more tears streaked down and his cheeks. 'I honestly have no idea *what* my daughter was doing, Inspector.'

'The drugs would explain the moods you mentioned she was prone to – that and her tiredness.'

Webster nodded. 'Yes, I guess it would. This is all my fault, Inspector.'

'You can't blame yourself, Mr Webster.'

'Can't I? I'm her father. How could I not know my own daughter was a drug addict? Looking back, it was obvious. If I'd been paying more attention and done something to stop it, she'd still be alive.'

'Mr Webster, please believe me, drugs are indiscriminate. They affect all kinds of people from all different backgrounds. Coming from a good home doesn't make one immune to them.'

Webster appeared lost in his grief now. Phillips wanted to leave it there, but she had one more question that needed answering. She hated to ask it, but it was important to know the answer, 'Do you know if Chantelle had a boyfriend or had an active sex life?'

Webster wiped his eyes with the hanky and shrugged. 'Not that me or her mother knew about, but I think we've already established that I hardly knew my daughter, Inspector.'

'Thank you, Mr Webster. That's all I needed to know.'

Silence filled the room for a long moment before Webster repeated his question from their first meeting. 'Did she suffer, Inspector?'

Phillips wanted to protect him from any more pain, so was careful in her choice of words. 'The pathologist report suggests that cold water shock would have set in almost as soon as she entered the water, and she'd have died soon after. I very much doubt she was aware of what was happening to her at the end.'

'She always hated the cold, just like her mother. The heating is always on full blast in our house, even in the summer.' Webster flashed a smile as he relished the memory. 'Can I go now?'

'Of course. Would you like me to drive you home?'

Webster stood and cleared his throat. 'No thank you, Inspector. I could do with the walk and some fresh air.'

'I understand,' said Phillips, and shook his outstretched hand.

She swallowed the lump in her throat as Webster walked through the exit doors and back into the main hospital. She waited a minute or so before calling Jones.

'Guv, how did it go?'

'Oh, you know, awful.'

'Sorry to hear that. Seeing a family's grief up close is the worst part of this job.'

'Yes it is. It *really* bloody is, Jonesy. That's why I'm calling. I know everything is pointing to suicide by drowning, but I'm not convinced. I've just watched a heartbroken parent identify his baby girl, and I won't be able to live with myself if I don't at least try and find out what really happened to Chantelle Webster.'

'Ok, Guv. So, what next?'

'I'm heading back to the station now.' Phillips checked her watch. 'I should be with you in half an hour. Pull the team together in my office. I want to have a closer look at Chantelle's movements on the night she died. The first thing we need to figure out is how she ended up in Miles Platting.'

'On it, Guv.'

'And do you know if her coat was ever recovered?'

'Not that I'm aware of, but I can double-check.'

'Yeah, do, because that's bothering me too. Why would anyone go out in this weather without a coat on?'

'I have to admit, it does seem a bit odd.'

'Suicidal more like.'

'Is that what you're thinking, Guv? It was suicide?'

Phillips blew her lips. 'I don't know, Jonesy. But, for the sake of her family, we need to find out.'

8

As Phillips rolled her squad car onto Oldham Road towards Ashton House, she gunned the engine without thinking. Her mind was stuck on Chantelle's missing coat. Had she really gone out that night without one, or had someone taken it from her? Maybe it had been stolen? 'What happened to your coat, Chantelle?' she mumbled under her breath as she stopped at a set of traffic lights on red. As the car idled, her mind wandered back to Miles Platting and the moment Chantelle's body was lifted from the canal. The image of her frozen body, soaking wet and lifeless, was clear in her memory. 'Did you drown or were you pushed, Chantelle?' Phillips said out loud as the lights turned to green.

Traffic was light and she was soon nudging the speed limit, repeating the question over and over: 'Drowned or pushed? Drowned or pushed?'

In that moment, she was reminded of a news story she had heard in the last few months. Hitting redial on her phone, she was soon reconnected to Jones.

'Everything ok, Guv?'

'Something popped into my head just now. I remember hearing about another drowning a few months back. A young girl went into the water around Halloween, if I recall. Could be a couple of weeks either side of it. If I'm remembering it right, that victim was found wearing very little as well. Could be nothing—'

'But it could be something.'

'Yeah, maybe. Worth a look, at least. Tell Entwistle to pull all the drowning files from the last two months and bring them to the meeting. I'll be with you in ten.'

PHILLIPS STRODE INTO HER OFFICE, where Jones and Bovalino sat opposite her empty chair. 'Where's Entwistle?' she asked.

'Printing off those files you requested,' said Jones.

Phillips glanced out into the main office and watched as Entwistle walked to the large printer on the other side of the room and began pulling together reams of paper, stapling them at the corners.

Phillips removed her rain-stained coat and scarf, and took a seat. A steaming cup of coffee was waiting for her on the desk. 'So, who made the brews?'

Bovalino patted himself on the shoulder. 'That'll be me, Guv. Your *star* detective.'

'Brown-noser,' sneered Jones playfully.

Phillips smiled and took a gulp from her hot Americano, savouring the flavour and the warmth for a moment. 'God, you do make the best coffee, Bov.'

The big man smiled. 'I'm Italian. What do you expect?' he replied before his nose disappeared into his own mug.

A few minutes later, Entwistle entered Phillips's office and dropped a thick file in front of each of them before perching his buttocks on top of a small filing cabinet. 'That's every drowning case since October, Guv.'

Setting the coffee down on the desk, Phillips picked up the file in both hands and began leafing through it as the team waited with bated breath. 'Right. We're looking for a drowning that looks like Webster's. I can't remember the name or exact location on the canal network, but I'm sure it was the Rochdale Canal. Like Chantelle, she was wearing next to nothing. I heard it on the radio when I was driving to a meeting at the town hall. It stood out to me because the heater in the squad car was playing up that day and it was bloody freezing. I remember thinking the poor cow must have been half-way to hypothermia before she even went into the canal.'

The men scanned the reports in front of them, each focused on finding the girl first. Phillips did the same. The dominant sound in the room was that of pages flicking over.

As was often the case, Entwistle was first to the mark. 'I think this could be it, Guv. Candice Roberts, aged twenty-three from Failsworth. Found on the sixth of November just up by Ancoats.' Entwistle folded the file on the correct page and handed it to Phillips. She scanned down the report.

She nodded. 'That looks like her, for sure.'

Entwistle smiled, his face filed with pride.

'Bloody teacher's pet,' teased Bovalino, throwing a ball of paper at Entwistle as Jones chuckled.

'Now, now, Bov,' Phillips chortled. She loved the team banter and actively encouraged it. She felt it was of vital importance to team morale, especially after the recent dark times they had shared under the oppressive leadership of their former boss, DCI Brown.

'Turn to page forty-three of your files.' Phillips waited for them to catch up before reading the relevant points out loud. 'Candice Roberts was found less than a mile from Webster.

Time of death was 1 a.m. She was wearing hot-pants, heels and a crop top but, just like Webster, no coat or jacket. She also had cash in her purse, but nowhere near as much as Webster. Official cause of death – *accidental drowning.*'

Bovalino chipped in. 'Nothing in the post mortem indicates she was unconscious when she went in, but then there's also no marks or abrasions on her hands or shoes. That would suggest that, like Webster, she didn't try to climb out.'

'Look at this, Guv – page forty-nine.' Jones had skipped ahead.

Phillips flipped forwards a couple of pages. 'Jesus.'

Jones presented the team with the image he had found. 'She was found with a circular bruise on the back of her neck.'

Phillips stared at the image for a long moment. 'What are the chances of both our victims suffering the same bruising after drowning in the same stretch of water?'

'Slim,' said Bovalino.

Phillips flicked through to the last page of the document and took a moment to find what she was looking for. 'That makes sense.'

Jones followed her lead and pulled up the final page of the report. 'What we looking at, Guv?'

'The pathologist who performed the post mortem was Doctor Murray. That would explain why Chakrabortty didn't make the connection between the bruising on Webster and that on Roberts.'

Entwistle's fingers danced loudly across the keyboard, his face fixed on the screen. 'I've found Roberts's full file, Guv. Even the first page doesn't make great reading.' He turned his laptop to face her.

Phillips began to read from the screen. 'Multiple convictions for prostitution, soliciting, possession of class A drugs. She was no angel, that's for sure.'

'Prostitution would explain the cash in her purse and the skimpy clothes,' said Bovalino.

Phillips nodded. 'Which, considering the similarities, begs the question: was Webster on the game too?'

Jones nodded. 'It would explain a lot, Guv. Leaving the house every night under the premise of going to work. Lying to her parents. The cash in her purse.'

'Agreed,' said Phillips. 'But there's one thing I still can't get my head round. Why, on such cold nights, was neither Roberts nor Webster wearing a coat or jacket?'

'Maybe they didn't want to hide their assets?' ventured Entwistle.

Bovalino scoffed. 'You can still show your "tits and ass" and wear a coat, lad.'

Entwistle shot him a look. 'Sorry, Bov. Unlike you, I'm not an expert on paying for sex.'

Before the bickering and insults derailed the discussion, Phillips raised her hand to signal a truce. 'Check CCTV in and around the area where the girls went into the water – as well as the city centre cameras – on the nights they drowned. See if you can spot either Roberts or Webster before they died. It'd be good to know if they took their coats off – or even had them removed – or whether they were daft enough to walk the streets in bugger-all clothes each night.'

As the team set off to tackle their various tasks, Phillips took a moment to finish her coffee and pull the file together.

A few minutes later, she began to prepare for her weekly one-to-one with Chief Superintendent Fox at 3 p.m. that afternoon. She expected to be pulled to task for adding Chantelle Webster's supposed run-of-the-mill drowning to MCU's already bulging caseload. The connection they had just discovered between Roberts and Webster would go some way to softening the blow, but Phillips knew there wasn't enough evidence for Fox to green-light a full investigation into Webster's death. Not yet, anyway. Still, she had a couple of hours to work out a way to sell it to her boss and keep the case alive.

Standing up from behind her desk, she walked across her office and closed the door before drawing the blinds. The clock was ticking and there was no time to lose.

9

Phillips sat on the large black leather sofa outside Fox's office under the watchful eye of her assistant, Ms Blair. In the last couple of hours, Phillips had pulled together as much information as she could to try and persuade the chief super to keep the Webster case open – at least for the time being. As ever, Entwistle, Jones and Bovalino had rallied round to help find the level of information Fox would expect to see at this stage, but on such short notice it was still thin. Phillips could only hope her boss was in a good mood. However, her heart had sunk when Ms Blair had informed her that Fox was running late, as she was locked in her office with Chief Constable Greenacre – a man Phillips knew she despised and whose job she craved. Phillips braced herself for the inevitable fallout of that meeting.

After reading through her files on the Webster case one more time, she made notes on the rest of the team's caseload and prepared to deliver as much good news as she could up front – in order to soften Fox up if such a thing was even possible.

Phillips checked her watch and glanced at Blair. 'Should I reschedule?'

Blair looked up from her computer and forced a thin smile. 'She won't be long.'

Phillips nodded and glanced at the door to Fox's office just as it opened and the chief constable strode out and across the space without acknowledging either Blair or Phillips. A moment later, Fox appeared, glasses perched on the end of her nose. Her sunbed tan and bleached blonde hair appeared incongruous for the time of year.

She passed Blair a large file. 'I need copies for me, the chief constable and the mayor.'

She turned her attention to Phillips. 'Come in, Jane,' she said, her tone flat.

Phillips followed her and took a seat. Fox's large smoked glass desk was covered in files, which appeared to be full of budget sheets, and a stack of local and national newspapers.

Fox busied herself without looking up before turning to face Phillips. 'Right, what have you got for me this week? Good news, I hope.'

During her twenty-year career, Phillips had faced-off against stone-cold killers, hitmen, gangsters and psychopaths, yet her weekly one-to-one with Fox terrified her more than any of those battles. She couldn't put her finger on why her boss made her so uncomfortable, but each time they met, Phillips felt the stomach-wrenching nerves of a naughty child facing their headmaster. Taking a deep breath, she started with the good news: a list of the convictions the team had delivered in quarter four. Of particular note was a case of human trafficking that had been hand-balled to MCU from another force from the south. The southern force had failed to make any mean-ingful progress on it, and when the gang moved into Manchester, the case was dumped at Phillips's door. After six months of dead-ends, Jones and Bovalino had finally made the breakthrough needed. After tracking an Eastern European haulage firm from Dover to Manchester, they had arrested the driver and seized the lorry. Inside, they'd uncovered thirty young women, all locked in a tiny container hidden behind a false wall in the trailer. Under interrogation, the driver had broken down and given up layer upon layer of detail about the organisation. The CPS had just charged three foreign nationals with trafficking, kidnapping, rape and prostitution.

Phillips passed Fox the file. She examined it without flinching, her cold black eyes scouring every detail on the page. 'Excellent work, Jane.' She dropped the file from a height onto her desk. 'Always nice to show Kent Police how it's done.'

'Thank you, Ma'am.'

'Now tell me, Jane. How many cases does the MCU have open as of today?'

Phillips glanced at her notes. She had been expecting the question. 'Thirteen, Ma'am.'

Fox reclined and tapped her pen on her teeth. 'Thirteen, thirteen. Unlucky for some.'

Phillips knew what was coming next.

'That's quite a lot, wouldn't you agree?'

'Look, I think I know where you're going with this, Ma—'

'So why, DCI Phillips, with so many open cases, are you taking on even more?

Phillips felt her neck blush as her heart rate rose. She pulled the two photos of Webster and Roberts from her file. 'Ma'am, if I may—'

'Do you know how far behind we are against our conviction rate targets, Phillips? Never mind how much money this department is haemorrhaging!'

Phillips held the pictures in her hand. 'Ma'am, if you'll just *look* at these photos.'

Fox ignored the request, instead sitting forwards to glare at Phillips. 'I've just spent the last two hours being bollocked and patronised by the chief constable. He's very unhappy with how far MCU is from the targets he set at the start of the year. It's the middle of December, with time and money running out before the end of the fiscal year. A time when every pound is a prisoner. So, what does my DCI do to help reduce our deficit? She ignores the *thirteen* open cases that need convictions against them and tries her best to open up *yet another* case. Spending even more money MCU can't afford on a fucking stone-cold drowning. Can you explain that to me, DCI Phillips? Can you? Because I'm lost. I really am.'

Phillips steadied herself before passing across a photo of Webster. A close-up shot of the bruising on her neck.

Fox made a fuss of turning the photo at different angles, as if trying to make sense of it. 'What in God's name is this?'

'It's the reason I brought the case into MCU. A perfect circular bruise on the back of the victim's neck. I've never seen anything like it.'

Fox's frustration was obvious as she threw the photo back at Phillips. 'You tied up valuable man-hours because of a fucking bruise? Have you lost your mind, Inspector?'

Phillips was doing everything she could to stay in control of her emotions, when all she wanted to do was reach across the desk and slap some sense into the silly bitch. Remaining as calm as she could, she pushed the second photo across the desk to Fox. 'This exact same bruising was found on another supposed drowning last month. Both were young women, and both were dressed inappropriately for the weather on the nights they died. Even though there were no obvious signs of a struggle, I'm not convinced either woman drowned. The similarities make me think their deaths could be linked.'

Fox let out a sardonic chuckle. 'Jesus Christ, Phillips. When are these bloody crusades of yours going to stop?'

Phillips frowned. 'I'm sorry, Ma'am. I'm not following you.'

'You have thirteen bona fide unsolved cases on your desk,

so why are you wasting time on two girls that obviously drowned. Seriously. Who cares if they wore skimpy clothes and had a similar bruise?'

'Ma'am. Roberts was a known sex worker, and Webster was lying to her parents about where she was going each night. I'm confident she was on the game too.'

Fox took another look at the photo for a long moment before turning it to face Phillips, 'Have you ever had cupping therapy, Inspector?'

'No, Ma'am. I don't go in for that sort of thing.'

'Well, you should. It might help you relax and get some perspective in life.' Fox threw the second picture back across the desk. 'Google it when you get back downstairs. These bruises might not look quite so sinister once you do.'

With reluctance, Phillips collated the pictures and put them back in her file.

'Now is there anything else we need to discuss, or are we done here, Inspector?'

Phillips said nothing for a moment. Her anger burned hot in the pit of her stomach. Where was the harm in digging just that little bit deeper if it meant they would know for certain how the girls had died? Surely Richard and Anya Webster deserved that much, and all she needed was a couple of days. She opened her mouth to speak, but Fox's face made it clear the conversation was over. 'There's nothing else, Ma'am.'

'Good,' said Fox with force. 'Dismissed.'

10

Jones tapped on the open door to Phillips' office. As she looked up from her computer screen, he stepped inside with her fresh morning coffee and a bacon roll, and placed them on her desk. He took a sip from his own cup before speaking. 'Everything ok, Guv? You look a bit pissed off.'

Phillips reclined in her chair and sighed. 'Have you ever heard of cupping therapy?'

Jones took a seat opposite. 'Can't say I have, but Bov might know what it is.'

'Bov?'

'Sure. He might look like a silverback gorilla, but he loves a good spa day.'

Phillips laughed. 'A six-foot-four Italian man-mountain who drives a rally car in his spare time, likes to spa? Jesus. And I thought I knew you lot inside out.'

'Believe me, Guv, he's never out of them. Says it's good for cleansing his Mediterranean skin. You want me to call him in?'

'No need. I've found what I was looking for online.' Phillips turned her screen to face Jones.

'What am I looking at?'

'Temporary scarring from cupping therapy. Look familiar?'

Jones leant forwards, his eyes squinting, 'Perfect circular bruising. Just like Roberts and Webster.'

Phillips took a large bite of her sandwich and chewed it for a moment before speaking again, 'Fox thinks both the girls had cupping therapy before they died.'

'She said that?'

'Not quite, but as good as.' She took another bite. 'Told me to forget them and concentrate on the rest of our caseload.'

'Maybe she's right, Guv. We don't have much else to go on.'

'I know, I know, but if you'd seen Richard Webster in the Chapel of Rest. It was heart-breaking. And I still don't believe any woman in the world would deliberately head out on a cold December night without a coat or jacket. I mean, I understand that the rest of the outfit would be scarce, but standing on a corner freezing your tits off wouldn't be the sexiest look to attract punters with, would it? Plus, I'm sure there's more to Chantelle Webster's story than her just lying to her parents.'

Jones took a gulp from his own drink. 'But what can we do if the super's not convinced there's anything to investigate?'

Phillips stared at the computer screen as she finished the last of her sandwich. 'We can have one more look. Unofficial, of course.'

'You sure that's a good idea, Guv? If Fox finds out, she won't like it.'

Phillips shrugged. 'With my track record, I may not be the best one to answer that. Look, my gut tells me there's something not right with this picture. You know me; I won't be able to rest until I know what happened.'

'And what about the other open cases? Fox is expecting movement on those before Christmas.'

'We can continue as normal, using the wider team for the legwork on the official cases, but run this investigation between just the four of us. If we double our efforts for a few days, then maybe something will fall out. You up for that?'

Jones drained his cup and chucked it in the bin. 'Always, Guv. Not sure the missus will be too pleased, but she knew what she was getting into when she married a detective.'

Phillips pushed her chair back and stood. 'Good. Let's keep this between you, me, Bov and Entwistle. No need to share with the wider support team. We'll commandeer the conference room. Grab the guys and bring your laptops. We've got some digging to do.'

Thirty minutes later found the four core members of Greater Manchester's Major Crimes Unit spread around the large conference-room table. The blinds surrounding it were half closed to the outside offices. Each of the team had a laptop in front of them, and a large whiteboard on wheels was positioned behind Bovalino. Yet another surprising element to the big man: he had perhaps the neatest handwriting on the planet, which meant he was their scribe.

'I know we've heard it all before, but Jonesy, remind us of what we have on Roberts. If there *is* a case to answer here, it's not obvious, which means that whatever we're looking for will be hidden in the small details.'

Jones glanced between his notes, his laptop screen and the team. 'Right. Her full name was Candice Roberts, no middle names. She was twenty-three, from Highgrove Avenue in Failsworth. A known sex worker with six convictions for soliciting, prostitution and possession. She was also a single mum to a twelve-year-old girl who is now in foster care due to the fact Roberts's next of kin, her mother, was deemed unfit to look after her.'

'Why was that?' asked Phillips

'A junkie and a sex worker too, Guv.'

'A family business,' said Bov facetiously.

Jones continued. 'She was last seen alive just after 9 p.m. on the 5th of November on CCTV in the city centre. She was spotted crossing Trinity Way just by the Arena before heading up the road to Cheetham Hill. Her body was discovered by a jogger at 7 a.m. on the morning of the 6th of November. It was partly submerged in the Rochdale Canal in Ancoats, just by Little Islington. Like Webster, the body was caught up in junk and reeds in the water, so was unable to sink.' Jones had already printed off several images of Roberts's dead body as it was found in the water, as well as after it had been moved to the towpath. He stuck them to the whiteboard now, under a magnetic block. The team took a moment to look over them as he pointed to each photo in turn. 'As you can see, like Webster, she was discovered wearing skimpy clothes and high-heels. And again, like Webster, no coat or jacket was ever recovered, but a purse containing forty pounds was slung across her torso.'

'Official cause of death, Jonesy?' asked Phillips.

'Drowning.'

'And has that been signed off by the coroner?'

'Not yet, Guv. With the cold snap, there's a backlog of deaths due to exposure. Without a grieving family demanding answers, she's been classified as low priority. We're expecting an update in the new year.'

'And it's worth noting,' Phillips interjected, 'Doctor Murray performed the post mortem as opposed to Chakrabortty who did the one on Webster. That would explain why the pattern of bruising to the neck wasn't spotted.'

The team nodded.

'Anything else, Jonesy?'

'Nothing of note, Guv, no.'

Phillips turned her chair to face Entwistle. 'So, what about Webster? What do you have on her?'

Being the computer geek of the group, Entwistle shared his

laptop screen with the room. Using the projector hanging from the ceiling, he beamed images onto the white wall opposite them.

'Close the blinds, Bov,' said Phillips, conscious of any wandering eyes in the outside office that might land on the enlarged images of a soaking wet and frozen Chantelle Webster.

Entwistle recapped the dead girl's background right up to, and including, her death, before presenting fresh information. Clicking on a folder on his laptop, he opened a PDF file. 'This is where it gets interesting. Digging through the system, Webster's name popped up on a report from Operation Roundup.'

'What's that?' said Bovalino.

Entwistle offered a smug grin. 'Exactly what it sounds like. An operation by the Sex Crimes and Trafficking Squad in November to round up the street-walkers and get them off the streets.'

Bovalino scoffed. 'What, literally?'

'Not quite, Bov, but not far off. The idea was to speak to the girls and offer them help to get off drugs. Shelter if they needed it, as well as safe havens for those that might be the victims of trafficking gangs.'

Phillips sat forwards and leaned on the desk. 'So, what did the report say about Webster?'

'Just that she was spoken to by the officers but denied being a prostitute. She had no convictions and was new to the streets. However, the report suggests she was more than likely a sex worker. Anyway, like each of the girls spoken to that night, she was offered support and shelter but refused it. Again, citing the fact she *wasn't* a prostitute or an addict.'

'If she wasn't a hooker, then what was she doing in Cheetham Hill at that time of night?' said Jones sarcastically. 'It's not quite Spinningfields, is it?'

Phillips drummed her fingers on the table. 'Ok. Even if we assume she was a prostitute, that in itself is not enough new information to make the case to Fox. So, what else have you got?'

'I'm not sure if this is helps, but Roberts was also spoken to as part of Operation Roundup in the exact same location at around the same time.'

'Meaning they may have known each other,' said Bovalino.

Phillips gazed at the projection on the wall for a long moment. It still wasn't anywhere near enough to warrant further investigation. Squinting, she strained to see the name of the officers who had filed the report. 'Can you blow up the names at the bottom, Entwistle?'

Entwistle obliged, and Phillips read the first name out loud for the benefit of the room. 'Detective Sergeant Rachel Gibson.'

'Oh, that's Gibbo,' said Bovalino.

'You know her?'

'No, Guv. But a mate of mine worked with her in the Tactical Aid Unit a few years back. Held her in very high regard.'

Phillips's gaze returned to the projection on the wall as she read the second name on the sheet. 'Detective Constable Don Mountfield. Anyone know him?'

The three heads around her shook, each face a blank.

'Well, we still don't have enough for me to take this to Fox. That said, my gut tells me that if we keep looking, something *will* come up. For now, you lot get back to your active cases whilst I take a walk over to Sex Crimes. Let's see if Gibson and Mountfield have anything that might help us.'

A chorus of 'Guv's followed, and the team began packing away their laptops and files.

'I know I don't need to tell you this,' Phillips said, 'but you know how paranoid I get. This stays with us, ok?'

'Yes, Guv.'

'Of course.'

'Not a word.'

Phillips smiled. 'Right. Let's clean up this room so that even SOCO wouldn't know what we've been up to.'

11

F letch curls into a ball in a vain attempt to limit the damage of the belt buckle as it strikes, over and over again. The mother is ranting, raging and almost incoherent. Her venomous behaviour sprang from nowhere just a moment ago as she returned to the bedsit. Fletch was watching television, but could see something was wrong as soon as she walked through the door – and knew better than to catch her eye in such a mood. Better to look anywhere but at her. But – as had been the case so many times before – the slightest movement from Fletch had been all the excuse the mother needed to unleash her venomous demons.

After a prolonged and frenzied attack with the belt, the mother runs out of steam and falls onto the bed, her breathing laboured. She's drenched in the grey sweat of exertion and heroin withdrawal. Fletch is semiconscious, fighting to stay alive. Fletch clings now, with lacerated hands, to the dirty carpet that covers the floor. It's no use. A moment later the world goes black.

After what feels like a lifetime, Fletch returns to consciousness. An eerie silence fills the grubby bedsit. It's never this quiet. Summoning every ounce of strength and courage left, Fletch manages to stand. Pain surges through every fibre and tissue; the urge to defecate is overwhelming. The television is off for the first time in a lifetime, and the mother is nowhere to be seen.

Careful with each step, Fletch moves through the tiny room to the bathroom and comes face to face with the mother. She's unconscious, half submerged in a bathtub full of water. Her arm hangs over the side of the plastic tub. Below it, a filthy hypodermic needle sticks out of the floor like a dagger. The mother's breathing is laboured and she looks grey all over, as if sinking into death.

'Please God, let her die so I can leave this place.' Fletch offers a silent prayer, then prods the mother's head. With little force, it flops sideways and slides closer to the water. Even though one side of her mouth is now submerged, the mother does not stir. Fletch pushes the mother's head farther into the water without response, then farther still, and farther again until the mother's mouth and nose are submerged and bubbles begin to form on the surface. Fletch gazes in awe as the bubbles continue to appear for the next few minutes. The expectation is the mother will soon wake, but she doesn't.

When morning comes and the monster remains under the water, Fletch can dream of freedom. The mother is dead.

12

Despite the Sex Crimes and Trafficking Squad also being based in Ashton House, Phillips and SCT's DCI Paul Atkins did not often cross paths or even speak to one another aside from a nod or the odd hello as they passed each other in the corridors or the car park. So it was no surprise Atkins looked suspicious when Phillips strode into his squad office. He was in the briefing room and had just finished the morning update. Phillips waited patiently by the door as the team filed out and Atkins finished up a conversation with his two-I-C, Detective Inspector Manushri Chaudry, who stared at Phillips for a moment as she walked past without saying a word.

Atkins was a tall, long-limbed man with a well-trimmed dark beard. He smiled. 'Detective Inspector Phillips. This is a surprise.'

'I've been reinstated, as well you know. It's detective chief inspector.'

'Just my little joke. Anyway, *DCI* Phillips. To what do we owe the pleasure of a visit from the GMP's celebrity copper?'

'Jesus. When will people let that shit go?'

Atkins raised his hands in mock defence. 'Getting a little sensitive in your old age are you, Phillips?'

'No, just tired of being reminded of the past. The Michaels case was a long time ago. I've paid my dues since then and put it behind me. Sadly, not everyone else has, it seems.' She stared at him, daring him to test her patience again.

Atkins took the hint and his tone softened. 'Ok, ok, I'm sorry. It was just a bit of banter, no offence intended. Let's start again, shall we?'

Phillips nodded.

'So how can Sex Crimes be of help to MCU?'

'Am I right in thinking you were the SIO in charge of Operation Roundup in October?'

Atkins raised an eyebrow. 'I was. Why do you ask?'

Phillips pulled a copy of the files relating to Roberts and Webster and passed it over. 'I'd like to speak to DS Gibson and DC Mountfield if I can.'

Atkins scanned the sheets. 'Oh. Why?'

'A potential double-homicide.'

He looked closer at the reports now, flicking between the two sheets. 'I don't know this Webster girl but everyone in SCT knew Roberts. She drowned, didn't she?'

'So the pathologist report suggests, but the other girl, Webster, turned up last week in almost identical circumstances. It could be a coincidence, but it could also be a double murder. I'd like to know either way.'

Atkins handed the files back. 'So how can Gibbo and Mountfield help with that?'

'Looking at their files, they've both worked the streets for a long time and may have some insight that can help us. I'd like a quick chat, that's all.'

'Well, Mountfield's a no-go today as he's on leave, but Gibbo is around. Although I'm not sure she'll give much away.'

Phillips eyed Atkins with suspicion. 'What do you mean by that?'

'Well. Like you said, she's worked the streets for a long time. She's seen some pretty harrowing things. All the team have, to be honest. Comes with the job, but Gibbo has seen more than most.'

'I know how she feels.'

'Do you? You ever found an eleven-month-old baby that's been dead for two weeks, lying next to its junkie mother's corpse?'

'Jesus. That's rough.'

Atkins nodded. 'That's Gibbo. She was tough before that, but now she's like concrete. Nothing gets through. So by all means ask her your questions, but don't be surprised if she's a bit frosty or hard to connect to. I think it's her way of coping.'

Phillips felt the fading gunshot wound twinge in her chest, a daily reminder of her own trauma suffered in the line of duty. 'I get it, Atkins, and at this stage I'll take whatever information I can get.'

Atkins chuckled. 'Bit thin on evidence, are we?'

'Wafer thin, but my gut's telling me to keep looking. You know how it is. But listen, not a word to anyone at the moment. Strictly speaking, the case is closed.'

He nodded and, based on his reputation in the force, Phillips believed he would be true to his word.

'Wait here. I'll go and get her.' Atkins strode out of the briefing room and to the door of the large open-plan SCT office, 'Gibbo. You've got a visitor.'

Phillips watched as a platinum blonde woman looked up. She nodded, stood up from the desk and walked over to Atkins. He said something out of Phillip's hearing before pointing in her direction. Gibson nodded and headed for the briefing room.

Phillips offered her outstretched hand, which Gibson shook

with force. She was quite tall up close, about five feet ten, with an athletic build. Her features were striking, with angular cheekbones and dark brown eyes which seemed even darker next to her bleached blonde hair.

'What can I do for you, Ma'am?'

Phillips gestured to a couple of chairs close by. 'Let's sit down, shall we?'

Gibson sat. Up close, her face was taut, eyes distant.

Phillips handed over the Roberts and Webster files and repeated what she'd just said to Atkins.

Gibson scanned the files. 'I heard about Webster drowning last week. It's so frustrating. We're constantly warning the girls to stay away from the canals. In particular during the winter months. It's so easy to fall in, even more so when they're wearing thick-soled high-heels.'

'So you believe she drowned?'

'Don't you?'

Phillips kept it vague for the moment. 'I'm not sure, so we're checking all avenues. Looking at your report, there's no concrete evidence she was a sex worker, but it seems to lean in that direction.'

'Like you say, there's nothing concrete on file, but from what I saw, I'm almost certain she was a pro – she just never got caught.'

'And do you know if she was using heroin?'

'One hundred per cent. Chantelle was a big-time junkie. In fact, I can't remember ever seeing her straight. That's why she worked so damn hard. She was getting high in between tricks.'

'And what about Roberts? Was she using?'

'All the girls do. It's a catch-22. They need money for drugs so they work the streets. Then they need drugs because working the streets is so fucking awful.'

Phillips sensed Gibson was beginning to soften. 'Sounds like you feel sorry for them?'

Gibson nodded. 'I guess it's hard not to. It's a vicious cycle. A lot of the girls' parents were junkies and on the game themselves, so it's all they know.'

'So what happened to Webster, then? She came from a loving family and had a son of her own.'

All of a sudden Gibson's expression turned stoic and she folded her arms tight against her chest. 'Those are the cases that make the least sense to me. I'll never understand why anyone from a background like hers ends up working the streets and hooked on smack.'

'You mentioned Webster worked a lot each night. What kind of money are we talking there?'

'Well, with the influx of trafficked girls from Eastern Europe, supply is much higher than demand. Sex is cheap these days. For oral, she maybe got fifteen to twenty quid. More if the guy wanted it without a condom. Full sex, twenty-five to thirty-five – anal is premium-rate, so I'd guess fifty for that. She was servicing five or six johns a night, so she'd have been doing all right if she didn't spend it all on smack.'

'What would it cost if someone wanted to hire her for the night?'

Gibson scoffed. 'This isn't *Pretty Woman*, Ma'am. Street girls don't end up in hotel suites.'

Phillips didn't appreciate the attitude and she fixed Gibson with a hard stare.

'Sorry, Ma'am, I didn't mean to be disrespectful.' Gibson realised her mistake.

'So, explain what you *did* mean?'

'Just that street girls are so high on crack and heroin that by the time they've done a couple of tricks, they look scuzzy physically. Then they start clucking for their next hit, scratching themselves and shaking. They're desperate to get high again. No man would want to spend a long time with a street-walker.'

Phillips passed two evidential photographs of Roberts's and

Webster's purses across, both containing ten- and twenty-pound notes. 'Both girls were found with cash on them when we pulled them out of the water. Roberts had forty pounds in her purse. Webster, on the other hand, had over a hundred and forty quid on her. I'm just wondering how long it would take a girl to earn that kind of cash?'

'I guess it depends on whether or not they have a pimp.'

'Did Webster have one?'

Gibson shook her head. 'No, I don't think so. I never saw anyone with her, and we've come across most of the pimps that are currently working the city limits. A hundred and forty quid was probably three or four hours work for Chantelle, but I'm surprised she had it all on her. Like I said, it was normal practice for her to get high between tricks.'

Phillips retrieved the photos and placed them back in the file. 'Are the canals often used by the girls for sex?'

'In the summer yes, but it's very rare in winter. It's freezing down there and most men don't like the cold when they're trying to perform. If you get my meaning?'

'So, any idea why they would be down there?'

'I'd say the most obvious reason would be to take a short-cut over the locks. Most of the punters will drive the girls to a secluded spot for sex, such as industrial areas that aren't used at night. There's a few of those around the canals. When they've finished, the punters often kick the girls straight out the car, or at best drop them off at the nearest main road. So, depending on where they last had sex, Roberts and Webster may have been trying to get back to their usual patch as fast as possible to pick up their next job. If the canal intersected their route, they could have tried to cross it over the locks. But as many a drunken punter has found out on a night out around Canal Street, they're very, very slippery. It's so easy to lose your footing – even easier if you're wearing six-inch heels.'

Phillips pictured the two girls trying to cross the thin

wooden barriers and had to admit it made sense. Yet something about this case gnawed at her. Still, there was no need to share her concerns with Gibson. 'You're probably right. I've taken up enough of your time already.' Phillips gathered the file and stood, offering her hand to Gibson. 'Thank you.'

Gibson stood and shook her hand. 'Anytime, Ma'am. And if there's anything else I can do to help, please let me know.'

Phillips nodded and made her way out of the office and headed back up to MCU.

She was no closer to a breakthrough she could take to Fox and time was running out. She knew full well she couldn't hide an off-the-books investigation for long. Ashton House was a hot-bed for gossip, and she was sure her visit to SCT would be fed up to Fox before long. She felt certain neither Atkins nor Gibson would say anything, but Fox had many informants in the building, each feeding her information in the hope of furthering their own careers. Taking that into account, she figured she had the remainder of the day to work on the case unhindered before Fox pulled her in for one of her infamous 'chats'.

With the clock ticking, it was time to pay another visit to Richard Webster.

13

The squeaking garden gate to the Webster's house announced Phillips and Jones's arrival. Once again the dog appeared at the bay window, barking ferociously. The growls and snarls increased in intensity as they approached the front door and rang the bell. They could hear Richard Webster shouting to the dog as he closed the front room door as per their last visit. A moment later, he opened the front door and peered out. He looked like he had aged ten years since Phillips last saw him at the Chapel of Rest, his eyes red and swollen.

'What do you lot want now?' he sneered. It was obvious he didn't appreciate the visit.

'Please may we come in, Mr Webster?' said Phillips.

'My wife is very upset. It's not a good time.'

Phillips knew the information she was about to share with the Websters would be heart-breaking for them, and for a moment she contemplated walking away from the investigation completely. Was it necessary for them to know what Chantelle's life had become? Jones coughed and glanced sideways at Phillips, before his gaze moved in the direction of the squad car.

She had worked with him for a very long time and could sense he was having the same thoughts.

'What do you want?' Webster repeated.

Just then Chantelle's son, Ajay, appeared from the lounge and stepped into the hall, stopping for a moment to stare at his grandfather, then at Phillips and Jones in turn. His big brown eyes seemed to bore into Phillips's soul. He continued to stare, biting his lip and hopping from foot to foot. A second later, his aunt Lisa appeared and whisked him away upstairs. Phillips's responsibilities became very clear to her; if somebody *had* murdered that little boy's mother, it was her job to bring them to justice. 'Can we speak inside, Mr Webster? It won't take long.'

Webster nodded and they followed him inside and into the lounge. Anya sat in the same spot as last time, on the sofa. Tissues were bunched together in her right hand and her face, like her husband's, was swollen from crying. Webster took a seat next to her and stared back at Phillips and Jones as they took an armchair each.

Phillips sat forwards and offered a sympathetic nod. Her voice was soft when she spoke, 'We've been looking into Chantelle's movements the night she died. We're hoping, with your help, we can work out how she ended up in the canal. We have a few more questions, and then I promise we'll leave you alone.'

Anya Webster was struggling to keep it together, her breathing shallow and noisy through her blocked nose.

Richard Webster held Phillips's gaze. 'Ask your questions and then please go.'

Jones retrieved his notepad.

Phillips pressed on. 'When we last spoke, you said Chantelle came here at 7.45 p.m. and left soon afterwards. At the time you believed she was going to the McVitie's factory, but as we now know, she lost that job back in October. Do you have any idea where she had been going each night since then?'

Webster shook his head. 'I can only imagine she was going back to her flat and, based on what you said, using drugs.'

'Her former boss at the factory told us she was a heavy user and he had no choice but to let her go. That kind of usage requires a lot of cash. Have you any idea how she would come by that kind of money?'

'Begging, maybe? You see a lot of them on the streets nowadays, don't you?' said Webster.

Phillips wasn't ready to share the full details of Chantelle's life just yet, so changed tack, hoping to soften the blow. 'Had Chantelle ever been in trouble with the police?'

Anya covered her mouth with a tissue, struggling to hold back the tears. Richard shook his head. 'No, Inspector. Shanny was always a good girl. We brought her up to know the difference between right and wrong.'

Jones glanced up from his notepad at Phillips. She knew what he was thinking; prolonging the inevitable wasn't helping. It was time to come clean. 'Mr and Mrs Webster. I'm afraid there's no easy way to say this, but we believe Chantelle was working as a prostitute.'

The room fell silent as Phillips's words landed. Richard Webster reacted first and jumped from the sofa. 'How dare you!'

Phillips recoiled in her chair. 'I know this can't be easy to hear, but Chantelle was listed in a police operation. It was undertaken in November by the Sex Crimes and Trafficking squad, and targeted known prostitutes. It happened not long after she lost her job.'

Richard Webster looked incredulous. 'Chantelle was *arrested?*'

'No. But as part of the operation, she was spoken to late at night alongside known prostitutes in Cheetham Hill. It's a notorious red-light district.'

'Just because she was there doesn't mean she was one of them, does it?'

'No, but it does increase the likelihood. Having spoken to the officers in charge of the operation, *they* believe she was a sex worker. It would go some way to explaining why she was dressed the way she was on the night she died, plus why she had cash in her purse.'

Webster dropped onto the sofa.

Phillips knew no father would ever want to believe their daughter was selling their body for sex, but the knowing look on his face suggested it was all starting to make sense to him. Anya could no longer control her emotions and once again turned to the sanctuary of her husband, sobbing into his chest.

Now reluctant, Phillips continued. 'If Chantelle was a sex worker, then, judging by the money we found in her purse, the likelihood is she came into contact with a number of people on the night she died. We'd like to speak to them. Is there anyone she was friends with that might help us do that?'

Webster swallowed hard. 'No, Inspector. Like I said to you before, Chantelle had become distant in recent months. She shared very little of her life with us. She rarely stayed long after dropping Ajay off, and had nothing to say when she picked him up. I just assumed she was tired after the night shift.'

Anya Webster pulled her head clear and turned to face Phillips, her lip trembled as she spoke. 'Are you saying my daughter's death wasn't an accident?'

'At this stage we don't know, Mrs Webster. Everything is pointing towards her having drowned, but her case is very similar to another girl's, who died in November. She was a sex worker, and they were both found with similar marks on their bodies. It could be a coincidence, but it's our job to find out if it's not and if somebody did harm her.'

Anya wiped her eyes with a tissue, stood up from the sofa and moved across the room and out of sight into the kitchen.

She returned a moment later and handed a key to Phillips. 'Chantelle's flat is two streets away. It's not been touched since she left it. Maybe you'll find what you're looking for in there.' She sat back down.

Phillips stared at the key in her hand and then back at Anya. She was overwhelmed by the strength of the woman in front of her. 'Thank you, Mrs Webster. I promise we'll leave everything just as we found it.'

Richard Webster stood. 'I'll show you out.'

As they reached the front door, he touched Phillips's wrist, 'Please, Inspector, be discreet. My wife and I are good Christians and active in the local church. If Chantelle was mixed up in everything you say, we'd rather the world didn't know. We want people to remember her as she was before all this happened.'

'You have my word, Mr Webster. No one will hear anything from us.'

Webster let out a faint smile. 'Thank you, Inspector. Thank you.'

PHILLIPS AND JONES braced themselves against the wind and rain as they walked the short distance to Chantelle Webster's flat. They unlocked the front door and climbed the stairs to the open-plan living space. It smelt musty and stale, in part due to a lack of fresh air but in the main because of the overflowing rubbish bin in the corner of the kitchen. A host of empty take-away boxes had been left on the small glass coffee table in the lounge area. Unlike her parents' elaborately decorated house, there wasn't a single Christmas decoration to be seen. Phillips imagined what little Ajay's Christmas day might be like without his mother; the poor kid.

As a precaution, they both slipped on latex gloves and

began their search. For what, they weren't sure. Whilst Jones started on the living room, Phillips took bedroom one, which had been Chantelle's. Inside, the double bed was unmade. The cable of an electric blanket led from the mattress to a wall socket. Underwear was strewn on most of the surfaces. On closer inspection, it was a mixture of clean and used. Any flat space that remained contained framed pictures of Chantelle and Ajay, from birth up to about a year ago. Opening the small IKEA wardrobe, she found the hanging rail packed with an array of tiny, provocative outfits on one side, juxtaposed by thick coats and jackets on the other. The floor of the wardrobe was covered by a mass of high-heeled shoes, but there was nothing of note. Checking the bedside cabinet, she found condoms and lubricant. Phillips wondered if Chantelle had brought clients home. Judging by the state of the flat, if she did, she guessed she hadn't done so of late.

When she was finished in the bedroom, she moved back into the living area, where she found Jones hunched over a laptop.

'Bingo,' he said with a grin.

'What you got?'

'Access to her laptop. I just cracked the password.'

'*You* have?' Phillips was surprised. Jones wasn't known for his technical prowess.

'I tried her first and last name, then her first name and date of birth. None of them worked. Then I tried putting her son's name in – you know, Ajay.'

Phillips smiled at the unnecessary explanation of the boy's name. Jones was enjoying his moment.

'Then I spotted this.' Jones handed her a framed picture of Chantelle, holding Ajay moments after he was born. Running along the bottom of the frame was the inscription, 'Ajay Webster, 25 October 2014'. So then I tried Ajay Webster 251014 – and hey presto.'

Phillips patted him on the shoulder. 'Well done, Jonesy. Entwistle better watch out – he's got some serious competition.'

A huge smile of satisfaction spread across Jones's face.

Phillips moved towards Ajay's bedroom. 'While you have a look at that, I'm gonna check the other room. Shout if you find anything of interest.'

'Will do, Guv.'

Inside, she was struck by the sparsity of the little boy's room. Aside from a Go-Jetters duvet cover and a few toys in one corner, there was very little to indicate it belonged to a child. It was cleaner than the rest of the flat, but the carpet was still in need of vacuuming. Like his mother's room, a mix of clean and dirty clothes littered the flat surfaces. Inside his small wardrobe, she found a few books and a pair of well-worn Peppa Pig wellingtons with a matching raincoat. 'For jumping in muddy puddles,' she found herself muttering before closing it again and heading back to Jones.

'Found anything?'

'A few bits of interest, but nothing significant, I'm afraid.'

Phillips stood behind him and looked at the screen as Jones moved through various windows.

'Based on her browsing history, she looks like quite a bright girl. I've gone back as far as October at the minute. Around the time she lost her job, she started looking into the typical punishment for soliciting and prostitution, as well as social service cases where sex workers had lost their kids.'

'Weighing up the risks, maybe?'

'Looks like that way. Then a bit later on, she's looking up symptoms of gonorrhoea before searching for treatments.'

'If she had an STD, then there's a chance she was playing fast and loose without a condom. Maybe for the extra cash?'

'Maybe. It's a helluva risk, though, in this day and age – and in particular for the punters. I mean, the majority of street-walkers do it to feed their habit. If they're taking heroin, there's a good chance it's injected and they're sharing needles. HIV is on the increase again, for God's sake. Why would anyone paying for or selling sex not use a rubber?'

Phillips sighed, 'I dunno Jonesy—'

Her phone rang. She flicked on the speaker phone. 'What's up, Entwistle?'

'It's Fox, Guv. She's just been down here looking for you.'

'To the squad room?'

'Yep. She left a couple of minutes ago.'

'What did you tell her?'

'Nothing. I lied and said I had no idea where you were. Made a joke about your movements being above my pay-grade.'

'Did she buy it?'

'I couldn't say. She just stared at me for a bit and then smiled, but in a way that kind of freaked me out.'

'Shit. She knows we're up to something. Did she say anything else?'

'No, Guv, just that she would track you down herself.'

'That's all I need.'

Fox never ventured down to the third floor without good reason. She must have found out about her visit to Atkins and Gibson. *Damn, that was quick.*

'Sorry, Guv.'

'Don't be sorry, Entwistle. She could squeeze a confession out of a dead man. You at least bought me some time to prepare.'

Just then, Phillip's phone began to beep, indicating another call. She could see on the screen it was Fox and her heart sank. 'She's calling me now. I'd better go.'

Clearing her throat, she switched calls, leaving it on speaker so Jones could hear. 'Ma'am, what can I do for you?'

Fox wasted no time on pleasantries. *'You can start by telling me where the hell you are, Chief Inspector.'*

Phillips decided to pretend she was working on another

open case. 'I'm following up on the McBride murder. A potential eyewitness.'

'*Who and where?*'

'Well, I say eyewitness. It's CCTV at one of the neighbour's houses. Turns out the kit's quite cheap and there's nothing that would stand up in court.'

Fox remained silent on the other end.

'So a bit of a dead end, Ma'am.'

'*Sounds familiar.*' If Fox believed her, Phillips couldn't tell.

Fox continued. '*I think it's time you and I sat down and prioritised MCU's caseload. We need to ensure you and the team are working on the cases we can crack the quickest. I have a meeting with the chief constable and the mayor next week. I'd like to be in a position to assure them we're making progress in the areas that matter.*'

'Yes, Ma'am, of course. I'll speak to Gillian and make an appointment for next week.'

'*I've already done it. You'll be glad to know she's allocated two hours for us at 10 a.m. tomorrow. As we're almost at year end, time is of the essence.*'

Phillips's heart sank. She had run out of time. Whatever had happened to Webster and Roberts would never see the light of day now. Fox would see to that.

'*You'll need to bring your full list of cases. Plus progress reports for each.*'

'Yes, Ma'am.'

'*I'll see you at ten o'clock sharp.*' Fox ended the call without waiting for a response.

Phillips's frustration was palpable.

'Looks like somebody told her about your visit to SCT, Guv,' said Jones.

'Sneaky bastards. She usually finds out in time, but this has to be a record.' Phillips blew her lips in frustration and scanned the room. 'Right. There's nothing else we can do here. Bring the laptop. Maybe Entwistle can find something on it.'

Jones looked disappointed by Phillips's unintentional snub.

'We'll drop the keys off back at the Websters and get back to the station. You never know, Bov or Entwistle might have uncovered something – *anything* – I can sell to Fox in the morning to keep this case open.'

14

A s my car slows, she steps out from under the lamppost, takes one last drag of her cigarette, which glows in the night air, then stubs it out under her heavy platformed shoe. The sound of the electric window whirring as it descends draws her towards me. Before I can say anything, her head is almost inside the car. I'm thankful she doesn't seem bothered by my appearance, but is quick to tell me anything kinky will cost extra. That's fine with me. I'll agree to whatever she wants right now. All that matters is getting her into the car. She tells me the price for what I want is thirty pounds, and my heart lifts when she explains there is no pimp to report back to. She's free to leave right away. She jumps into the seat next to me and a moment later I pull away from the curb. The police scanner is buzzing on a low volume near the central console. She asks why I have it. I tell her it's to ensure we don't get arrested, and she appears to accept this.

I have a secluded spot in mind for us, and she's happy to go wherever I want. It's very cold tonight and she seems to enjoy the warmth of my car.

She pulls a cigarette from the packet, but I shake my head. I hate the smell of cigarettes and I don't want that stench in here. This is a pool car. There would be big trouble at work if I was accused of smoking in it.

For the next ten minutes, we make steady progress towards our destination. I could get there quicker, of course, but the main roads are filled with police cameras, which I'm keen to avoid. I duck down one of the grimy back streets that make up Ancoats, just north of Manchester city centre, then zip through a maze of weather-beaten and ancient cobbled roads. I connect with Lower Vickers Street in Miles Platting and pull the car over to the right. When we park up, we're not far from Victoria Mills Park.

The girl's name is Sasha Adams. I know her, of course. I've been watching her for some time. She's a heavy drug user, which means she doesn't remember me. If she did, she would have thought twice about getting into the car tonight. Sat as close as she is to me now, I can see how heroin has ravaged her twenty-three-year-old skin. She has natural pretty features, but at the rate she's shooting up, her looks won't last much longer. Like so many girls before her, the heroin will ruin her teeth and cause her jaw to sink, and she'll come to resemble a pensioner with missing teeth. Once that happens, her earning potential will shrink to almost nothing. It's frustrating to witness someone so young wasting their life. I almost feel sorry for her. The truth is, though, she's had plenty of chances to get off the street and start again – but she *keeps* coming back. It cannot be allowed to continue – the cycle has to end.

As time passes, I begin to sense she's clucking in the seat next to me, rubbing her thighs and chattering inanely. All of a sudden, she appears impatient. Eager to get on with this job so she can score her next hit. 'So, what d'ya wanna do?' she asks, her accent unmistakably Mancunian, her words very nasal and drawn out.

I point through the windscreen into the distance. 'I wanna take you down to the canal.'

She doesn't look too pleased with my request. I'm not surprised; it's minus six outside.

'Come on. It's a fantasy of mine.' I smile and open my wallet so she can see the crisp, fresh notes. 'I'll pay you an extra tenner.'

She wants an extra twenty. For the sake of expedience, I agree.

I get out of the car and watch as she steps awkwardly onto the frozen ground. Her thick-soled high-heeled shoes are not appropriate footwear for the short walk down to the canal. I walk ahead, forcing my head down against the bone-chilling wind. From time to time I turn back and watch her hobbling along like a baby giraffe. She looks ridiculous in her skimpy outfit and high heels. I can hear her whingeing and cursing. She's cold, but I don't care.

As I reach the opening to the towpath, I stop. She's going to need my help to make it down to the water without breaking her neck on the slippery, moss-covered steps. As she reaches my position, I hold out my hand and guide her down each step, slow and deliberate. It's almost pitch-black down at the bottom. At last she plants her heels on the cobbles and waits for a moment, letting her eyes adjust to the darkness.

When she's ready, and still holding her hand, I guide her under the bridge.

'Is it much fucking farther?' Her words echo around the curved underside of the bridge.

'Just a few more steps. It'll all make sense when we get there. I promise.'

She's not happy. 'I should have charged you an extra thirty, for fuck's sake.'

We reach the spot I want.

'What kind of fantasy involves having sex under a fucking bridge in the middle of winter?'

Her language leaves much to be desired, but then, what can I expect? She's a junkie-whore.

She stands in front of me shivering, hopping from foot to foot, rubbing her arms in an attempt to keep warm. 'So what you want me to do then?' Her words bounce off the walls around us.

I stare in silence at her for a long moment. I'm downwind of her and it smells like she's not washed her genitals for some time. *What kind of low-life punters are happy to pay for a stinking vagina?*

Her teeth have started chattering. 'Can we get on with his? It's bloody freezing down here,' she spits.

'Get in the water,' I say, my tone unflinching.

She laughs.

I repeat myself.

'What the fuck are you talking about?' Her face screws up in a ball.

Then I press the silenced Glock 19 9mm beneath her ribs. Her eyes widen. She opens her mouth to scream, but I clamp my hand over it just in time.

'Shut your dirty fucking mouth and get in the water, *Sasha*.'

Her eyes widen and she stares at me in horror. I can almost hear her thoughts. *How do I know her name?* I move my face as close to hers as I can stand, and dig the gun harder into her ribs. 'I'm not kidding. Get in the water *now*.'

She grimaces, then with some reluctance turns and totters towards the canal. She looks ridiculous in the skimpy outfit with skin on show everywhere. Stopping at the water's edge, she turns back to look at me.

'Keep your shoes on but remove your coat,' I tell her.

She starts to cry. 'Why are you doing this?'

It's too late for tears. 'Do as you're told, Sasha. Remove the coat.'

She complies.

'Now jump in.'

'Please don't do this!'

I'm beginning to lose my patience. I step forwards and press the gun against her forehead, 'Shut your fucking mouth, bitch!'

Tears streak down her swollen cheeks. The cheap black mascara gives her the look of a wet panda, and she whimpers like an injured animal as I cock the pistol.

'It's your choice. Either you get into the water or I put a bullet in your skull. What's it gonna be?'

She looks at me. Then down at the water. Then back to me.

'Do it now!' I roar.

She half jumps, half slips, then falls into the water. There is a loud crack as she hits the ice, followed by a satisfying splash as she breaks through it.

Time is of the essence. I put the gun back in my pocket and retrieve the animal control pole I stashed in the large bush at the base of the bridge yesterday. Holding it in both hands, I walk back to where Sasha is now flailing in the ice-cold filthy water. She tries to speak, but nothing is coming out.

It's taken hours and hours of practice, but I'm now able to hook the rubber loop around her neck and tighten its grip in one smooth movement. Following her instincts, she grabs at the pole behind her, but I yank it out of her reach, then force her head under the water, which silences her splashing. I hold her under for fifteen seconds, and when I pull her back above the surface, she coughs up water as she gasps for air.

'I'm sure you want to scream, Sasha, but I'm afraid you can't. You see, your body is experiencing cold water shock, causing your lungs to tighten and your heart to beat at almost twice it's normal rate. In a few minutes, hypothermia will set in and your body will begin to shut down as it draws blood away from your skin to your vital organs, attempting to keep you alive.'

I dunk her once more, this time for thirty seconds.

As she resurfaces, I'm forced to shout above the noise of her flailing arms splashing in the water. 'Do you know why I'm doing this, Sasha?'

She's struggling to stay afloat. Her heavy shoes aren't helping. I'm not surprised when she doesn't answer me.

'You, Sasha, are a junkie and a whore. A stain on the world that needs to be eradicated. To be wiped out and destroyed. There is no place for your kind in decent society.'

I force her under the water once more. This time I count to forty-five before letting her back up for air. Her breaths are short, and her arm and leg movements have slowed to almost nothing. Only the pole is keeping her afloat.

It's time to complete the ceremony. I close my eyes and open myself up to a higher power, summoning the strength to finish the job. When I open my eyes again, I look upon her flailing body, consumed with abject fear and panic. I hold the pole in my left hand as I bend down and place my right hand on top of her frozen head. 'I am The Baptist, here to deliver *you, Sasha Adams,* to the reckoning. The time has come for you to leave this life and make your peace with God.'

Her mouth opens and closes like a fish out of water. Her teeth chatter, and she tries calling for help one last time. Nothing comes out. I can see she's not far from death.

It's time to let her go.

I press the release button at the end of the pole and the rubber loop becomes slack once again, which allows me to remove the animal control pole from her neck. She is unable to stop herself swallowing water and sinks below the surface. As she disappears into the dark waters, bubbles appear on the surface for a few seconds and then cease, leaving nothing but tiny waves blowing over the surface of the water.

I stare at the spot where she went under for a long moment. I'm filled with a mix of emotions; anger, mixed with a sense of relief and justice.

The world is a better place without Sasha Adams. At least now her four-year-old daughter has a fighting chance at life.

15

Phillips poured herself a strong black coffee and took a seat at the kitchen bench overlooking the garden. The rain lashed the floor-to-ceiling windows at the back of the house. The dark grey sky outside didn't help her mood. She took a deep breath and released it with a low, frustrated growl. She and the team had so far been unable to find anything that would warrant a full investigation into the deaths of Roberts and Webster. She took a long drink, then pulled the folder of the MCUs outstanding case notes across the bench. She opened the Manila folder to reveal a one-inch-thick stack of reports and updates. It was 7.30 a.m., and she was due to meet Fox at 10 a.m. A meeting she dreaded.

These days Phillips considered herself pretty battle-hardened. With over fifteen years of experience dealing with some of Manchester's most horrific crimes, very little intimidated her. With one exception: Chief Superintendent Fox. Phillips had fought off killers in her own home and even survived being shot at point blank range, so a one-to-one with her boss should be a walk in the park. But there was something very unnerving about Fox. Her black soulless eyes, the fake Cheshire Cat grin that oozed disingenuity. Perhaps it was the never-ceasing rumours circulating around Ashton House that she was a functioning sociopath – a woman always plotting and planning. Happy to say *whatever* was required to deliver the exact outcome she wanted. Regardless, Fox brought Phillip's anxiety back to the fore whenever they met.

Just over a year ago – not long after the shooting that almost killed her – Phillips had been diagnosed with PTSD. In the months that followed, she had struggled in silence as she and the team waded through the endless devastation and destruction that formed the basis of investigations for the GMP's Major Crimes Unit. She had, for a time, managed to hide her mental health problems until she had once again come face to face with a killer. In the heat of that battle she had frozen and, to her eternal regret, her inaction had allowed the killer to inflict life-threatening injuries on DC Entwistle. From that moment she had vowed to seek help, and been lucky enough to be referred to the renowned Manchester psychologist, Dr Scott Hogan. Together, over many painful and profound sessions, they had found a way for her to manage her inner demons each day, to enable her to live a normal life again – if there was such a thing in the MCU.

Since working with Hogan, she had been reinstated as DCI. Leading her beloved team, and with the help of meditation, exercise and diet, she had found a balance she had never known before. Yet, despite all the mental-health work and self-help, Chief Superintendent Fox still made her feel vulnerable and, somehow, unsafe.

She drained her cup. 'Why the fuck am I still doing this to myself?'

Gathering up the case notes, she grabbed her car keys. Just then, her iPhone rang, vibrating on the bench as her ring tone – Tom Jones's 'What's New Pussycat?' – filled the kitchen. The music was silenced a moment later as she accepted the call.

'Jonesy, what's up?'

'We've got another one, Guv.'

Phillips was attempting to pull on her coat with one hand. 'Another what?'

'Another dead girl in the canal. Scantily dressed, no coat. No signs of trauma.'

Phillips dropped the file back on the bench. He had her full attention now. 'Any bruising to the neck?'

'I asked the same question, but she's still in the water at the moment. A fire crew will be on scene in the next few minutes.'

'Who called it in?'

'A city centre uniform crew.'

'Where and when was she found?'

'This morning, just after six. A jogger spotted her in the Rochdale Canal near Victoria Mills Park.'

'I take it Evans is on his way?'

'As far as I know, Guv.'

'Ok. Text me the exact location and I'll head over there myself.'

'Will do.'

Phillips's attention was drawn back to the copies of MCU's case files on the bench. 'Shit. Fox.'

'What about her?'

'I'm due in her office in two hours.'

'Lucky you. Seriously, don't stress about it. Me and Bov can handle this one.'

'Oh, I know you can. It's just that I suspect Fox has called me in because she's trying to shut down the Webster investigation. Another dead girl with a circular bruise on her neck would be a good thing right now. If that was the case, then Fox would have little choice but to let us carry on looking into Webster's death.'

'So what do you wanna do?'

Phillips considered her options for a moment. Deliberately

missing a meeting with Fox was never a good idea, but her gut told her the similarities Jones had just described were no coincidence. She had to see the body for herself. 'Send me the location, Jonesy. I'm on my way.'

'If you're sure, Guv?'

Phillips closed her eyes and took a couple of long, deep breaths. It was a technique she used every day to manage her anxiety.

'I'm sure, Jonesy,' she lied. 'Pick up Bovalino and meet me at the scene as soon as you can. Tell Entwistle to get over to the office and wait for instructions. We're going to need to dig quick and fast into this one before Fox finds out what I'm doing.'

She ended the call and sat back at the bench for a moment, absentmindedly tapping her phone against her teeth as she considered the consequences of going behind Fox's back. Was getting to the bottom of Roberts's and Webster's deaths worth risking her career for? For a split second she contemplated ringing Jonesy back to call the whole thing off, but then she thought of little Ajay growing up without his mum; the missed birthdays and Christmases, his wedding, the birth of his own children, even. She pictured a young boy turning into a man, never knowing what his mum was like or how she felt about him. Would he spend his life wondering, 'Did she fall into the canal or did she jump to her death?' He deserved to know the truth, and whatever the risk to herself, Phillips knew she had to take it.

EVANS and his team arrived just before Phillips did. A crash on the elevated stretch of Manchester's inner ring-road, the Mancunian Way, had delayed her by twenty minutes. Travelling from the opposite side of town, so able to avoid the congestion, Jones and Bovalino were also on scene by the time Phillips walked down the icy, worn steps to the towpath. Up ahead, both men stood with their backs to her, keeping watch as the SOCO team pulled on their white overalls. The rain had stopped, but the wind still howled over the water. Small wavelets broke against the mossy walls of the canal. Thanks to this morning's heavy rain, the water level was high.

'Morning gents,' she said as she approached.

Jones and Bovalino turned in unison. 'Guv.'

'Anything yet?'

Jones pointed to the mass of uniformed bodies up ahead. A mix of police, paramedics and firemen surrounded the body, now resting on a plastic sheet on the towpath. 'The paramedics are just confirming extinction of life and then she's all ours.'

A few minutes passed with no-one saying anything before a uniformed officer broke ranks and walked towards them. As he came closer, Phillips noted it was the same sergeant who was on the scene when Webster was fished out.

'Ma'am,' he said before nodding to Jones and Bovalino. 'Paramedics confirm extinction. Over to you now. From what we can see, it's almost identical to the last one.'

'Any bruising to the neck?' asked Phillips

'Nothing at the front. I couldn't see the back as she was facing upwards.'

'Ok. Which uniform team was first on scene?'

The sergeant looked a little coy. 'Er. Same as the last time, Ma'am.'

'The young kid?' asked Jones.

'Yes. By pure coincidence, he and his partner were closest when the call came in. I'm grateful he'd learnt his lesson and called me first this time so I could decide on whether or not to contact you. As you can imagine, I wouldn't ordinarily bother MCU with a drowning, but it was so similar to the last one, I thought you'd want to know.'

'And where's the kid now?' asked Phillips.

'I sent him back at the station when the medics and fire crews turned up. No sense him hanging around if I was here.'

'Thank you, Sergeant,' said Phillips, indicating the conversation was over.

The officer turned and walked back towards the body, where Evans and his team were putting the finishing touches to the white tent that would cover the dead girl.

After suiting up themselves, Jones, Bovalino and Phillips entered the SOCO tent and looked at the dead girl for the first time. She couldn't have been more than twenty years old. Like Roberts and Webster, she was wearing a short miniskirt and crop top with thick-soled high heels – the kind a pole dancer would wear. Kneeling down, Phillips could see her skin was marked with the sores and scars of heavy drug use, and her hands and fingernails were black around the edges. Evans passed over a small purse which Jones opened, peering inside. 'Twenty quid cash, Guv. So, like the others, it doesn't look like she was robbed.'

Phillips nodded. 'Can we see the back of her neck please, Evans?'

With the help of one of his assistants, Evans rolled the girl onto her side and pulled back her matted bleach-blonde hair, revealing a perfect circular bruise. It was identical to those found on Roberts and Webster.

Phillips let out an audible sigh of relief and grinned. 'We've got it. That's what we needed.'

'The bank card here says her name is Sasha Adams,' said Jones, handing it to Phillips, who examined it for a moment.

Phillips checked her watch. It was 9.30 a.m. 'Get Entwistle to find out everything there is to know about her. And I mean *everything*. I'm due to meet with Fox in half an hour and she's gonna be majorly pissed off when I don't turn up. Which means I need to ensure I'm well armed when I do see her. With three identical bodies found in the same stretch of water, these deaths *have* to be connected. Now all we have to do is find something to convince our beloved chief super of that.'

Jones and Bovalino looked at each other, then back at their DCI. Their expressions said everything: Phillips was once again skating on very, very thin ice.

16

E ntwistle was ready with a large folder of information
on Sasha Adams as Phillips rushed into the MCU
squad room. 'Here you go, Guv.'

'Anything conclusive?' she asked, hopefully.

'Sorry, Guv, I'm sure I can find something more in time, but
I've got nothing concrete just yet.'

Phillips hefted the heavy Manila folder in her hands. 'Then
what's in here? It's as thick as a brick.'

'Background on Sasha Adams. She's got quite a record.'

'Walk with me. I'm very late for Fox as it is.'

As they moved through the corridors of Ashton House,
Entwistle brought Phillips up to speed on the information she
was carrying. Adams, like Roberts and Webster, was a street-
walker with a serious drug addiction. She was just twenty-four
years old when she died, but had been working the streets since
she was fifteen. After being brought up in part by a heroin-
addicted mother – also a sex worker – she later passed through
various children's homes across the North West of England until
she was old enough by law to look after herself. Her first arrest

had come at just sixteen, and over the next four years she'd served various short-term prison sentences, even giving birth to her daughter Isobel four years ago as a remand inmate of Henning House Prison just south of Manchester. Since her release, she had managed to stay free from arrest. However, her name was listed as one of those contacted during Operation Roundup, so there was a very good chance she was still an active sex worker.

Phillips stopped for a moment to digest the information. The connections between the girls were starting to fall into place. 'Anything else that could help?'

Entwistle took the file from Phillips and pulled out a series of red bills. 'It might be nothing, but all of the girls who drowned were in deep financial trouble. Each was served with an eviction notice a couple of weeks before they died.'

'Private or council landlords?'

'Private, Guv.'

'Please tell me they all rented from the same guy?'

''Fraid not.'

'That would be too easy, wouldn't it?'

Entwistle handed her another printout. 'But there is a connection. I haven't had chance to look into yet, but I did notice that each of the landlords used the same maintenance company – Manford Estates based in Longsight.'

Phillips raised an eyebrow. 'Did I ever tell you I don't believe in coincidences? You could be onto something there.'

Entwistle smiled triumphantly as Phillips gathered everything back into the folder. 'Dig into Manford. I want to know everything about them. Right, wish me luck. It's time to walk into the lion's den – or should that be the Fox's hole?'

A few minutes later, Phillips walked into the reception area to Fox's office. Ms Blair looked up, her expression grave. 'You were due two hours ago.'

Phillips didn't have the energy to respond. The outcome

would be the same whether she explained her absence or not. 'Is she in?' she asked.

Blair looked unimpressed. She was used to people in Phillips's position begging forgiveness, somehow hoping it would curry favour with Fox. Blair pursed her lips and buzzed through to her boss.

The door opened and Fox stood in silence, staring at Phillips – one of her favoured intimidation techniques. Phillips steeled herself.

'You'd better come in. Sandra, hold my calls and cancel my next appointment. DCI Phillips and I have a lot to discuss.' Fox motioned her inside before walking back behind her desk, where she stood, fingertips on the smoked glass. 'So what the actual fuck have you been doing now? MCU conducting yet another investigation into a straightforward drowning?'

Fox's spies had once again been busy.

'As I have already explained, I have a very important meeting next week with the chief constable, the mayor and the leader of the city council. I like to be prepared for them well in advance and have all my facts in place before I go in. Our one-to-one this morning was a vital part of that planning process. A one-to-one you failed to appear for, and furthermore for which you have made no attempt to explain your absence. Let me ask you, DCI Phillips, do I look like an idiot to you?'

The question caught Phillips off guard. 'No Ma'am.'

'Well, why are you treating me like one? Do you think I was born yesterday? That I don't know what you're up to? I'm pretty sure I can guess what happened this morning. Let's see if I'm right, shall we? So another drowning came in that looked similar to the other two you've been obsessing over. *You* know *I* don't believe anything other than that they drowned. That any further investigations would constitute a deliberate waste of time and money. So, rather than bring me into the loop, you set off on yet another of your bloody crusades and waste more of

MCU's valuable time, before I had time to shut you down. How am I doing so far, Inspector?'

There's a good reason she made detective chief superintendent, thought Phillips.

'Judging by the look on your face, Inspector, I'd say I'm pretty close.'

Phillips produced the folder. 'Ma'am. I'm sorry I didn't bring you into the loop, but we have found a connection between the three dead girls. If you'll indulge me, I can show you.'

Fox dropped down into the large leather chair. 'This has better be good, Inspector.'

Phillips took her seat opposite and spread the documents out in front of her. She spent the next several minutes walking Fox through the similarities of each of the deaths, including the fact they were all single mothers. She had researched cupping treatments online to compare the marks to the bruises on the girls' necks. They had not come from cupping.

The image of the big Italian having such a treatment seemed to amuse Fox. She was softening.

Finally, Phillips pulled out the rental arrears statements and pushed them across the table. 'Entwistle has found one more connection that I believe could be key.'

Fox reviewed the pages.

'Each of the properties rented by the girls used the same maintenance company, Manford Estates in Longsight.'

'And what does that prove?'

'That they are all *somehow* connected, Ma'am.'

Fox stared back at the printout once more. 'It's a bit thin, Phillips.'

She was back to using her name. Phillips felt a tingle of excitement. Fox was softening.

'I know, Ma'am. But with the identical bruising, each drowning having been in the Rochdale Canal, the similar clothes, and now the maintenance connection, these deaths aren't random. I believe someone is pushing the girls into the canals.'

'If that is the case, how do you explain the fact none of them made any attempt to climb back out?'

'The walls are vertical and slippery. Maybe they tried and failed?'

'Come on, Phillips. I've read the post mortem results. None of them had any marks on their fingers or the front of their shoes that indicated they tried to climb out. If your theory is true, then someone forced the girls into the water, where it appears they stayed of their own volition until they drowned.'

Phillips had to admit that, when she put it like that, it did sound implausible. 'Ok, but what about the identical bruising on the victims' necks? How do you explain that?'

'Probably just a coincidence. Or maybe it's drug related. After all, each of the girls had high levels of heroin in their blood post mortem. Maybe the bruising was caused by the way they were taking the heroin? God knows there's always something new for us to contend with when it comes to drugs.'

'Maybe you're right, but shouldn't we know for sure?'

Fox's tone softened. 'Look, Jane. I can see merit in your thinking, I really can – and I'd be happy to sanction a small investigation in January. Once we hit the new financial year and can reset the targets. But opening one up now, with our unsolved cases way above what we promised to deliver to the chief constable and the city officials – it doesn't look good.'

Phillips suspected she was being played. Fox's transition from super-bitch to supportive parent had been seamless. So she decided to play a game of her own.

'As you wish, Ma'am. I understand.'

Fox's sinister Cheshire Cat smile returned. 'Good. That settles it.'

Phillips gathered the papers and put them away in the

folder. 'Do you still have connections in the press, Ma'am?'

Fox looked surprised. 'I do. Why do you ask?'

'It's the journalist, Don Townsend. He's been calling me non-stop this morning. I've not answered, but in his voicemails he mentions he wants to talk to me about the drownings. Could be nothing, of course, but in my experience he's only ever interested in sensational, headline-worthy stories.'

Fox's smile vanished. 'That's all we need. You'd better find out what he wants. The last thing I need before my meeting next week is that arsehole stirring things up in the press.'

Fox had taken the bait. It took all of Phillips's strength to fight off the grin that threatened to spread across her face. 'What about the rest of the cases, Ma'am? Would you like me to talk you through them ahead of your meeting?'

'Just leave them on the desk. I'll read them later.'

Phillips placed the thick folder back on the smoked glass. 'Of course, Ma'am.'

'Right. Make sure you find out what Townsend wants as a priority. Dismissed.'

'Of course, Ma'am.'

A few minutes later, Phillips breathed a sigh of relief and punched the air as she made her way back towards the squad room. En route, she ducked into one of the empty meeting rooms and pulled out her phone. It took a moment to find the number and press dial. It rang a few times before being answered.

The leering voice on the other end of the call made her skin crawl. 'DCI Phillips. Long time no speak. What can I do for the long arm of the law today?'

'I need a favour, Don.'

'Go on?

'Can you put a call in to Chief Superintendent Fox's office this afternoon?'

'What about?'

'Tell her PA you want to talk about three recent drownings in the Rochdale Canal.'

'And then what am I supposed to do?'

'Nothing. I can guarantee Fox will avoid your call.'

'But what if she doesn't? What if she answers?'

'If that happens, just ask her if the deaths of Candice Roberts, Chantelle Webster and Sasha Adams are connected. She'll panic and fob you off. She has no desire to talk about them, I can assure you of that.'

Don Townsend remained silent for a moment as he wrote down the names. 'And *are* they connected?'

'I don't know at this stage.'

'But they might be?'

'All in good time, Don.'

'What are you up to, Phillips?'

'I don't have time to explain right now. Will you do it?'

'Well, I must admit, I'm intrigued. So what's in it for me?'

'If they are connected, an exclusive story that I'll *only* share with you. And don't ask me for details. I can't say. Not yet. But I will.'

Townsend chuckled. 'Sounds interesting. Ok, I'll do it. But you'd better come through for me on this, or you know what I'll do?'

'Don't worry, Don. I'm very familiar with how you operate. I'll come through. Just make sure you call Fox this afternoon, ok?'

'Well, I'm just about to head out and get some lunch. I'll do it when I get back.'

'Thanks, Don.'

Phillips ended the call and stepped out of the meeting room. She took a moment to check each way for anyone who might have overheard, but it was all clear.

Now all she had to do was wait for Don to play his part, and Fox to react.

17

Phillips was in her office, working through a file Entwistle had handed to her just a few moments ago on Manford Estates. It was a preliminary report he had rushed through for her, and she was hopeful more detailed information would be available tomorrow.

Her desk phone rang. Phillips checked her watch. It was two hours since she'd asked Don Townsend to call Fox. She hoped this was the call she had been waiting for.

'MCU. This is Phillips.'

'For arguments' sake,' said Fox without an introduction, 'if I *did* sanction an investigation into these three deaths, how soon do you think you could rule out homicide?'

'Well, there's no guarantees, Ma'am, but if it *isn't* murder, then I would hope it would be obvious quite quickly. As long as I have the authority and budget to dig where I want, that is.'

There was a pause at the other end of the phone before Fox spoke again. 'Ok, you've got your investigation. But I want it closed before the end of the year, which gives you three weeks.'

'Thank you, Ma'am. With such a tight time frame, I wonder if it would be possible to second DS Gibson from SCT?'

'Is that necessary? It'll mean paying overtime to cover her cases.'

'She knows the streets and the girls better than most. I think her experience would expedite the investigation, Ma'am.'

Fox took a moment to mull it over. 'Ok. Do it. You can have her for three weeks, but not a day longer. I'll speak to DCI Atkins to make sure she's made available to you.'

Phillips grinned into the phone. 'Thank you Ma'am.'

'Just don't fuck it up or there'll be hell to pay.'

'I won't, Ma'am.'

'Oh, and Jane. No heroics on this one, please?'

'You have my word on it, Ma'am.'

Fox ended the call without saying goodbye and Phillips clapped her hands with glee. Townsend must have played a blinder. She had her investigation and an extra pair of hands, but she also now owed an exclusive to one of the toughest hacks in the UK press. She prayed to God she could find one or there really *would* be hell to pay.

THE NEXT MORNING, Phillips was working her way through the staff records of Manford Estates. She was so engrossed she didn't notice Detective Sergeant Gibson standing at the door to her office until she cleared her throat.

Phillips looked up. 'DS Gibson. I didn't hear you come in.'

'Please, Ma'am, I prefer Gibbo.'

'And I prefer Guv. I'm not a bloody spinster.' Phillips grinned as she stood to shake Gibson's hand. 'Come on. Let's go meet the team.'

Out in the squad room, Jones and Bovalino were both busy on their phones, chasing down various avenues of enquiry into the deaths. Thanks to Fox's paranoia that Don Townsend was ready to blow the story wide open, the three deaths were

MCU's main priority. The desks surrounding Jones and Bovalino were now filled with uniformed support staff, all engrossed in their tasks. Phillips and Gibson arrived at Jones's desk just as he finished his call.

Phillips made the introductions. 'DS Jones, this is DS Gibson – or Gibbo as she prefers to be called.'

The two sergeants shook hands.

'Call me Jonesy.'

'And this big lump—' Phillips patted Bovalino on the shoulder as he continued on his call. '—is Bovalino, or Bov.' The big Italian shook Gibson's outstretched hand in silence and nodded.

'Don't worry, he's not usually this quiet,' joked Jones.

'Where's Entwistle?' said Phillips.

Jones pointed to the small kitchen at the end of the squad room. 'Gone to make the coffees, Guv.'

A moment later, Entwistle wandered back with a tray of four steaming cups. Phillips turned to face him. 'Just in time, Entwistle. I hope you have a drink for DS Gibson?'

Entwistle appeared flustered as he placed the drinks on the desk in front of Phillips. 'No. Sorry, Guv,' he said. His gaze was fixed on Gibson. 'I'm DC Entwistle, it's a pleasure to meet you. Would you like me to make you a brew?'

Gibson shook her head. 'I'm fine, thank you. I don't drink tea or coffee.'

Entwistle hadn't taken his eyes off the newest member of the team. Standing at almost six feet tall with an athletic frame and short peroxide blonde hair, Gibson was very striking. 'That must take some will-power,' he said. 'I wish I could give up coffee. I drink far too much.'

Phillips noted his tone, which was reminiscent of a doe-eyed teenager's. Jones, noticing it too, sat back and folded his arms as he watched the exchange, a lopsided grin spreading across his face.

As Bovalino finished his call and put the phone down, Phillips took the opportunity to address the wider room. 'Right, guys. Can I have your attention please? I'd like to formally introduce Detective Sergeant Gibson – or Gibbo – to the team. She's been seconded into MCU for the rest of the month to help us find out what happened to Roberts, Webster and Adams. As of yesterday, these are now on our priority case list. Chief Superintendent Fox wants the truth of what happened to these girls ASAP.'

'What changed her mind, Guv?' asked one of the support team.

'I simply expressed the PR benefits of getting to the bottom of these cases *before* anything got out to the press.'

Jones laughed. 'You mean before someone *leaked* it to them, Guv.'

Phillips shot him a look that wiped the smile off his face. Knowing the speed at which information could get back to Fox in Ashton House, she didn't want him making jokes like that in front of the wider team.

'DS Gibson joins us from the Sex Crimes and Trafficking squad. She's our eyes and ears on the street, in particular Cheetham Hill, Ancoats and Miles Platting, where we believe young girls are being picked up and then forced into the canals and drowned. Entwistle, can you pull up the images for us, please?'

A large screen behind Phillips clicked into life before an image of Candice Roberts – taken in the morgue during her post mortem – appeared.

'This is Candice Roberts. She was twenty-three and from Failsworth. A known sex worker found in the Rochdale Canal in October. Unfortunately, we don't have any images of her at the time her body was discovered, as it was assumed she had drowned, but we do know she went into the water wearing a short miniskirt, a crop top and stacked heels. So far, no coat has been recovered, which is very strange considering the time of year.'

Another image appeared, this time the back of her head and neck.

'This picture was taken during the post mortem. Notice the large bruise on the back of her neck; a perfect circle. I want you all to remember how it looks; it could be very important going forward. The next image is of Chantelle Webster as she was pulled from the water. She was twenty-three years of age and from Stretford. Thanks to the quick thinking of a junior PC, MCU was called in to oversee the recovery of her body. Like Roberts, at first it was believed she had drowned and, like Roberts, there were no signs of trauma to the body, which would suggest that once she was in the water, she didn't try to climb out. She too was found in what are considered clubbing clothes, and without a coat.'

Phillips flicked through the images until she found the one she was looking for from the post mortem. 'You'll notice she too has the same bruise on the back of her neck.'

The image of a different girl appeared on screen.

'Finally, this is Sasha Adams, aged twenty-four and from Rusholme. Another street-walker. Adams was also found dead in the Rochdale Canal, with identical bruising and wearing almost the same outfit as the other two girls – as yet no coat or jacket has been found for her either. Again, we found no signs of trauma marks on her head, shoulders or arms. Plus, just like the other girls, there were no signs on her fingers or shoes to suggest she tried to get out of the water. Please note that each girl had money in their purses, so we can rule out robbery. All three were heroin addicts and they were all single mothers. We're not sure if that has any bearing on the case, but it's worth you knowing everything we have so far. Now, as many of you know, I do not believe in coincidence. So, when three girls, all sex workers in the same patch – Cheetham Hill – end up dead in the Rochdale Canal, all with identical bruising and similar outfits, we have to assume these deaths are somehow connected.'

'Are we looking at a potential serial killer then, Guv?' asked Bovalino.

'It's far too soon to tell, I'm afraid.' Phillips cast her gaze around the room. All eyes were on her. 'The clock is ticking on this one guys. The gap between Webster's and Adams's deaths was just a few days. If someone *is* killing these girls, there's a strong chance they'll do it again *and soon*. And as we know, Manchester has one of the largest canal networks in the country with miles and miles of waterways. So far the dead girls have all been found in the same stretch of water, but that doesn't mean we shouldn't look at other locations across the network. I want to hear about anything of interest anywhere on the canals, understood?'

A chorus of 'Yes Guv's filled the room.

'Good. You've each got your assignments. Heads down please and don't come up until you have something.'

As the wider team got back to work, Phillips took a moment to pull her core team together in her office.

Bovalino was last in and closed the door behind him. 'I've been thinking, Guv.'

'Careful, big fella. You know it doesn't agree with you,' joked Jonesy.

Bovalino flipped Jones a V-sign. 'You mentioned that each of the victims had kids, and that maybe that could somehow be a link...'

'Yeah. So what?' said Phillips.

'Well, I think you might be right. I mean, they were all single mothers and they all lived alone.'

Phillips dropped into her chair and placed her hands on the side of her face. 'That's true, but if the kids are the link, how are they linked?'

Bovalino continued, 'Well, I was wondering if it could it be through Social Services?'

Phillips rubbed her open palms over her face, causing her skin to redden. 'Maybe, but again, how, Bov?'

'Could our killer have access to Social Service records?' Gibson chipped in.

Phillips looked incredulous. 'You think our killer is *working* for Social Services?'

'Maybe,' said Gibson.

Phillips wasn't buying it. 'So, someone whose job it is to protect kids is killing their mothers? That doesn't make any sense.'

'What if that's exactly why they're doing it, Guv? To protect the kids,' said Jones.

Phillips turned to him. 'You've lost me now.'

Jones sat forwards. 'Hear me out. As we know, each of the kids has been taken into care since their mothers were killed. What if that's what our killer wanted all along: the kids away from their drug addict mothers?'

'What? A killer with a conscience?' said Gibson.

'I know it sounds far-fetched,' Jones continued enthusiastically, 'but as we've got bugger-all else to go on, maybe it's worth a look?'

Phillips knew he was reaching, but he was right about one thing: it was worth a look. 'Well, it can't hurt. Entwistle, see if any of the girls are connected in any way through Social Services.'

Sitting opposite Phillips, Entwistle opened his laptop screen on his knees but said nothing for a moment, as if lost in thought. The team waited for him to acknowledge the request.

'Did you hear me?' prompted Phillips.

Entwistle was aware of all eyes on him. 'Sorry, Guv. I was just trying to figure out how I'd do that. There's no way I can access Social Service records without clearance from the organisation, and with strict safeguarding protocols to follow, that will take time.'

Phillips leant across the desk and stared Entwistle straight in the eye. 'Bureaucracy has never stopped you before. Come on. There must be a workaround we can access quickly.'

A second later, something seemed to spark in Entwistle as he sat to attention and began typing. 'Well, I may not have access to Social Service records, but I can at least cross-check the girls addresses against the different Social Service catchment areas. Let's see if they're all covered by one office or were allocated to different locations.'

Phillips smiled. 'Sounds like a good place to start.'

It took Entwistle a couple of minutes. 'Right, I've got something, but it's not good news, I'm afraid. Based on their home addresses, it looks like each of the girls would have been attached to different Social Services offices, so it's doubtful that could be the link.'

Jones shook his head. 'Bugger. That's a shame. I thought we might have been on to something there.'

Phillips placed both hands flat on the desk in front of her. 'It is a stretch, but let's not discard it completely. Not just yet, anyway. We need to keep an open mind on every possible angle.'

Each of the team nodded in unison.

'In the meantime, Jones and Bovalino, you go and see Candice Roberts's mum. See what you can find out from her. Did she have a boyfriend? Any changes in behaviour recently, etc.? I'll take Gibbo to see Adams's mum.'

'What about me, Guv?' said Entwistle.

'You stay here and keep digging into Social Services, see if there are any other ways they could be linked. And find out as much as you can on Manford Estates. Let's see if there's a more concrete connection than just the fact they were responsible for maintaining the girls' flats.'

Entwistle looked dejected, and Phillips suspected he wanted to spend more time with his new crush, Gibson. Sadly for love's young dream, they worked for the Major Crimes Unit, not a dating agency.

She checked her watch. 'It's 10 a.m. now. We'll aim to meet back here at 1 p.m. to debrief. Okay?'

They nodded, then each set off to complete their assignments.

18

The path to Fiona Adams's flat was covered with rubbish. There was even an old armchair, now sodden with rain, and a small rusted pink child's bike. The curtains were drawn behind the rotting ground-floor windows, and the front door looked like it had been repaired at some point. A large piece of chipboard had been screwed on to it, likely to cover a hole. With Gibson at her side, Phillips pressed the doorbell, but it made no sound. After a long moment, she banged on the door, repeating the process for several minutes. Finally they heard the lock move, and the door creaked open as a dishevelled older lady peeped out.

'Fiona Adams?'

'Who wants to know?'

Phillips flashed her ID, followed by Gibson. 'Detective Chief Inspector Phillips. This is Detective Sergeant Gibson.'

'I know who *she* is,' spat Adams.

Phillips continued, 'We're from the Major Crimes Unit and we'd like to talk to you about Sasha. May we come in?'

'Do I have a choice?' Adams left the door open as she retreated into the darkness.

The small flat was no more salubrious inside. Dirty plates and takeaway containers covered most of the surfaces, alongside overflowing ash trays and a homemade crack pipe. Adams didn't seem to care less that it was on show. She sat back in the battered old armchair and rolled a cigarette between her blackened fingernails before lifting it to her mouth. As she lit it with a match, her face was illuminated, bringing her ravaged features into focus – her skin, covered in spots and sores, her jaw sunken after losing most of her teeth. The few that remained were black and gnarled.

Phillips and Gibson took a seat next to each other on the small two-seater sofa which, having long since lost its springs, caused them to sink low into the frame. Adjusting her weight, Phillips sat forwards and pulled out her notepad and pen. 'When did you last see Sasha?'

Adams took a long drag from her cigarette and blew a plume of smoke across the room before shrugging her shoulders. 'Dunno. Last week I guess.'

'Could you be more specific?'

'Why does it matter? She's dead.'

'You don't seem overly upset, Fiona,' said Gibson.

Adams shot her a look of pure distain. 'Better her than me.'

Phillips couldn't believe it. 'Don't you care that your daughter is dead? That your granddaughter has been taken into care?'

Adams took another drag from her cigarette before answering. 'She's better off in care. Better than living like this.'

Phillips had to admit she had a point. 'We'd like to find out what Sasha was doing and who she was with the day she died.'

'Why does that matter? She drowned, didn't she?'

Phillips had no desire to share any of her suspicions with Adams. 'Yes she did, but we'd still like to know how she ended up in the water.'

'She was probably taking a shortcut. All the girls do it.'

Gibson cut in now. 'How long have you been working the streets, Fiona?'

'Too bloody long.'

'And have you ever taken that shortcut at Miles Platting?'

'Maybe, at some point. I can't remember, to be honest. It all looks the same up there.'

Phillips stepped back in and changed tack. 'Did Sasha have a pimp?'

'No. Neither of us did. Not worth the hassle. They're supposed to protect you, but they end up hurting you more than the punters. It's all Eastern Europeans now, and they're nasty bastards. No, she her took her chances on her own, just like I do.'

'These Eastern Europeans you mentioned. Do you know if they ever threatened Sasha?' said Phillips.

'No, but only cos she *didn't* work for 'em. They're full of charm when they're trying to get you on-side. Well known for it. It's once you're in their crew that they start beating on you.'

'And what about you? Have they tried to recruit you?'

Adams scoffed. 'They're not interested in old meat like me. They couldn't give a fuck about anyone over the age of thirty.'

Phillips's interest was piqued. 'And how old are you, Fiona?'

Adams blew out another plume of smoke. 'Forty-two.'

Thanks to the crack and life on the streets, she looked almost double that.

Phillips pressed on. 'Going back to Sasha's last few days. Is there anything you can recall, or think of, that might help us find out who she was with?'

Adams stubbed out her cigarette and began rolling another. 'Nothing. To be honest, we'd had a bit of a falling out a few months back and we'd not spoken since. I've seen her around like, up by the shops, but never said owt to her.'

'And what about your granddaughter?'

'What about her?'

'Have you seen her recently?

'No. I'm not good with kids, like.'

'Is that why you've not been assigned as her guardian?'

Adams shrugged her shoulder again. 'Probably.'

They were getting nowhere, so Phillips decided to cut her losses for the moment. She handed Adams her card. 'If you do think of anything that might help us, my number's on there. Please call me day or night, ok?'

Adams inspected the card without saying anything.

Phillips stood, and Gibson followed. 'Well, thank you for your time. We'll see ourselves out.'

Outside, as they walked back to the car, Phillips stopped and took a moment to look back at the grotty flat. 'It's no life, is it Gibbo?'

'No, Guv. It's bloody awful. She was right about one thing in there; at least the granddaughter has a chance at something better now.'

Phillips nodded. 'I hope so, I really do. But how many kids in care end up back on the streets, hey?'

Gibson looked forlorn. 'Too many, Guv. Far too many.'

19

Phillips and Gibson arrived back in the squad room just as Jones and Bovalino were taking off their thick winter coats. Jones hung his on the back of the chair. 'Bloody hell. I don't envy those girls being out in weather like this.'

Bovalino did the same, giving a shudder as he released his coat. 'Can you imagine how cold it must have been for them in the water?'

Whilst the wider team occupied the majority of the room, Phillips's core team had maintained their usual position in the corner just next to Phillips's office. Phillips strode into the space rubbing her hands together, followed by Gibson. 'Is someone gonna sort out a brew? I'm bloody freezing.'

Everyone looked at Entwistle, who took the hint. He blushed as he looked over at Gibson. 'Despite how it looks, Gibbo, I'm more than just a tea-boy, you know.'

Bovalino threw a ball of waste paper at him. 'Shut up and get the drinks in, lad.'

Five minutes later, Entwistle returned with a tray of hot drinks. Gibson had already dispensed a glass of water from the cooler and sat cradling it at the spare desk opposite Jones.

Phillips stuck a picture of Adams's dead body on the white-board outside her office and turned back to the team. 'So, what did you get from Roberts's mother?'

Bovalino took the initiative. 'She's a junkie like her daughter, but not a sex worker. She makes her money from begging up at Piccadilly each day.'

'And how has she taken Candice's death?' asked Phillips.

'Quite upset, but Jonesy and I got the sense it was more to do with the money she was losing as opposed to the fact her daughter had died. It seems Candice was paying the rent on the flat. Although, by the sounds of it she'd run into trouble of late and was in arrears.'

Entwistle chipped in. 'I looked into her finances. She was flat broke and had been threatened with eviction.'

Bovalino continued. 'The mother's terrified she's gonna be evicted herself now. She kept asking if we could put a word in with her landlord for her. It was quite sad, if truth be told.'

'Anything that might help us understand how Candice ended up in Miles Platting that night?'

'Nothing much, Guv. She said Candice went out as normal at around 9 p.m. but never came home. She did confirm she was wearing a coat when she left the house, though. With her description, we can at least start looking for it now. It might tell us something.'

Phillips nodded. 'Any lead's a *good* lead right now. Bov, get uniform up to Miles Platting and start the search for it, will you?'

'Consider it done, Guv.'

'Anything else?'

Jones shook his head. 'Nothing of any substance, Guv. Just that Candice's daughter had been taken into temporary care until the grandmother could get clean.'

'That'll never happen,' said Gibson. 'Once a junkie, always a junkie.'

Phillips tapped her pen on her teeth as she pondered what she'd heard. Eventually, she let out a loud sigh. 'Getting anything out of the mothers was always gonna be a long shot. Drug addicts aren't known for their razor-sharp memories after all.'

'So where next, Guv?' asked Jones.

'Let's start trawling CCTV footage of the red-light areas. See if we can turn up any useful footage from the nights the girls died.'

Jones raised his hand. 'I'll do that.'

'Thanks Jonesy.

'Entwistle, I need you to check the ANPR cameras. We're looking for all the cars that were in those areas the nights the girls died. Let's pull together a list and work our way through the drivers. See if any of them have form. In particular, we're looking for anyone with a record of sex crimes or violence against women. And get the girls' phones to the digital forensics team. I want all calls and text records since September, plus details of any social media activity. That's often a good window into someone's life.'

'Yes Guv.'

Phillips looked at her watch. 'It's two o'clock now. How fast can you pull that together?'

'Should have it by the end of the day.'

'Ok. Let's reconvene at 5 p.m. and see what we've got. Gibbo, can we talk in my office?'

A MOMENT LATER, as Phillips closed her office door, Entwistle caught Jones's attention. 'Gibbo seems nice, doesn't she?'

Jones nodded. 'Yeah. Bit tall for me, like. Probably more Bovalino's cup of tea.'

The big man looked up from his computer screen. 'What you saying about me?'

'Entwistle was just saying he fancies Gibbo—'

'I didn't say that *exactly*.'

'And I said she's too tall for me. She's more *your* type, you big lump.'

Bovalino smiled and shook his head. 'Not me mate. From what I hear, she's into black guys.'

Entwistle's eyes widened. 'Is she?'

'Yeah. And in particular, mixed-race.'

'So you gonna ask her out, then?' said Jones.

Entwistle blushed, a half smile on his face. 'Nar. Work relationships aren't good, are they?' His question sounded more hopeful than damning.

Jones sat forwards, his voice a conspiratorial whisper. 'Ordinarily I'd agree with you, but she's on secondment. So she'll be out of here in a month. If you fancy her, you should go for it.'

'But what about the Guv?'

'What about her?'

'Won't she be pissed off?'

'Well, *she* doesn't fancy you,' joked Bovalino.

'Piss off! *I mean,* won't she be angry if two of her squad started dating?'

'Not a bit,' said Jones, glancing at Bovalino. 'She won't mind, will she, Bov?'

'Not at all. She'll be totally fine with it.'

Entwistle looked over towards Phillips's office, where she and Gibbo were deep in conversation. He smiled and nodded, then turned his attention back to his screen. He whistled cheerfully as he began typing.

Jones and Bovalino exchanged winks and wide grins. He'd played right into their hands.

∿

AFTER HOURS GLUED to her desk, Phillips noticed a number of the uniformed support team had begun switching off their PCs and started putting on their coats. She checked her watch. It was coming up to 6 p.m. She had been so engrossed in her work she'd lost track of time. She wandered back into the main office and nodded as each of the uniformed officers passed her with a 'Night Ma'am.'

In the heart of the room, Jones, Bovalino, Gibson and Entwistle remained engrossed in their work.

'How you getting on with that list, Entwistle?'

'So far I have fifty vehicles spotted on the ANPR cameras in the red-light zones the nights they died.'

'Well, let's start with them, shall we. Can you print them off?'

Whilst the team waited for the list of names, Phillips walked back to her office to fetch her laptop, and returned a moment later. She perched on the end of the desk next to Entwistle. 'Let's take ten names each and see what we can find on them.'

Entwistle divided up the sheets and handed them out ten apiece.

'I don't need to tell you guys that, so far, all the evidence suggests nothing more than that the girls drowned. Even though these cases are a priority, Fox will only let the investigation continue for so long. When you check these names, the smallest detail on the driver history could be the difference between the cases being closed and catching a killer. So, look hard and highlight anything unusual. Anything at all.'

The team nodded and turned their attention back to their respective computer screens.

An hour of intense silence followed, punctuated by the sound of fingers tapping on keyboards and computer mice clicking back and forth.

'Guv, take a look at this.'

Phillips got up, walked over to Jones's desk and leaned in to get a look at his screen.

Jones pointed to the data. 'This number plate appeared on the night Roberts was killed.'

'And?'

'Well, if you look at the cameras, you can see it's attached to a Ford Mondeo, right?'

Phillips nodded.

'If you click on the vehicle details, that plate is registered to a Volkswagen Jetta.'

'Fake plates,' said Phillips.

Bovalino, Entwistle and Gibson stopped what they were doing and looked over towards Phillips.

'Not only that,' Jones continued, 'but the Jetta is officially registered as off the road. Look – it has a SORN against it.'

'Now we're getting somewhere. Entwistle, can you cross-check all the cars on the list against the SORN database? Let's see if this is the only one.'

Entwistle wasted no time accessing the Statutory Off Road Notification database, and within a few minutes had found two more. He turned his screen to face Phillips and Jones before clicking on the two registrations. 'Both these plates belong to cars that are officially off the road.' He clicked the screen again. 'And yet they appeared on the nights Adams and Webster died. This one, M-J-64, was captured in Cheetham Hill when Adams went missing, whereas Y-T-12 was on the inner ring road in the early hours of the morning when Webster was found.'

Phillips leaned in closer to have a better look. 'Can you pull up the images of the vehicles they were attached to. Let's see what make of cars we have.'

A flurry of movement followed, and two grainy images appeared on Entwistle's screen – both of a blue Ford Mondeo.

'Bloody hell! It looks like the same car using different plates,' said Jones.

Phillips slammed her hand on the desk in front of her. 'Guys, I think we've just found our killer.' A wide grin spread across her face as she stared at the screen in front of her. 'Entwistle, print out the different images of the cars, will you?'

Entwistle did as requested and handed them to Phillips. She examined them closely. Based on the quality of the images and the fact the pictures had been taken at night, it was difficult to make out too much detail. 'I agree with Jonesy. Looks like the same car with different plates. What do you think?' Phillips handed the printouts to Gibson, who inspected them in silence.

'So, what happened to the original cars the plates came from?' said Bovalino.

'I can soon find out.' Entwistle began tapping away on his laptop.

Gibson finished looking at the images and handed them to Jones. 'It looks like the same car to me. Hard to tell for sure, though.'

'Well, here's a coincidence,' said Entwistle. 'The plates are all registered to cars that were bought by Adders Scrap Metal Merchants in Ancoats.'

'And what do I always say about coincidence?' asked Phillips.

'No such thing, Guv,' Jones, Bovalino and Entwistle answered in unison and with gusto.

'No-such-fucking-thing,' repeated Phillips.

'I know the guy who owns that scrap yard,' Gibson cut in. 'Adwadil Bahmani. Everyone calls him Adders for short. SCT have been watching him for a long time. We suspect the business is a front for drugs and sex-trafficking, but so far we've not been able to prove a thing. Word on the street is Bahmani is a bad man.'

'Maybe you and I should pay him a visit tomorrow. See what he has to say about the plates?'

Gibson shook her head. 'No point, Guv. He's a grade-A misogynist. He doesn't speak to women. He's far more inclined to talk to Jones and Bovalino, and in particular Bov. It's a Pakistani cultural thing. They respect masculine men.'

'Are you saying I'm not masculine enough, Gibbo?' Jones faked appearing upset and affected a camp voice, drawing laughs from the room.

'Not at all, Jonesy. I can see you're *all man*.'

Jones grinned.

Phillips turned to Gibson. 'Is this Adders guy under SCT surveillance at the minute?'

'Nothing active, Guv, so it's safe to go in.'

'Ok. In that case, Jonesy and Bov, first thing tomorrow I want you up at that scrap yard. Shake his tree a little and let's see if anything falls out.'

Jones and Bovalino nodded.

Phillips tapped Jonesy on the shoulder and locked eyes with Entwistle. 'Good work, you two. I knew these cases had to be linked, and we're getting closer to finding out how.' She picked up her laptop and headed for her office.

Gibson stood up. 'I need a cigarette.'

Entwistle's eyes followed her as she walked across the room and stepped out into the corridor.

'You gonna ask her out or what?' said Jones.

Entwistle's head shot round to face him. 'You really think I should?'

'Get it done, lad,' said Bovalino.

Jones pointed to the doorway. '*Carpe Diem*, son. Seize the day.'

Entwistle said nothing for a moment, clearly deep in thought. Then a wide grin spread across his face and he leapt from his chair. 'You're right, Jonesy. *Carpe Diem*. I'm gonna do it.' A moment later, he left the room.

PHILLIPS SAW Entwistle shoot past her door just before she heard loud cackles from Jones and Bovalino. Curious, she walked back into the squad room to find them huddling against the window that overlooked the car park. She stood behind them for a moment, watching.

'He's doing it, Bov, he's bloody doing it.'

'The gullible bastard,' said Bovalino.

'What are you two up to now?'

Both men turned to face Phillips. With their wide grins, they resembled naughty schoolboys.

Jones laughed. 'We persuaded Entwistle to ask Gibbo on a date, Guv.'

'As in *DS Gibson*?'

'Yeah,' said Bovalino.

'DS Gibson who's *gay*?'

Jones nodded and giggled before turning back to look out the window. 'Shit. They're coming back up.'

Both men shot back to their desks and tried their best to look as if they had no idea what had just taken place in the car park. Their heaving shoulders and barely disguised grins said otherwise.

Phillips stood with her arms folded and watched as Gibson walked confidently into the squad room and sat down. She said nothing.

A moment later, Entwistle crept in looking a little embarrassed, and took a seat at his desk.

No one said a word. Phillips broke the ice. 'Everything all right, Entwistle?' she asked.

Jones and Bovalino couldn't contain themselves any longer.

They both cracked up, guffawing loudly. Gibson followed suit, and all three turned to look at Entwistle.

'You total bastards!' he said, sulking before finally beginning to laugh himself.

Phillips joined in too, before walking over and patting him on the shoulder. 'Aww, Entwistle. I think you need to work on your skills as a detective, sunshine.'

Gibson laughed. 'I couldn't agree more, Guv. I mean, come on Entwistle. I'm flattered, but how could you not tell I'm gay?'

20

Bovalino pulled the unmarked squad car up to the open gates of Adders Scrap Metal Merchants. With Jones beside him in the passenger seat, they surveyed the site for a few moments, taking in the high fences with the heavy curls of razor wire looping along the top.

'Do you get the feeling Mr Bahmani doesn't like unexpected visitors, Bov?'

Bovalino leaned forwards over the steering wheel and looked up at the foreboding entrance, 'Certainly looks that way, Jonesy. I just hope he hasn't got a bloody big dog.'

Jones chuckled. 'Or worse still; *two* bloody big dogs.'

Bovalino drove through the gate and the car pitched and bounced from side to side across the rough terrain, accompanied by the soundtrack of dirty rainwater splashing up from the puddles below. They stopped just in front of a grubby Portakabin, parking up next to a large white Range Rover with blackened windows and sparkling metal rims. As they stepped out onto the oil-stained, weather-beaten asphalt, two large German Shepherds ran out from the side of the makeshift building and began barking. Mercifully they were tethered on thick ropes that kept Jones and Bovalino just out of reach.

'What is it with scrap merchants and big dogs?' Bovalino complained, 'I bloody *hate* big dogs!'

Both men stood motionless, watching the powerful barking beasts for some time before a heavily built man appeared at the open door. He shouted something in Urdu at the dogs and they circled back round to the rear of the building.

An unexpected full grin spread across the man's thick-bearded face. 'Gentlemen. What can I do for the Greater Manchester Police?' His accent was a mixture of Pakistani and thick Mancunian.

'How do you know we're police?'

'Cars are my business, sir, and I can spot a cop car a mile off. Plus, you don't look like my usual customers. I mean, no one wears shoes like yours in a place as mucky as this, do they?'

In spite of himself, Jones glanced down at his feet and noted the man had a point; his black brogues were covered up the sides and across the toes in mud and salt. 'Are you Mr Bahmani?'

He nodded. 'Aye, but everyone calls me Adders.'

Jones stepped forwards and flashed his ID. 'DS Jones and DC Bovalino. Can we ask you few questions?'

Bahmani eyed them with suspicion. 'What about?'

'Fake plates,' said Bovalino.

Bahmani glanced at Bovalino. 'I don't sell fake plates. *That's illegal.*'

Jones opted to lie. 'We're not investigating you, Mr Bahmani, but we believe someone has stolen plates from a couple of your decommissioned cars. We'd like to see those cars, if we can.'

Bahmani remained defiant, his large frame filling the door. 'You got a warrant? I know my rights, like.'

Jones had to bite his tongue. If he had a pound for every

wannabe gangster who'd watched an American cop show and now believed they knew the law, he'd have retired years ago.

It was cold in the wind and he was getting pissed off. He looked over at Bovalino and sensed he felt the same. 'We're not here to search your offices. We're just seeking information on vehicles that are registered to this business. All we need is ten minutes of your time and then we'll be on our way.'

Bahmani stared at Jones in silence for a moment, then nodded. 'You'd better come in, lads.'

The office inside was surprisingly warm and well presented. In contrast to the filthy yard outside, it was clean and well decorated with modern office furniture and artistic black and white photos of Bahmani surrounded by several children, with an attractive looking woman smiling beside him.

'My wife and kids.'

'Looks like a big brood,' said Jones.

The grin returned. 'Three boys and two girls, plus another due any day now.'

Jones exhaled theatrically. 'Wow. You're a glutton for punishment.'

'Naw. The wife and her mother look after them. I just earn the money. Keeps me out of the house.' Bahmani took a seat and signalled for Jones and Bovalino to take the chairs opposite him.

Bovalino took out his notepad.

'Is the scrapyard your only source of income?' Jones asked

'Naw, mate. I have a few houses and a couple of phone shops too. I like to keep the money coming in from different businesses, just in case one of the others doesn't work out. It's the Pakistani way.'

'How many people do you have working for you across each of the businesses?'

Bahmani thought for a moment. 'I dunno. Maybe ten in total. Mainly family.'

'And how many in the yard?'

'Just me and my cousin Tahir. I buy the cars and he pulls them apart.' He pointed through the window behind Jones. 'That's him driving the forklift'

Jones and Bovalino turned in unison and watched for a moment as an old Honda was raised from the ground on the arms of the forklift. Jones turned back to Bahmani. 'Do you keep records of all the cars you buy and dispose of?'

'Got to. It's illegal not to, innit?' He tapped the wafer-thin monitor attached to his state-of-the-art PC. 'It's all on here.'

'Great. Would you mind checking a couple of registrations for us?' said Jones.

Bahmani pulled the keyboard closer, and Jones noted the heavy gold rings on his fingers and the large-linked gold chain fastened loosely around his right wrist. 'What's the first one?'

As Jones read out the registration, Bahmani typed, the chain clinking against the desk as he did. They repeated the process until all three cars had been located in the files. 'Sorry lads; those cars have all been scrapped,' said Bahmani. He looked pleased with that fact.

Jones did his best to hide his frustration. 'When was that?'

'Looks like it was just last week.'

'And did you know the plates were missing when you scrapped them?'

'I don't often see the cars once I've paid for 'em. Tahir does all that.'

'Can we speak to Tahir, then?' Bovalino asked.

'He doesn't speak English.'

Bovalino stared Bahmani straight in the eye. 'Then you can translate, can't you?'

Bahmani stared back for a moment before getting up and walking over to the open door. He whistled and shouted something in Urdu, and the forklift engine died. A moment later, Tahir appeared in front of the office but remained outside.

Another blast of Urdu followed. Jones could see Tahir shaking his head and shrugging his shoulders before turning away and walking back to the forklift. The noisy engine burst into life once more. Bahmani returned to his chair. 'He can't remember.'

Jones found it hard to believe that was the sum total of the interaction they'd just witnessed, but again contained his frustration. 'So he doesn't remember scrapping the cars, or he doesn't remember seeing the registration plates?'

Bahmani sat forwards and tapped his right temple with his index finger. 'My cousin isn't very bright, I'm afraid. I only gave him this job because my mother asked me to, as a favour to her sister. Don't get me wrong; he's good at it. He's a strong boy. But he's not blessed with brains. Plus, he's come here straight from Islamabad and doesn't speak a word of English. He couldn't tell one British plate from another. It's a big yard and customers are free to roam looking for parts as they wish. Obviously I can't sell second-hand plates, so they just get chucked in the bins at the back of the site. The bins aren't locked and are out of sight of the office. Any one of my customers could have picked them up. The plates could be anywhere by now.'

Jones suspected Bahmani knew far more than he was letting on, but without due cause, there was nothing they could do to compel him to share whatever information he was keeping to himself.

'What about CCTV? I notice you have cameras on the main street.'

Bahmani placed his finger against his thick lips. 'Don't tell anyone, but they're dummies.'

The man had an answer for everything.

'So why are you so interested in these plates? What have they been used for?

Jones played it cool. 'They were recently spotted on the Automatic Number Plate Registration cameras, but the vehicles didn't match what we had on file.'

Bahmani appeared intrigued. 'You can see all that through the cameras, can you?'

'Yes. In some cases we can even see who's driving,' Jones said, studying Bahmani's face for any changes or movements that would indicate guilt or fear. He saw nothing aside from his lop-sided grin.

'I'd better make sure I stick to the speed limits then, hadn't I?' Bahmani checked his chunky, glistening gold watch. Jones saw that it was a Rolex. 'If there's nothing else, lads, I've gotta get on. All them kids to feed. You know how it is.'

Outside, Jones and Bovalino stood by the squad car and scanned the yard. It looked like any one of the scrap merchant yards littered around the city, but Jones suspected there was lot more going on here than met the eye. They climbed into the car together, shutting out the cold and the noise of the forklift.

'What d'ya reckon, Jonesy?'

'I can see why SCT are interested in him. You can just tell he's crooked. That watch he was wearing is worth about twenty grand and that's a hundred-grand Range Rover he's driving. The scrap metal trade is lucrative, but I doubt the yard makes that kind of cash.'

'Ok. So he's crooked. But is he a killer?'

'I dunno, Bov. I just don't know. If he's into trafficking, as SCT suspect, then maybe the girls' deaths are linked to that. But how do we prove it?'

'Feels like we're finding more dead ends than answers on this one.'

Jones nodded and stared out the window towards the Portakabin. 'Come on. Let's get back to the station and update the guys. Let's hope they've had a more successful morning than we have.'

21

Phillips sat in her office, looking out at the trees blowing in the wind. Bruce Springsteen's 'Santa Claus Is Coming To Town' played on the small radio on her desk.

Little Ajay Webster was on her mind once again. He was lucky enough to have his grandparents to look after him now, and she hoped he would soon adjust to life without his mother – without needing to go into care.

Jones and Bovalino walking back into the squad room caught her attention, and she called them over. Neither looked happy. 'How'd you get on?'

'Nothing on the plates, Guv. All three cars were scrapped last week and he has no idea what happened to the plates after that.'

Phillips dropped her clenched fist on the desk. 'Bollocks, bollocks, bollocks.'

Just then, Gibbo walked in. 'So how was the charming Adders Bahmani?'

Bovalino dropped into one of the chairs opposite Phillips. 'He's a proper smarmy bastard, isn't he?'

'Yep. And I bet he had an answer for everything?' said Gibson.

Jones hitched his buttocks onto a small filing cabinet behind him. 'He's crooked, that's for sure, but you can tell he's good at covering his tracks.'

Gibson folded her arms, standing tall with her feet wide apart. 'We've been after him for years now. Drugs, prostitution, trafficking, money laundering. You name it, we believe he's up to his eyeballs in it. Proving it, however; that's a very different matter.'

'How the hell do these guys manage to keep the trails behind them so clean?' said Bovalino.

'Well, with Adders, he's the master of utilising his own culture to keep outsiders *out*. You never see him with anyone other than his trusted lieutenants or his family. We've used all manner of snitches over the years, but none could get near him. It's a closed shop. And he's a nasty bastard too. Again, we can't prove anything, but the one person who did break rank and spoke to us was found dead. Hanged in his garage with his tongue missing. We never did find it.'

'Maybe he fed it to those bloody big dogs of his,' said Bovalino.

Gibson chuckled. 'I wouldn't put it past him.'

Entwistle walked into the office holding a pile of papers, and Phillips opened her arms dramatically. 'Here he is. MCU's very own Lothario, DC Entwistle.'

The team laughed along.

Entwistle blushed. 'I'm never gonna live this down, am I?'

Jones patted him on the shoulder. 'Don't worry, son. We'll soon forget. Just give it a couple of years.'

Phillips grinned. 'So, lover-boy. What you got for us?'

'Well, the digital forensics have come back on Roberts's and Adams's phones. Webster's was too damaged.' Entwistle laid a number of pages out across Phillips's desk. They were printouts from social media accounts. 'These were posted on Candice Roberts's Facebook account a couple of years ago.'

Bovalino leaned in to get a better look. 'Seems like any other twenty-something's social media. Pouting and posing for selfies.'

'Check Bov out, knowing all the lingo,' said Phillips.

He smiled at her. 'What can I say? I'm down with the kids, Guv.'

'I don't doubt it, Bov. So, why are these images important?'

Entwistle tapped his finger on one of the pictures. It was of Candice Roberts drinking in a bar or club with her arms wrapped round a good-looking blond guy. He looked to be about the same age as her. 'This fella has been tagged on this picture. You can see his name at the bottom there – Billy Armitage.'

Phillips took a closer look.

'Billy Armitage is one of the few people she bothered to tag, so I figured he must have been important to her. I ran all the Billy Armitages we had in the system, but none of them look like this guy.'

Phillips couldn't hide her disappointment.

'But then I had an idea to run that name through the ANPR database. Guess whose car comes up night after night in the red-light districts – including the night Webster died?'

'Please tell me it's Billy Armitage?'

A grin spread across Entwistle's face, making him look like the cat that had got the cream. 'It is, Guv.'

Phillips clapped her hands. 'Entwistle, I could kiss you!'

'Steady on, Guv. You know what he's like with the ladies,' joked Bovalino

Phillips grabbed the printout and studied it for a long moment. 'So, what about his car? Is it a Mondeo?'

Entwistle handed over another image. It was a grainy picture of a car taken by one of the ANPR cameras. 'I'm afraid not. He drives a twenty-year-old Audi A4. Metallic silver.'

'That's a shame. But he could still have been driving the Mondeo. It's easy enough to swap cars without being seen in those areas. Ok. What else do we know about him?'

Entwistle read down the file in front of him. 'He's twenty-six. Lives in East Manchester and works as a painter and decorator. He was arrested for assault when he was twenty-one, but the charges were later dropped because of insufficient evidence.'

'Was the assault against a man or a woman?' said Gibson.

Entwistle checked the file. 'Erm, a man. Armitage and another guy got into a fight in a pub after a Man City – Man United derby game.'

Gibson seemed satisfied with the answer.

'Anything else?' said Phillips.

'Er, just that he's single and lives alone, Guv.'

Jones drummed the side of the filing cabinet with his fingers. 'When was his car last spotted on the cameras?'

Entwistle pointed to the picture on the desk in front of Phillips. 'That image is from last night, but he's been captured up there every night in the last couple of weeks.'

Phillips sat to attention. 'Right, if he is our guy, it looks like he's searching for his next victim. There's no time to waste. I want surveillance on him tonight. Whatever you had planned, cancel it.'

Each of the team agreed.

'We'll use a relay formation and split into three teams. Gibbo, you take someone from the support team and go first. Jones and Bovalino, you take the second leg. Entwistle, you're with me on the final leg. Everyone happy with that?'

It seemed as though Gibbo wasn't.

'Something on your mind, Gibson?' asked Phillips.

'If it's all right with you, could I call in one of the guys from

SCT? No offence to the wider team, but if this is our killer, I'd rather have experience in the car when I'm tailing him.'

'Do you have anyone in mind?'

'Don Mountfield. Over twenty years on the job, ten of those in SCT.'

Phillips thought it over for a moment. 'It's a shame not to expose one of the wider team to this kind of operation, but I take your point on experience. I'll call Atkins and see if we can get Mountfield for the night.'

Gibson smiled. 'Thanks, Guv. I'd appreciate it.'

Phillips clapped her hands together. 'Right guys. Call home if you need to and make your excuses. Get something to eat and let's get ready to catch this bastard. We'll reconvene for the briefing at five.'

22

It was just before 9.30 p.m. and the three unmarked squad cars were parked up, waiting for the surveillance operation on Billy Armitage to begin. As planned, Gibson would take the first leg of the relay-formation, so she was positioned outside Armitage's flat on a small council estate in Salford, just west of Manchester city centre. Thanks to DCI Atkins, she had her colleague from SCT, DC Don Mountfield, with her for the operation.

Phillips and Entwistle had pulled up half a mile from Armitage's flat. Jones and Bovalino were parked next to them, ready for the off. Once the operation started, each team would follow at a distance. When Gibson had tailed Armitage for about five minutes, she would leave the pursuit at a natural junction and allow Jones and Bovalino to move up behind the target. The same manoeuvre would be repeated with Phillips and Entwistle five minutes after that. If the surveillance continued for a long period of time, then they would rotate through the team for as long as necessary. However, according to Entwistle's detailed ANPR data, Armitage was a creature of habit, navigating the same route each night before parking up in Cheetham Hill. If he followed his usual routine, they anticipated he would arrive at his destination within fifteen minutes of leaving his home.

Phillips picked up the radio. 'Ok guys. We're hoping for eyes on Armitage any minute now. Is everyone ready?' She glanced sideways and noted Jones and Bovalino nodding in time with their verbal response.

'Ready and willing, Guv,' said Jones.

There was no response from Gibson. Phillips waited a moment before speaking again, 'Gibson, do you copy?'

Silence.

'What the fuck?' Phillips mumbled as she pulled out her mobile phone to call Gibson.

'Sorry, Guv. I'm here.'

'Gibbo! Is everything ok?'

'We've got a problem, Guv. It's Mountfield. He's really sick.'

'What do you mean "he's really sick"?'

'He's just this minute hurled himself out of the car and started projectile vomiting.'

'Vomiting?'

'Yes, Guv. He seemed fine when I picked him up an hour ago.'

'Has anyone seen you? Has your position been compromised?'

There was a pause at the other end. Gibson finally spoke again. *'No Guv. I don't think so.'*

Phillips checked her watch. It was now past 9.30 p.m. and they expected Armitage to make his move any second now. *Shit.* 'Do what you have to to contain Mountfield and keep your eyes on Armitage. I'm coming over with Entwistle to replace you. We'll have to operate with a two-car relay.'

Gibson sounded embarrassed and harassed. *'I'm sorry. This doesn't paint the best picture of SCT.'*

'Do you want us to follow you, Guv?' Jones chimed in.

Phillips looked over to him and nodded. 'Armitage's flat,' she said to Entwistle. 'Fast as you can. Go, go, go.'

Just as the cars moved away, Gibson resurfaced. *'Guv. I have eyes on Armitage and he's on the move.'*

'Shit. That's all we need.' Phillips indicated for Entwistle to stop the car whilst she figured out their next move. Jones and Bovalino passed by a moment later. 'Can you follow him Gibbo?'

'Mountfield is still being sick.'

'Fuck Mountfield!' Phillips was struggling to sympathise with the man jeopardising their chance to catch their prime suspect. 'If he's not well enough to travel, leave him behind. We'll send a uniform car for him. *Just don't lose Armitage.'*

'Roger, Guv. Mountfield's a mess. He's gonna have to stay here.'

'Do you still have eyes on the target?'

There was another frustrating pause, and Phillips's heart began to pound.

Gibson broke the tension a moment later. *'Armitage is on the move and so am I. We're heading out of his estate now, turning left onto Seedly Terrace.'* There was silence for a moment. *'He's indicating left onto Langworthy Road, just by the medical centre.'*

'We'll follow the route as planned, guys,' Phillips announced, and Entwistle set off, ready for their turn in the relay.

Radio silence followed for about a minute. Gibson broke the silence. *'He's taking a right onto Eccles Old Road and heading down towards Broad Street.'*

'He's following his usual route, Guv,' said Entwistle as they raced to catch up with Gibson. Jones and Bovalino were about two hundred metres ahead of them.

'Jonesy, do you have eyes on Gibson and the target?'

'Yes, Guv. They've stopped at traffic lights so we're staying a safe distance back. But it's a clear road, so we can see them.'

Phillips's heart rate began to settle, and she relaxed as far as her nerves would allow on a surveillance operation. With so many unknown variables, she was alert and acutely aware of everything that might cause an issue.

She then remembered Mountfield and the fact he needed picking up. Now the operation was back on track, she felt a pang of guilt for the way she had reacted earlier. She called it in and arranged for a uniformed team to pick him up, then returned her full focus to the operation.

'I'm stepping down. Jones, do you have the target in sight?' asked Gibson, coming to the end of her leg of the surveillance.

'Target is in sight,' Jones responded. *'You're green for go, Gibbo. We are now taking the lead.'*

'Roger that, Jones. I'm looping round and back behind the Guv,' said Gibson.

The next five minutes passed without incident, and then it was Phillips and Entwistle's turn to take the lead when Jones and Bovalino pulled off the road at the junction of Great Cheetham Street East and Bury New Road.

'We have eyes on Armitage,' said Phillips as they moved in behind his car. 'If he sticks to his normal routine, we can expect him to pull up in the next few minutes. Stay close but stay back. We don't want to spook him.'

As expected, Armitage followed the road round to the right as it became Elizabeth Street, before merging left onto Queens Road, then heading up to Cheetham Hill, where he began to slow but continued moving.

'Ok, guys, looks like he's slowing down. We'll stay with him. Jones and Bovalino, I want you guys to switch places with Gibbo. If he moves off, you take the lead and Entwistle and I will follow you. Gibbo, you park up out of sight and wait in case we need you again. I'd rather not put you at risk on your own, but I don't want to lose this guy either. Everybody clear?'

'Yes Guv,' said Jones.

'*Received and understood. I'm standing by, Guv,*' added Gibson.

Phillips closed the link to the radio and took a deep breath for a moment. She let it out before returning to the radio. 'Right, guys. Stay sharp. I want Armitage in custody *tonight*.'

23

There's nothing random about who I pick up and where I find them. It's all part of my well-crafted plan. Each one has been selected to meet God in the *next* life so they can answer for their sins from *this* life. Estelle Henderson is where she always stands. She's wearing a cheap fake fur coat over a micro mini skirt. Her long, pale, blotchy white legs run into prerequisite street-walker footwear: almost vertical high heels with platform soles. Her greasy home-dyed hair has changed colour again. It's bright red now.

I pull the car up and roll down the window, the universal signal that I'm 'looking for business.'

'Twenty quid for oral and thirty for full sex,' she says, chewing gum. I can't be sure if she thinks it's sexy or whether she's just ignorant. Looking at her up close, and hearing her speak, I presume it's both.

I tell her I want full oral and open the door for her. She jumps in beside me and the interior light casts a warm glow across her face. For a split second I forget where I am and what I'm here to do. *She almost looks human.*

'I know a nice quiet little place.' I tell her as she closes the door and darkness returns to the car.

ARMITAGE'S CAR crawled to a stop about two hundred meters ahead of Phillips and Entwistle, who reacted and pulled to the side of the road to remain undetected. Phillips radioed through to Jones and Bovalino, who followed suit and parked up in the shadows, awaiting further instructions.

Up ahead, a young girl stood on the pavement to the left of Armitage. The glow of the street light accentuated the angles of her face. She moved towards the car and bent down to speak through the open window. The conversation lasted no more than a minute before she opened the passenger door and got in. The interior of the car illuminated as she did so, but soon faded away.

Phillips's heart raced as her adrenaline spiked. 'She's in the car, guys. Jones and Bovalino, standby.'

'*Roger that, Guv. Standing by,*' said Jones.

THE FIRST FEW minutes after I pick up a girl are without doubt the most nerve-wracking. When I stop to agree the price, I always try to keep one eye on my surroundings, but it's very difficult on the dark streets in this part of town. It's in these fleeting moments while the car is stationary that the police can adopt radio-silence and sneak up on you.

As I pull the car away from the curb, my heart pounds and my eyes dart from my wing mirrors to the rear-view mirror, looking for any signs that I am being followed. I see nothing, but it always pays to be cautious. I zig-zag through the streets for a few more minutes, then double back on myself, just to be sure, before heading off towards the canal.

'Jesus!' Estelle jumps with fright in her seat as a thin voice crackles through the small speaker. 'What the fuck's that?'

'A police scanner,' I reply coolly, keeping my eyes on my mirrors.

'What do you need that for?' She sounds tense.

'Curb crawling is a crime. And I don't know about you, but I'd prefer *not* to get caught.'

This seems to satisfy her for a few minutes and she quietens, listening to the radio and yet another bloody Christmas song.

As ever, my route is mapped in advance to avoid the ANPR cameras, but if you use any well-maintained road, there is still a chance a mobile camera fixed in a squad car can catch you unawares. Thank God I've not seen any so far tonight. When we turn onto the back streets near the canal, I feel a sense of relief. I've already recced this area and I'm certain there are no ANPR cameras down here. And with no occupied offices or industrial units to worry about, CCTV won't be an issue either.

The car lops from side to side across the rough cobbles and potholes for a few minutes. Estelle is getting nervous again. 'Where are we going?'

I smile at her. 'I told you; somewhere quiet.'

She's agitated, glancing around at the dark world that surrounds the car. 'There was loads of places back there we could have used. What the fuck are we doing all the way down here?'

'This place is special,' I say, without looking at her.

⁓

BOVALINO LOVES cars and loves to drive. It's what he does in his spare time. He's also been trained to the highest level of advanced and tactical driving with the police.

Jones was grateful for his exceptional skills as they tracked Armitage through the back streets of Manchester. Their target had driven with caution since picking up the girl, evidently trying to avoid being noticed by any passing patrol cars.

Armitage indicated left and pulled off the main road, heading towards the industrial units near Miles Platting.

Bovalino followed his car, keeping at a safe distance and switching off his headlights to avoid detection.

Up ahead, Armitage pulled his car to a stop. The brake lights glowed in the darkness for a moment before all the car's lights were turned off.

'He's stopped and parked up, Guv,' said Jones over the radio.

'What's your location?' asked Phillips.

Bovalino slowed down and pulled the car left and out of sight in the shadows of one of the derelict industrial units, coming to a stop.

'He's taken her to the canal near Ancoats. The same place Candice Roberts's body was found,' said Jones.

'Do you have eyes on him?'

Jones raised his night-vision binoculars to his face. 'Yes, Guv. He's with the girl. Nothing's happening at the moment. They're talking. Looks like it's getting a bit heated.'

'Maybe the girl's got spooked by the location. We're en route to you now. We'll approach from the south and stay out of sight, ready to go in as soon as you give us the signal.'

'Roger that, Guv.'

I PARK the car and kill the engine, which turns off the radio. Silence fills the car, aside from the odd burst of activity on the police scanner, but I've turned it down so it's just about audible. I stare at Estelle for a long moment, saying nothing. I can tell she's nervous and unsure of both me and her surroundings.

'Why the fuck have you brought me all the way down here?'

I remain silent and continue to stare at her.

'Look, I've changed my mind. I don't want to do this.'

'Don't you need the money, Estelle?'

Shock spreads across her face. 'How do you know my name?'

'Oh, I know all about you, Estelle. Who you fuck each night, where you buy your drugs, where you live with your son, Cooper.'

Fear is etched across her face. Even in the darkness, I can see her eyes bulging.

She begins yanking at the door handle. It's no use. I control the central locking and it's locked from my side.

'Let me out! Let me out!' she screams hysterically.

'Don't worry, Estelle, I'll let you out. You see, we're going for a little walk down to the canal.' I pull my gun and jam it into her ribs.

She panics now, throwing herself back against the passenger door, desperate to open it.

'*Ok, guys. We're in position about a hundred meters to your rear. We can see you, and Armitage in the distance,*' Phillips's voice chimed over the radio.

Jones sensed the tension mounting in the car they watched as he continued observing Armitage through the night-vision binoculars he held in his left hand; the radio in his right. A moment later, his instincts were proven right. 'Fuck! She's just lashed out at him, Guv. Looks like she's trying to get out of the car, but it's locked. We're going in!'

'*Go! Go! Go!*' replied Phillips.

Bovalino gunned the engine and the sound of screeching tyres filled the night air. Activating full beam on the headlights, he raced the car up the street and skidded sideways, blocking Armitage's car from moving. Phillips and Entwistle arrived a split second later, just as Jones and Bovalino rushed from their vehicle. Bovalino pulled his baton as he reached the driver's door. Jones arrived at the passenger door a second later, a heavy-duty flashlight trained on the two occupants.

'Out of the car now!' Jones commanded.

Both passengers raised their hands in surrender before the driver released the central locking and they each climbed out.

Phillips and Entwistle arrived just as Jones began cautioning Armitage.

'Billy Armitage, I am arresting you on suspicion of the murders of Candice Roberts, Chantelle Webster and Sasha Adams...'

Bovalino pressed Armitage up against the car and began to pat him down as he protested, 'You don't know what you're talking about. I haven't done anything!'

Phillips approached the girl and prepared to search her. 'You got any needles on you?'

The girl didn't speak, but shook her head.

Phillips frisked her and pulled a bank card from her small purse. 'Chloe Barnes. Is that you?'

The girl remained silent.

'Look, you can play that game all you like, but it won't take long for us to figure out who you are. So why not just co-operate and make it easier on yourself, huh? So I'll ask you again. Are you Chloe Barnes?'

The girl nodded.

'See. That wasn't so difficult, was it,' said Phillips, and handed her over to Entwistle. 'Put her in our car. She's coming back to Ashton House with us.'

Entwistle obliged, then jumped in the driver's seat.

Armitage continued to protest his innocence, but Bovalino paid him no attention as he slapped him in handcuffs and frog-marched him to their waiting car.

Phillips followed them. 'Good job, guys.'

'Thanks, Guv, but it was a team effort.'

'Oh shit. Thanks for the reminder, Jonesy.' Phillips pulled out her radio. 'We've got him Gibbo,' she said triumphantly.

There was a pause before Gibson chimed through. *'Thank God! I was worried losing Don might have messed things up.'*

'A minor hiccup,' said Phillips, feeling somewhat relieved. 'So we've picked Armitage up with a girl named Chloe Barnes. Do you know her?'

'I do, Guv. She's a regular on the streets.'

'Well, in that case I'd like you to interview her. There's more chance she'll to talk to you.'

'No problem.'

'Great. We'll see you back at Ashton House within the hour.'

'On my way now, Guv.'

24

Gibson was waiting in the squad room when Phillips
and Entwistle arrived back from the operation.
Downstairs, Billy Armitage and Chloe Barnes had
been processed and now sat in separate cells in the custody
suite, waiting to be interviewed.

'Any news on Mountfield?' asked Phillips as she walked into
the incident room.

Gibson shrugged. 'I checked with uniform whilst I was
waiting for you guys. They said by the time they arrived at
Armitage's flat to pick him up, he'd disappeared. So I tried his
mobile to see where he'd gone, but it's going straight to voicemail. I'm guessing he must have gone home. Mind you, he was
in a bad way when I left him, projectile vomiting onto the car
park of the flats.'

'Any ideas what might have caused that?'

'I'm pretty sure it was food poisoning. When we were
waiting for the op to start, he said he wasn't feeling great. He'd
even thought about calling me earlier to drop out. Said he'd
eaten something at lunchtime that hadn't agreed with him, and

he'd been feeling nauseous ever since. Then a minute later, without warning, he opened the car door and started being sick. It was bloody everywhere. I'm just glad he managed to keep it out of the car. The stench was disgusting.'

Phillips nodded. 'Ok, well, at least you tried to get in touch with him. We've covered our duty of care on that. If he's not answering his phone, there's not much we can do tonight. And besides, we have far more important things to deal with right now, like interviewing Armitage and Barnes.'

Jones and Bovalino wandered in, looking pleased with their night's work, and took seats.

Phillips was keen to get on. 'Right. Good work tonight, guys, but the hard work starts now. Billy Armitage is our only suspect in this case, and so far, aside from his altercation in the car with Barnes, all we have to link him to the canal murders are some photos on Facebook. So, to say we need something concrete in a hurry is an understatement. He's already asked for a lawyer, so as soon as one arrives, we'll get started. Jones, I want you to interview Armitage with me. Gibson, as you already know Chloe Barnes, I want you and Bovalino to find out what happened in that car with Armitage tonight. Technically she's not under arrest and is just helping us with our enquiries. No matter what we think of her and what she does for a living, we should remember that she was almost the victim tonight. Having said that, if she starts messing you about or trying to be clever, don't hesitate to charge her for solicitation and put the frighteners on her. We haven't got time for anyone to get in the way of this investigation.'

Entwistle raised his hand. 'What do you want me to do, Guv?'

'Sit in the observation suite and take notes on Armitage. Anything you hear that doesn't add up, dig into it and let us know.' Phillips moved her gaze across her team. 'Right, is everyone clear on what they're doing?'

'Yes, Guv' was the response she got from all of them.

Phillips checked her watch. 'It's coming up to midnight. Let's see if we can crack this before dawn.'

She stood and led the team out of the room and down towards the interview suites on the ground floor.

25

Billy Armitage sat behind a dark wooden table in Interview Room Two. Up close, he was a well-built young man who looked like he spent a lot of time in the gym. His large, calloused hands reflected his manual job. His file stated he was twenty-seven years old and had lived in Salford his entire life, moving to his current address just twelve months ago where, according to council tax records, he lived alone. Sitting next to him on a red plastic chair was his solicitor, Patrick Singleton, a scrawny, dishevelled man in a shiny silver suit, sporting thick glasses and lank, greasy hair. Phillips had met him many times during her investigations and felt confident he was neither bright nor particularly effective in his role as a Legal Aid lawyer, which was good news for her.

Phillips took her seat opposite Armitage as Jones sat across from Singleton. She explained the formalities regarding the use of video and the DIR – digital interview recorder – and activated the machine. It made a loud, prolonged beep to indicate it was working.

Phillips took the lead. 'Billy, can you tell us what you were doing with Chloe Barnes this evening when we arrested you?'

'We were just talking, that's all.'

'You drove from Cheetham Hill all the way to Ancoats for a chat?'

Armitage took a sip of water from the cup in front of him. He seemed completely unfazed. 'That's correct.'

'And what, exactly, were you talking about, Billy?'

'Life choices.'

Phillips raised her eyebrows. 'Life choices? What do you mean by that?'

Armitage sat forwards now. 'A couple of months ago, I gave her some money. It was to help her give up the life. To make a fresh start with her daughter, Zoe.'

'And did she?' asked Phillips.

Armitage shook his head. 'She managed to stay off the streets and packed in the drugs for a couple of weeks, but old habits die hard. It wasn't long before she was back on heroin, and back selling herself to feed her habit.'

Jones cut in. 'How much did you give her, Billy?'

'A grand. I'd have given her more, but it was all I had. The silly bitch went and shot the lot up her veins.'

Phillips folded her arms and gazed at Armitage for a long moment. 'So, why the Good Samaritan act? And why Chloe?'

'She was my sister's best mate. Life on the street killed Candy, and I wanted to try and stop it from happening to Chloe.'

That name rang an alarm bell in Phillips's head. 'Wait. You had a sister called Candy?'

'Yeah.'

'What was her full name?'

'Candice.'

'Your sister was Candice Roberts?'

Armitage looked surprised. 'That's her. Did you know her?'

Phillips kept her cards close to her chest. 'No, no. I just

remember reading about her death in the paper. She drowned in the canal, didn't she?'

Armitage scoffed. 'That's what you lot said, but I don't believe it. I think someone pushed her into that canal.'

'Are you saying she was murdered, Billy?'

'That's *exactly* what I'm saying, yeah.'

Phillips unfolded her arms and leaned in closer, her voice softer now. 'Why would you think that?'

'Candice was scared of water and she couldn't swim. There was no way she would've taken a shortcut by the canal. No way at all. She freaked out anywhere near water.'

Jones put down his pen. 'Yeah, but she was a drug addict, wasn't she?'

Armitage shot him an angry look, 'What's that got to do with it?'

Jones continued. 'Well, if she was desperate for her next hit, she'd probably take all kinds of risks, wouldn't she?'

'I know my sister, and even smacked off her tits or clucking for a hit, she was still terrified of water.'

Jones didn't respond, and Phillips resumed control of the interview. She passed a number of large images, printed in black and white, across to Armitage. 'Do you recognise the car in these pictures?'

Armitage glanced down and seemed to pause for a moment as he processed what he was looking at.

'Is that your car in each of the images, Billy?' said Phillips.

He continued to scan the black and white shots before looking up at Phillips. 'Er, yeah. Where did you get these?'

Phillips tapped the image closest to her with an index finger. 'They were captured by the automatic number plate recognition cameras – also known as ANPR – over the last couple of months in Cheetham Hill, Ancoats and Miles Platting. Areas known to be frequented by sex workers and their clients. Can you explain what you were doing around those areas so often, and so late at night, Billy?'

Armitage seemed to stumble. He opened his mouth, but appeared unable to speak.

Phillips passed across two more black and white images of his car. 'These two shots were taken on the nights Chantelle Webster and Sasha Adams died. Both within a mile of where their bodies were found.' She paused to let the full import sink in.

'Are you familiar with those names, Billy?'

Armitage nodded. 'I saw it in the news. They both died, like Candice.'

Phillips pressed him. 'Did you see it in the news, or did you, in fact, kill them along with Candice, Billy?'

Panic filled Armitage's face.

'I'd like a moment with my client, please,' his lawyer finally spoke up

Phillips was in no mood to stop. She fixed Singleton with an icy glare. 'Of course. When I'm finished, you can have all the time you need.'

As expected, Singleton backed down without a fight. Turning her gaze back to Armitage, she repeated the question. 'Billy, did *you* kill Candice Roberts, Chantelle Webster and Sasha Adams?'

Armitage looked up from the images. His words tumbled from his mouth in staccato. 'It was the car. The car. I was looking for the car.'

'What car?' said Jones.

'The one Candice got into before she died.'

'Come on, you can do better than that, Billy,' goaded Phillips.

Armitage managed to compose himself. 'I'm telling you the truth. Candice was last seen getting into a Ford Mondeo. It was the last time anyone saw her alive.'

Phillips resisted the urge to look at Jones. Billy had mentioned the make and model of the car they'd seen on the ANPR cameras.'

'What colour was this Mondeo?' asked Phillips.

'I dunno. Chloe reckons it was either black or blue, or maybe green. It's hard to tell at night.'

'Chloe – as in the girl you were with tonight?'

'Yeah, she was the last one to see Candice alive. She was next to her on the street when she was picked up. Told me she got in with the punter after a bit of chat at the car window. Next morning, Candice turned up dead.'

'Why didn't you report this to the police?' said Phillips.

'I did, honestly I did. Check your visitors' logs. A week after Candice died, I came in to speak to someone in charge to tell them, but I was told to leave a message and I'd get a call back. I never did, so I came back again a week later. That time I was told no-one from CID was available to take my statement, so I gave it to a uniformed copper. Again, I didn't hear anything back, so I got tired of waiting and decided to look for the car myself.'

Jones cut back in. 'That still doesn't explain why *you* were parked up with a sex worker tonight, just a few metres from the stretch of canal where Candice's body was found.'

Armitage exhaled loudly. 'I was trying to shock Chloe into giving up the life. I thought taking her there would scare her into realising the danger she faces each night she's on the streets.'

Jones nodded for a moment before continuing. 'So why do you care so much about Chloe? What's in it for you, Billy?'

'Candice and I were super close growing up, and it broke my heart when she got into drugs. I tried everything to get her off the junk and keep my niece, Katie, out of care. So when she died and Katie was placed in foster care, it felt like I'd failed. I wanted to make up for that. Chloe's a good person, and she's not stupid. She could have a real chance at a happy life without the drugs. She's still got custody of her daughter Zoe, but if she gets arrested one more time, she's been told Zoe will be taken into care too. I was trying to stop that from happening. I thought it might, somehow, make up for what happened to Candice and Katie.'

'I'm not sure I buy that, Billy,' Jones was quick to dismiss him. 'When we moved in to arrest you, it was because I saw Chloe hit you in your car. If you care about her so much, why would she do that?'

Armitage let out a loud sigh as he rubbed his large hands down his face, causing his cheeks to redden. 'Because right before you lot arrived, she told me she wasn't going to give up hooking. She was determined to take her chances. I lost my temper and called her a stupid fucking whore. She took exception to that and slapped my face. The next thing I knew, lights were flashing and cars were screeching in all around us.'

Phillips glanced down at her own notepad, which was full of scribbles, then across at Jones's, which looked almost identical to hers. She'd heard enough. The more they dug, the more questions they seemed to uncover. She reasoned it was time to pause the interview and regroup, see if Chloe Barnes's version of events matched Armitage's. She closed her notepad and nodded to Jones. 'For the purpose of the tape, Detective Chief Inspector Phillips is pausing this interview. The time is one-oh-five-a.m.' The DIR beeped, indicating it had stopped. She smiled at Singleton as she stood. 'Feel free to have that catch up with your client now, Mr Singleton.'

Singleton attempted to reply, but Phillips paid him no attention. She wasted no time in getting out of the room, with Jones following behind, and headed for the observation room at the end of the corridor.

26

E ntwistle caught the brunt of Phillips's anger as she strode into the observation room with Jones at her back. 'How the hell did we not know Armitage was Roberts's sister? Jesus, Entwistle, we looked like a bunch of amateurs in there!'

'I'm sorry, Guv. After hearing what he said, I had a quick look into their backgrounds. Strictly speaking, they're not. *His* mum – Mary Armitage – and *her* dad – Richard Roberts – were partners for many years, but they never married. That's why nothing showed up on the preliminary searches. Scanning through council tax records and the voting register, it looks like Richard and Mary got together in 1997, when Billy and Candice would've been toddlers. They'd both been married before, but were widowed when their kids were babies. It appears that the four of them lived together as a family until Richard Armitage died from a heart attack four years ago. Not long after that, Billy moved out. Candice followed him out of the family home about twelve months later. That was just after her first arrest for drug possession. She was arrested and charged again six months later for soliciting. She got three months inside that time.'

'What about the car? Does ANPR back up Armitage's story?'

Entwistle turned his laptop to face Phillips. A host of images were displayed on the screen. 'It does. A blue Ford Mondeo with fake SORN plates registered to a car from Adders Scrap Metal Merchants.'

Phillips looked at the images, then back at the observation monitor. 'Shit,' she said, frustrated. 'It looks like he's telling the truth.'

Jones appeared more optimistic. 'Guv, even if it's not Armitage, we do at least have a fresh lead on the mystery Mondeo. And all roads point back to Adders Bahmani. As you always say, there's no such things as a coincidence.' A hopeful smirk spread across his face.

'That's true, Jonesy.' Phillips turned and pointed to the observation monitor. 'How are Gibbo and Bovalino getting along with Barnes?'

'I dunno, Guv, I've been watching your interview since we started.'

Entwistle pressed a button to change the video feed to Interview Room Three. The back of Gibbo's and Bovalino's heads appeared. Chloe Barnes looked like she was in desperate need of a hit, hugging her arms and rocking back and forth in her chair.

Entwistle turned up the volume so they could hear what was being said. Gibson was talking,

'...but I still don't get why Billy gave you a thousand pounds, Chloe.'

Chloe Barnes looked agitated as she rocked in her chair. 'I told you, to get me off the gear.'

Gibson responded. 'Come on, Chloe, he's a painter and decorator. He doesn't earn enough money to chuck a grand at a street-walker just to help you detox. So stop messing about and tell us why he really gave you the money?'

Barnes shot an angry look at Gibson. 'Are you fucking deaf? Like I already said, it was to help me get clean.'

Gibson sat back and folded her arms, glancing at Bovalino. 'I'm not buying it. Are you Bov?'

'Sounds like bullshit to me, Gibbo.'

The room fell silent for a moment as Gibson and Bovalino stared at Barnes. This seemed to make her even more agitated.

'The sooner you tell us what we want to know, the sooner you can leave, Chloe.' said Gibson.

'This is ridiculous. I don't even know why I'm here. You didn't arrest me, so you can't keep me here.'

Gibson sighed. 'Chloe, how long have we known each other?'

Barnes shrugged her shoulders. 'I dunno.'

'Four years, Chloe. For four long years I've watched you working the streets, listening to all your bullshit stories and lies. I'm an expert at knowing when you're bullshitting, and you're lying to us right now. I can see it in your face. You can't look me in the eye, can you?'

As if to prove Gibson right, Barnes shifted in her seat and glanced down at the table.

'Here's the deal, Chloe. You tell us the real reason Billy gave you the money and we'll let you go tonight. If you keep lying to us, I'm gonna arrest you for soliciting right here, right now. With your record, that'll mean prison time. Is that what you want?'

Silence filled the room once more. After about a minute, Barnes relented. 'Fuck it. You'll find out anyway.' She sounded like a petulant teenager. 'Billy gave me the money for my daughter Zoe.'

'Zoe?' Gibson sounded shocked. 'I thought she was in foster care?'

Barnes rocked even harder in her chair now as she spoke, the drug withdrawal getting worse with each minute. 'She was.

But I got clean back in the summer and social services said I was ok to look after her.'

Gibson ran her hands through her peroxide-blonde hair. 'Jesus, how the hell did that happen? *You're* not fit to look after a child.'

'Fuck you!' spat Barnes.

Bovalino broke up the fight. 'Is Billy the father, Chloe?'

Barnes scoffed as if it was the most ridiculous idea she had ever heard. 'God no. He's so not my type.'

'Well, I've heard *everything* now,' said Gibson sarcastically.

Barnes scowled. 'Anyone can fuck me when they're paying for it, but when it's on my own time, I happen to be very choosy.'

Gibson let out an ironic chuckle as Bovalino spoke. 'So if he's *not* the father and you're *not* sleeping with him, why is Billy Armitage giving you a thousand pounds for your daughter?'

'Because Candice's daughter was taken into care. He feels guilty for it. I guess giving me the money for Zoe makes him feel better about himself. And if he wanted to give me his money, then I wasn't complaining.'

'And did Zoe see any of that money?' asked Bovalino.

'A bit.'

Gibson lost her cool now, slamming her hand down on the table. 'Cut the crap, Chloe! She got nothing. The whole lot went into your veins, didn't it?'

Watching on the monitors, Phillips scoffed. 'And the award for mother of the year goes to Chloe Barnes.' She turned to Jones and Entwistle. 'So Armitage has been lying to us, the sneaky little shit. I want to know why. Jones, come with me.'

A minute later, Phillips burst into Interview Room Two. She stood in front of the table opposite Armitage and his lawyer, and waited for Jones to close the door. 'Billy, why don't you tell us about Zoe Barnes. We know she's the real reason you gave Chloe the money.'

Armitage looked startled.

'Why have you been lying to us, Billy?' Phillips growled.

Singleton interjected. 'Is this an official line of enquiry, Inspector? Because if it is, shouldn't it be on tape?'

Phillips glared at him. He shrank back into his chair. She turned her attention back to Armitage, leaning on the table in front of him. 'What else are you lying about, Billy?'

Armitage stuttered. 'N-n-nothing, I swear.'

'So why lie about the money? Why not just tell us the truth?'

Armitage raised his hands in surrender. 'I'm sorry, I made a mistake. I should have told you. But I was scared.'

'Scared of what?'

'Social services finding out.'

Phillips took a seat and Jones followed. 'What has any of this got to do with social services?'

Armitage appeared nervous. 'Look, it was obvious when I saw Chloe tonight that she was using again. A blind man could see it. Because of that, I didn't want to bring the fact she had a daughter to your attention. I lost my niece Katie into foster care and I didn't want the same to happen to Zoe. I knew if I told you about her, with Chloe being back on the streets and using, you could take her away too. I figured if I kept quiet and you didn't know, you'd leave her alone.'

'And you think she's better off with a junkie street-walker?' said Jones.

Armitage dropped his chin to his chest. 'I was just trying to help.' Tears welled in his eyes as he stared at the table for a long moment. 'So are you going to tell social services, then?'

Phillips considered her options for a moment. Her main priority was to ensure Zoe's safety. At the same time, she took no pleasure from separating a child from its mother. Deep down, she hoped that would only be necessary as a last resort. Her tone softened. 'Billy, if Chloe *is* using, then her daughter is better off in foster care. I mean, who is looking after Zoe when Chloe's on the street?'

Armitage looked back up and appeared embarrassed. 'I don't know.'

Phillips was incredulous, 'Jesus, Billy. She could be at home on her own right now for all we know.'

Phillips and Jones exchanged a look. The child needed protecting.

Phillips knew Armitage was an idiot, but she had little to charge him with. She turned to Patrick Singleton. 'Your client is free to go home for the *time being*.' Her gaze moved to Armitage. 'But the vigilantism stops as of now. And if I so much as see your number plate on even a single camera within a mile radius of the red-light districts, I'll nick you for obstruction of justice. Am I making myself clear?'

Both Singleton and Armitage nodded with relief.

'Right, now piss off the pair of you.' Phillips stood and hurried out of the room and down the corridor. A moment later, she opened the door to Interview Room Three. 'Gibbo, Bovalino. Can I have word?'

The full team gathered a few minutes later in the observation suite. 'I'm letting Armitage go.' Phillips pointed to the monitor showing Chloe Barnes sitting alone a few rooms down the corridor. 'We can cut her loose too. But before we do, I want a uniform team round to her flat ASAP. If she's got custody of that little girl, God only knows what kind of state she's in.'

'I'll go with them,' said Gibson.

'Are you sure? It's late?'

'Yes, Guv. I've met Zoe before, so she may remember me. Seeing a familiar face might make it less distressing for her.'

'Ok, thank you Gibbo.' Phillips turned to Jones and Bovalino, standing next to each other as always. 'It's time to pay another visit to Mr Bahmani and find out exactly where he was the night Candice Roberts died. And this time I'm coming with you.'

Gibson cut in. 'He won't talk to you, Guv. Like I said, he hates women.'

Phillips gave Gibson a hard stare. 'I don't give a flying fuck whether he likes me or not. I'm a detective chief inspector investigating three murders. If he doesn't talk to me, I'll nick the bastard for obstruction. Entwistle, I need you to find me anything I can use for leverage with him.'

'On it, Guv.'

Phillips checked her watch. It was 3 a.m. 'All right, Gibbo, away you go with uniform. The rest of you, get home, grab some food and get a wash. I want us all back on deck first thing this morning. The clock is ticking and our guy is still out there. He could strike again at any moment.'

27

S now had fallen overnight, partially covering the sign that covered the locked gates to Adders Scrap Metal Merchants. Parked up across the road, Phillips sat in the passenger seat of the unmarked squad car with Bovalino at the wheel. Jones was in the back, leaning forwards with his head through the front seats. Agitated and anxious due to their lack of progress and sleep, Phillips checked the clock on the dash: 9.45 a.m. 'I thought this place opened at nine?'

'That's what it says on the website, Guv,' said Jones.

'If he's as crooked as Gibbo reckons, and this place *is* a front for his shady dealings, then I doubt our man cares much about passing trade,' added Bovalino.

Phillips rubbed her hands to fend off the cold. 'It'd be nice for something to go right in this bloody investigation, just for once. I'm really starting to wish I'd left it all well alone.'

'Don't stress, Guv,' Jones chimed in cheerily from the back. 'We're onto something here with Bahmani, I can feel it. And you're gonna love the man himself. Isn't she, Bov?'

Bovalino glanced left at Phillips and chortled. 'Oh yeah. He's a real charmer. Right up your street.'

'He can be Genghis-bloody-Khan for all I care. As long as he turns up soon and his office is warm.' Phillips rubbed her hands again, 'Is that heater actually working, Bov?'

'Jesus, Guv, how can you *still* be cold?' said Bovalino. 'It's on full blast and like a bloody sauna in here. In fact, I was just about to open a window. I'm suffocating.'

'Don't you dare,' laughed Phillips.

At that moment, a white Range Rover approached the gates and stopped. A large Asian man got out of the driver's seat.

'That's him,' said Bovalino.

They watched as Bahmani unlocked the gates and opened them wide before climbing back into the SUV and driving into the yard.

'In we go, Bov,' ordered Phillips.

A minute later, the team moved carefully across the snowy ground towards the office. Phillips was first into the Portakabin, drawing an angry look from Bahmani, who had turned to face her.

'Er, what the fuck are you doing? There's no *women* allowed in here.'

Bovalino stepped inside with Jones just behind him. 'She's with us,' said the Italian.

Phillips walked to within a foot of Bahmani and held up her ID. '*Detective Chief Inspector* Phillips. I'd like a word.'

Bahmani forced a thin smile. 'Well, I'd like to be Brad Pitt, but we can't have everything we want now, can we, love?'

Phillips returned his fake smile. 'I'll get straight to the point.'

'That'd be a first for a woman,' he said sarcastically.

Ignoring the jibe, Phillips continued. 'We have reason to believe that decommissioned number plates from cars registered to this yard have been used to commit serious crimes across Manchester.'

Bahmani walked round to the other side of his desk,

dropped into the large leather chair, and pointed at Jones and Bovalino. 'Like I told these two the other day, I don't mess about with bad plates. *That's illegal.*' His delivery was slow and deliberate, as though he were slow-witted and had been taught the words to say.

Phillips wasn't buying the act and moved towards his desk, flanked by Jones, whilst Bovalino remained by the door. 'Word on the street is you're a bit of a gangster.'

Bahmani continued to play dumb. 'Me? No love. I'm just a businessman trying to feed my family.' He pointed to the photographs of his wife and kids on the wall behind him.

Phillips gestured towards the window where the Range Rover was parked. 'Is that your only car?'

'Oh, that's not *my* car. That's my wife's. I just borrow it from time to time.'

'Where's your car, then?' said Phillips.

'Me? I don't have one. Too expensive, like. After all, I'm just a humble man with simple tastes.'

Observing the garish gilt-framed animal print decorations adorning the walls, Phillips believed the exact opposite to be true.

'Have you ever driven a Ford Mondeo?'

'A Mondeo? Maybe, but then I see that many cars every day, I don't remember.' A lopsided grin spread across Bahmani's face. He was giving her the runaround and they both knew it.

Phillips took a different approach. 'Where were you on the night of the 6th of November?'

Bahmani pretended to consider the question for a moment, repeating the date under his breath. 'What day was that?'

'A Tuesday.'

'In that case, I was at home with the wife and kids, and my in-laws.'

'And they can vouch for that, can they?'

'Oh yes,' he said confidently.

'What about Friday the 16th of November?'

Bahmani didn't flinch. 'I was at home with the wife and kids, and my in-laws.'

'Funny. You didn't need to think about that one,' said Phillips

The lopsided grin returned. 'No. The first one must have jogged my memory.'

At that moment, Phillips's phone rang. It was Gibson. She diverted the call to voicemail and continued, 'I'm sure I know what the answer will be, but can you also tell me where you were on Sunday the 9th of December.'

'Easy. I was at home with the wife and kids...*and my in-laws.*'

'You seem to spend a lot of time with your in-laws, Mr Bahmani.'

He guffawed. 'It's hard not to. They bloody live in my house.' He seemed very pleased with his performance so far.

Gibson called again. Phillips knew Bahmani was winning their head-to-head and figured a distraction might be enough for him to drop his guard, so she decided to take the call. 'Will you excuse me a moment?'

'Be my guest, love,' Bahamni said, smiling.

Phillips listened for a moment. 'You're kidding, where? ... Ok. We're on our way.'

Jones gave Phillips a quizzical look.

'Bov, turn the car around. We've got to go.' She headed for the door.

The big man stepped outside with Jones on his tail. As Phillips reached the door, she stopped and turned back to Bahmani. 'Out of interest, where were you *last night*?'

He took a moment to ponder the question before acting as if he had just remembered. 'Oh yes, I was at home with the wife and kids, and my in-laws.'

'Of course you were.' Phillips nodded before pushing open the door and heading for the car.

When she jumped in the passenger seat, Jones and Bovalino were eager for news. 'We've got another dead girl in the canal.'

'Another *fake drowning*?' asked Jones.

'Looks like it, only this time they found the body on the other side of town, in Pomona.'

'Jesus. He's branching out.'

'Exactly, Jonesy. And if he's changing his hunting ground to the wider canal network, it could make catching him almost impossible.'

Bovalino moved the car steadily over the rough terrain towards the main gate as Adders Bahmani opened the door to the Portakabin. He stood watching them, arms folded across his chest. The smile was gone, his eyes now cold, his face unflinching.

Phillips locked eyes with him and held his gaze until he was out of view, before turning her attention back to Bovalino and Jones. 'That slippery bastard is involved in all this somehow. I can feel it.'

A smile crept across Bovalino's face. 'You didn't fall for his charms then, Guv?'

'Was it that obvious?' she replied.

'Do you want us to check out his alibis, Guv?' Jones quipped from the back seat.

Phillips didn't bother to turn around. 'No. Get the support team to do it. I want us all focused on the new girl. And besides, trying to crack his alibi is a waste of time. Even if he *is* lying, there's no way his family would rat on him.'

28

No one in Phillips's core team had managed to get any sleep in the last forty-eight hours; way too much had happened. Now, huddled together in the incident room, they all looked exhausted and ready to drop.

Phillips pinned photos up on the board of the body that had been found that morning. 'I know we still can't prove this victim was murdered, but everything matches the others. So, I think it's safe to assume she met her fate at the hands of the same guy.' She turned back to face the team. 'Entwistle, what do we know about her?'

Entwistle positioned his laptop so the screen faced his colleagues. 'Ok. Her name is Estelle Henderson. She's twenty-five and from West Gorton. She was single and lived with her five-year-old son, Lewis. He was found at home today on his own when a uniformed team searched her flat. Apparently the poor kid was crying his eyes out when they go to him. Social services have since taken him into care.'

'Jesus. That's exactly the same as Chloe Barnes's daughter,' said Gibson.

Jones was incensed. 'What planet are these women on,

leaving their kids at home alone? I mean, what kind of parent does that to a five-year-old?'

Gibson looked sad. 'They're desperate for money to buy drugs. We see it time and time again in SCT. Feeding their habit is more important to them than feeding their kids. It's heart-breaking.'

Phillips shook her head in disbelief and took a seat at the spare desk. 'It really is.' She fell silent and zoned out, allowing her thoughts to crystallise.

The team sat in silence for a moment before Bovalino jabbed his elbow into Jones's ribs. 'She's got the look again.'

Jones looked over at Phillips and a grin spread across his face, drawing a confused expression from Gibson. 'What look?'

'When the Guv is putting something together in her head, she gets the thousand-yard stare,' Bovalino explained, pointing at Phillips,

Gibson followed his finger just as Phillips turned her attention back to the team. 'Something quite disturbing has just occurred to me. If I'm right, the unthinkable could be happening.'

'What is it, Guv?' said Jones.

'I really hope I'm wrong on this one,' said Phillips. 'Based on Evans's estimate of the time of death, we believe Henderson was killed between 10 p.m. and midnight last night, right?'

Jones nodded. 'Right.'

'Well. Is it a coincidence that our victim was abducted and murdered at the exact same time an MCU surveillance operation was in play, on the complete opposite side of town?'

Bovalino grinned. 'You don't believe in coincidences, Guv.'

'No I don't, Bov.'

'So what are you saying?' asked Gibson.

'I'm saying that either our killer is the luckiest man on the planet, *or* he had insight into our operation last night.'

Gibson looked incredulous. 'Jesus. You think the killer is someone on the force?'

Phillips took her time before nodding. 'Either that, or connected in some way. How else would they have known to move their hunting ground across town on the very night *we* were on surveillance in Ancoats?'

The room fell silent as everyone absorbed Phillips's theory.

Jones shook his head. 'Look, we know better than anyone that there are bent coppers in the world. But police officers kidnapping and drowning street-walkers? I'm sorry, but I'm not buying that.'

Phillips shuddered at the implications. 'I understand that, Jonesy, and I hate to do this, but I want background on each member of the wider team. That's the first place to start. Divvy the group up between you and let's see if there's anything suspicious on any of them, including that young copper who discovered two of the girls.'

The team nodded in turn.

Phillips stood and looked at her watch. 'Right. We've been awake for almost two days straight now. I suggest we get some sleep. That way we can be back at our desks first thing tomorrow morning. If we are looking for one of our own, we must be very careful. Catching someone this clever and hiding in plain sight will take fresh eyes.'

29

Phillips let the exit door to the morgue close gently behind her. The automatic lock clicked into place. She stood for a moment in the quiet corridor in the basement of the Manchester Royal Infirmary. The silence was deafening, in stark contrast to the noise of her mind, which whirred with questions. Estelle Henderson's post mortem had produced the exact same results as the previous three deaths: death by drowning. 'What are you missing, Jane?' she whispered to the empty space before walking back to the car.

Opting against using the elevator, she pushed open the thick fire door that lead to the stairs. She took them two at a time up to the ground floor, then exited out onto a rainy Oxford Road. Pulling her collar up against the weather, she walked at pace back to the car park before paying for her ticket and taking the elevator to the sixth floor. Earlier, when she had parked up, she had been so focused on the case and the constant questions running through her mind that she'd forgotten to make a mental note of her car's location, so it took a few minutes to find it.

Finally, as she jumped in the driver's seat, she repeated her question. 'What are you missing here, Jane?' When she fired the ignition, the radio burst into life and the tail end of Elton John's 'Step Into Christmas' filled the car. She normally enjoyed the festive season, but with four unexplained deaths weighing on her shoulders, this year it didn't feel right. Putting the car in gear, she moved out of the parking space and headed for the exit.

Phillips drove the first few miles on autopilot as she ran the facts of the case over in her mind: four identical deaths, four prostitutes – all drug addicts – and each of them single mothers living alone. Why were they being targeted? Her mind soon wandered to her latest theory – that the killer was actually a police officer – and she wondered if the team had found anything whilst she'd been away. Based on the lack of contact since she had left earlier, she assumed they had yet to make a breakthrough.

As she pulled the car onto Oldham Road, her attention was drawn back to the radio and a promotional trailer for the radio station's breakfast show. It featured a cast of bland presenters attempting to sound interesting. 'Seriously, who cares?' she said, annoyed, and leaned over to switch stations. The next channel was no better and she continued to flick through until a commercial playing on one of the stations caught her attention. The loud booming male voiceover filling the car.

'Have you suffered long-term sickness at work? Do you worry about paying the bills if it happened to you? If the answer's yes, then you need to call the friendly team at Robbins and Co Insurance on 0800—'

The commercial brought DC Mountfield and his sickness during the operation to mind. She switched off the radio and drove in silence for a moment. Mountfield's sickness had seen him removed from the surveillance team the night Henderson was killed. When Gibson had spoken to the uniformed team sent to pick him up, they'd reported he was nowhere to be found. *Could he have faked it to get out of the op?* It wasn't beyond the realms of possibility. He knew the full details of the operation, and if he had kept his police radio switched on, he'd also have known the exact location of the team at all times. Plus, as a detective, he would know how to avoid ANPR cameras. 'Jesus, could Mountfield be our killer?' she said out loud.

She hit the accelerator and the rest of the journey passed in a blur. Soon she pulled into the Ashton House Police Headquarters' car park and raced upstairs to her office.

Since they now had concerns that someone in the wider team could be involved in the deaths, Jones, Bovalino, Entwistle and Gibson had set themselves up in the meeting room at the end of the office and closed the blinds. Phillips wasted no time joining them. Her abrupt entrance caused the team to look up from their computer screens with expectant looks on their faces.

'Entwistle, I need you to come to my office. Bring your laptop.'

Jones locked eyes with Phillips and his brow furrowed. 'Is everything ok, Guv? Did something happen at the post mortem?'

Phillips already had one foot out of the room. 'Everything's fine, Jonesy. I just need Entwistle for something. I'll explain later.'

She walked briskly back to her office, unlocked it and stepped inside. Entwistle followed her a moment later.

'What's up, Guv?'

She walked around her desk and removed her coat. 'I need you to search the police motor vehicle records. I want to know what cars are allocated to the Sex Crimes and Trafficking squad. Can you do that?'

'Not with this.' Entwistle pointed to his laptop. 'We're not connected to their network. I could always ask them for temporary access, though.'

'And how long would that take?'

'Knowing IT, a couple of days.'

'That's too long. I need that information now.'

Entwistle looked puzzled. 'What's this about, Guv?'

Phillips dropped into her chair and ran her hand through her hair. 'I don't want to say just yet. Not until I get more proof. But I really need to know what cars are being used by SCT. Do you know anyone down in vehicles?'

'I'm afraid I don't, Guv.'

Phillips said nothing for a minute as she considered her next move. A moment later, she stood and walked back round her desk. Placing her hand on Entwistle's shoulder, she began steering him out of her office towards the corridor. 'I think it's about time you made friends with the vehicle team. Get yourself down there and get me that information ASAP.'

'But what if they won't give it to me? I'm only a DC.'

Phillips smiled thinly. 'Well, you'd just better make sure they do, Entwistle, hadn't you?'

He nodded as he opened the door to the corridor.

Phillips shouted after him, 'And Entwistle, you speak to no one about this but me. Got that?'

'Got it, Guv.'

ALMOST TWO YEARS AGO NOW, Phillips had been shot in the line of duty, leading to many months' convalescence in Wythenshawe Hospital. Her treatment had involved a series of painful operations as well as therapy sessions to help her deal with the mental trauma. In the months leading up to her return to work, she had been in constant contact with the Greater Manchester Police's HR team as they monitored her progress. During that time, she had grown close to one member of the team, Sandra Roden.

Roden sat alone at her desk in the small open-plan office when Phillips walked in. 'Knock knock.'

Roden looked up from her computer screen and smiled. 'Hello stranger. What brings you down here? Is everything ok?'

Phillips took a seat opposite her. 'Everything's fine, Sandra. I'm enjoying being back as DCI and the team are doing really well. Life's good.'

'That's great. I'm pleased to hear that.'

Phillips scanned the three empty desks. 'So where is everybody?'

'On an IPD training course over in Media City. They've left me holding the fort.'

'Didn't you fancy doing the course yourself, then?'

Roden shook her head. 'Not really. Since I had the kids, I'm only here three days a week, so it hardly seems worth the effort.'

'Fair enough. I guess you have different priorities now.'

'Indeed I do.' Roden sat back in her chair and folded her arms, a lopsided grin spreading across her face. 'So now you've ensured we're not going to be disturbed, why don't you tell me why you're *really* here, Jane.'

Phillips chuckled. 'Am I that obvious?'

'I'm afraid so.'

In spite of the empty room, Phillips leaned forwards. 'I need a favour.' She spoke in a whisper.

Roden laughed. 'That much I guessed.'

'Can you check a sickness record for me?'

'That really depends on who it's for.'

'Don Mountfield from Sex Crimes.'

'And what's his rank?'

'DC.'

Roden eyed Phillips with suspicion. 'Does DCI Atkins know you're looking at his team's sickness records?'

'Strictly speaking, no, but it's important, and I won't share them with anyone else...'

Roden put her hands up in mock surrender. 'Don't tell me anymore. I don't want to know.'

'Look, Sandra, I know this is a bit unorthodox, but I wouldn't ask unless it was very important. Please.'

Roden said nothing for a moment as she decided what to do. Phillips flashed a warm smile and held her breath.

Roden relented. 'Ok, as it's you. But I have two conditions.'

'Name them.'

'Well firstly, you didn't get them from me. If anyone asks, I'll deny everything.'

'Agreed.'

'And secondly, you destroy them when you've looked at them. Because if you do find something you may need for a case, you'll have to come back through the proper channels, ok?'

Phillips placed her fingers over her heart. 'I promise, Sandra. If I find anything, I'll do it by the book from that point on.'

Roden smiled as she began pulling up the records on her PC. 'It's a good job I like you. I don't do this sort of thing for everyone, you know.'

Half an hour later, Phillips was back in her office cross-checking Mountfield's sickness records against the dates of the four murders. She couldn't believe what she was seeing. She already knew he was taken sick the night of Henderson's murder, but to her amazement, he had also been on annual leave on each of the nights Roberts, Webster and Adams had been killed. 'Fuck, *it's Mountfield.*'

'What is Mountfield?' asked Entwistle as he entered the room.

Startled, Phillips instinctively closed the files on her desk and coughed nervously, 'Any luck on the SCT vehicles?'

Entwistle grinned. 'Yes, Guv. I got chatting to the bloke in charge, Dennis, and it turns out he went to school with my older sister and he—'

'So what did you find?' she interrupted. She wasn't interested in Dennis's life story,

Entwistle looked down at the sheet in his hand. 'Well, according to Dennis, they change vehicles every twelve months—'

Phillips lost her patience. 'Jesus Christ, Entwistle! What cars have they been driving?

Entwistle appeared a little affronted. 'I was getting to that. Er, one Vauxhall Astra, two Vauxhall Insignias and three Ford Mondeos.'

Phillips's heart rate quickened. 'Do we know what colour the Mondeos were?'

Entwistle scanned the page in his hand. 'Maroon, silver and, er—' He looked up, realising what she had been looking for. '—*blue*, Guv.'

'We've got him!' Phillips slammed her fist onto her desk, before leaping to her feet. Entwistle looked on, bemused. 'Come with me. I need to be brief the team.'

THE MEETING ROOM was silent as Phillips spent the next five minutes walking the team through the evidence she believed was stacking up against Mountfield.

Gibson appeared to be struggling.

'Jesus, Guv,' said Jones. 'I don't want to believe it, but you make a compelling argument.'

Entwistle nodded his agreement. 'Plus, from what we can see, the rest of the wider team is completely clean; not so much as a parking ticket.'

Gibson finally spoke. 'What about the young beat-copper who found the two dead girls?'

'Clean as a whistle,' said Entwistle.

Gibson nodded slowly, almost sinking into her chair. It was no surprise the enormity of the accusation against Mountfield had hit her hard.

Bovalino exhaled loudly. 'It could be just a coincidence though, couldn't it? You know, him being on leave when the girls died?'

'Yes, it could,' said Phillips. 'But, you know I don't believe in coincidence, Bov. Especially not when the guy we're looking at has access to a blue Ford Mondeo, the one car that appears on ANPR cameras in Miles Platting and Ancoats each night the girls were killed.'

Bovalino wasn't ready to convict a fellow officer just yet. 'I hear what you're saying, but even though he had access to *a* blue Mondeo, it doesn't mean it was the same car we've been looking for, does it? I mean, they're pretty common, Guv.'

'I know that, Bov, and none of us wants our killer to be a copper. But the fact that Mountfield is on the force means we can't ignore the facts either.' Phillips turned her attention to Gibson now. 'I know this must be hard for you, Gibbo, but you know him better than anyone. What do you think? Could it be Mountfield?'

Gibson ran both hands through her short hair and held them on top of her head as she spoke, her face strained. 'There has been the odd rumour about him taking his work home sometimes, but *nothing* like this.'

Phillips looked puzzled. 'How do you mean "taking his work home"?'

'You know, using the girls for free sex in exchange for not nicking them. But I never believed any of that shit myself. I've always found him to be a decent fella. He's happily married and got two kids of his own.'

'So, these rumours; who was spreading them?' asked Phillips.

'Just some of the girls on the street. But they're always blaming SCT for something, and never stop talking shit about us. I don't pay any attention to them, to be honest.'

'Probably worth a follow-up conversation based on what we know now, though?' said Phillips.

Gibson nodded.

'So how do you wanna play this one, Guv?' asked Jones.

Phillips held her fingers over her mouth for a moment as she considered her options. 'Well, based on the evidence so far, it's all circumstantial and we don't have enough for a warrant. We could watch him and see where he goes, but if he spots us and thinks we're onto him, he'll destroy every shred of evidence before we can get to it. So for now I suggest we gather more intel on him and see if we can get enough evidence to search his house *and* the Mondeo issued to SCT. Let's look for card transactions in the area around the time of the murders, go back over CCTV, recheck ANPR, see if you can make him out driving the Mondeo – we know the drill, guys.'

Each of the men nodded in turn as Phillips stood and placed her hand on Gibson's shoulder. 'You got a minute?'

Gibson nodded and followed her to her office, where Phillips closed the door. 'I think we need to discuss the elephant in the room, Gibbo. If you feel you need to leave the team, I'll understand. Mountfield as our prime suspect can't be easy.'

Gibson folded her arms defensively. 'To be honest, Guv, I'd prefer to stay if you're ok with it. I'm still struggling to believe it's Don. It's just not the man I know. So, if by investigating him it proves it wasn't him, as I hope, then I'll be doing him a favour by staying on.'

Phillips eyed her for a moment. 'Ok, I understand, but I must have your full cooperation and full disclosure.'

'That goes without saying, Guv.'

'And if you feel compromised at any point, you talk to me immediately. Are we clear?'

'Crystal.'

'Needless to say, no one outside of this team can know any of this. If word gets out we're investigating one of our own, a whole world of shit will be coming our way.'

'They won't hear anything from me.'

Phillips took a seat behind her desk. 'Good. Well, whoever our guy is, he's still out there and likely stalking his next victim. So let's see what we can find and in double-quick time, shall we?'

'On it,' said Gibson as she turned and headed back to the meeting room.

30

Tonight's target was never one of the original ones on my list, but I realise now she's as bad as the rest. I feel compelled to deliver her to judgment in the next life. I drive around cautiously for twenty minutes, getting more frustrated as I struggle to locate her. Then my heart lifts as she steps under a street light just ahead of me. The rain is bouncing off the pavements, so she's hiding under a small black umbrella, a cigarette glowing between her lips. I slow the car to a crawl and move along beside her. I let down my window and signal for her to join me. I'm wearing a baseball cap, so she doesn't recognise me at first as she totters over on high heels and bends down to greet me with her best fake smile.

'You looking for business, love?'

'No, Chloe, I'm looking for *you*.'

Her face contorts as she finally sees my face and recognises me. 'What the fuck do you want?'

With each kill that passes, I'm finding it easier and easier to lie. It comes natural to me now. 'I just want to talk, Chloe, nothing more.'

'I'm busy. Piss off.' She turns to walk away.

I hold up five folded ten-pound notes. 'Fifty quid, Chloe, just to talk, out of the rain.' It's an offer I know she can't refuse.

Her eyes lock onto the cash and I can almost hear her mind calculating how many hits she can get with it. She steps back towards the open window as the rain worsens. 'Just to talk, nothing else?'

I produce my warmest smile. 'I promise, Chloe.'

Nodding, she snatches the cash from my grip and closes the umbrella. She opens the car door and jumps in the passenger seat as the electric window whirs closed, shutting out the noise of the street and the rain outside, which continues to do battle with the car's windscreen wipers. I quickly scan my mirrors to ensure we're not being watched. When I'm satisfied it's all clear, I pull the car away. As usual, I loop around various roads in Cheetham Hill, to try and flush out anyone who might try and follow us, before making my way along the usual back roads towards Miles Platting.

We drive in silence for a few minutes before Chloe thinks to ask where we're going.

'I know a quiet spot,' I explain, but she doesn't seem convinced.

'If we're just talking, why do we need to go anywhere? Why couldn't we just sit in the car where you picked me up?'

This makes me laugh out loud. 'Do you really want the other girls to see you with *me*?'

I'm guessing she must be in withdrawal and not thinking straight. The reality of what I'm saying seems to dawn on her. 'Shit, no. I hadn't thought of that.'

'And I certainly have no intention of being seen with you either. Sitting in a car in the red-light district is asking for unwanted attention. That's why we need to go somewhere quiet.'

The low volume police scanner crackles into life, but Chloe seems oblivious to its presence. Conversely, I listen intently to everything that's being said. I'm pleased to note there's nothing coming through that need concern me.

I leave the main road at the first opportunity and begin zig-zagging through the darkened streets of a derelict Ancoats.

Before she moves to the next life, I need to know more about the child she will leave behind. 'How old is Zoe now?'

'Why do you want to know about her?'

'I'm interested, that's all.'

'She's two.'

'And did you know her father, or was she a "consequence of the job"?'

Chloe scowls at me. 'None of your fucking business, mate.'

I continue to press the point. 'So, it *was* a punter then?'

She shoots me another filthy look. 'I thought you wanted to talk about the girls and the punters. Not my bloody daughter.'

'It's my money, Chloe, so I get to choose the questions.'

She huffs, folds her arms sulkily and stares out of the passenger window into the darkness. Snow has begun to fall.

'Where is Zoe tonight?'

Chloe ignores me, so I repeat the question, slower and louder this time, which agitates her even more. *'She's at home.'*

'And who is she at home with?'

She glares at me through bloodshot eyes. 'Why the fuck do you care?'

'Just answer the question. Who is she at home with tonight?'

There's silence once more as we hit the abandoned broken roads that lead to the canal. As the car begins to lurch over the rough terrain, I ask again, 'Who is Zoe with tonight, Chloe? I'll keep asking until you tell me.'

'Jesus Christ! She's with her grandma. Now drop it, will you?'

I pull the car to a stop as we reach our destination, and

switch off the engine. The snow is falling heavily now. I turn to face her. 'I have to say, I really don't believe you, Chloe.'

'Believe what you like, I don't care.' She spits the words out before turning away from me.

I reach into my pocket for what I need, and a moment later a loud click echoes around the car as I cock the Glock and point it at Chloe's head. She instinctively turns to face me. Terror fills her eyes as she comes face to face with the barrel of a loaded gun. Her hands shoot up in surrender as her mouth opens, but she does not speak.

'I'll ask you one more time. Who is Zoe with tonight?'

She stutters and mumbles for a moment, but no actual words make it from her mouth.

'Tell me the truth or I will shoot you, right here, right now.'

She nods frantically and tears, blackened by her cheap eyeliner, streak down her face, giving her the look of a gaunt panda. 'Sh-sh-she's alone...'

Anger wells in the pit of my stomach. 'You left a two-year-old girl at home *alone* in that shit-hole you call a flat?'

She's crying like a child now. 'She was asleep when I left. What else was I supposed to do?'

'Be a fucking mother to your daughter, you silly little bitch. Mothers are supposed to protect their children, not abandon them so they can fuck men for drug money. You make me sick.'

I can hear her speaking and I know she's making excuses, but I no longer have any interest in what's she's saying. 'Get out of the car,' I order.

She looks shocked, but doesn't move.

I push the barrel of the gun against her forehead. 'Out of the fucking car now!'

She turns her head away and begins fumbling with the door handle. I'm tempted to pull the trigger and kill her now, but that would remove an essential part of the process. As she climbs out into the snow, I open my door and step out, my gun still trained on her. 'Walk over towards the canal. It's time to make your peace with God.'

'What's down there?'

I chuckle at her naïvety. 'Water, Chloe. Lots of water.'

'What are you going to do to me?'

'Me? I'm going to baptise you in the canal, just like I did your bestie Candice.'

A look of recognition crosses her face. 'Jesus! Billy was right. Candice *was* murdered, and *you* killed her.'

I scoff at her simplistic view of the world. 'I didn't kill her. I sent her to God.'

'You're fucking crazy.'

'No Chloe. *I* am the Baptist! Now get over by the canal.'

'Please don't do this—'

'I said, now!'

She complies, but struggles to walk on her heels towards the steps that lead down to the towpath and canal. The snow lies thick on the ground now, illuminating the area under the moonlight. I follow close behind, keeping the gun trained on her back. She stops at the top of the steps and turns to face me.

'Keep going,' I shout, waving the gun in my hand for effect, just as my foot drops into a large pothole, knocking me off balance. I tumble forwards. My instincts are to put my hands up to break my fall. As I hit the wet ground, I drop the gun and it skids across the ice and snow. Chloe wastes no time and, seeing me floundering on the ground, pulls off her heels and takes off running towards the canal.

It takes a moment for me to get back to my feet. I grab the gun and head after her. I can't see her, but she can't have got far. As I move through the darkness, I step on something loose but solid, causing me to fall forwards again, landing hard on my elbow. I cry out in pain and fumble back to my knees. I can see what tripped me up: a pair of size five, thick-soled stiletto heels that once belonged to Chloe. I regain my feet and survey the area, comforting myself with the fact she won't be hard to find; she's leaving tiny footprints in the snow.

A burst of traffic on the scanner filters out of the open car door, catching my attention. I'm sure I just heard the word 'Ancoats' mentioned. I walk back to the car and turn up the volume. It's not good news. A uniform team has been despatched to a potential break-in at one of the local businesses, which means they'll pass close by within the next five minutes. I have to get away from here.

I jump back in the car and discover Chloe has left her mobile phone on the seat. At least she won't be calling for help anytime soon. I reverse away from the canal before spinning the car around and gunning the engine. I head back towards the main road.

I chastise myself for losing Chloe. How could I have been so sloppy? In truth, however, all it does is slow things down a little. It won't stop me from sending her to God. After all, I have her phone, and *I know where she lives*.

31

When the Greater Manchester Police closed down its original headquarters located on Bootle Street in the heart of Manchester, they moved the bulk of their operations to the new Ashton House HQ in Failsworth. Since then, the city centre satellite station has been located on the ground floor of the historic Town Hall building in St Peter's Square. In stark contrast to its city-centre predecessor, the new unit is small and manned with just a few officers per shift.

Chloe limped into the city-centre station's reception, soaking wet, frozen, with eyes puffy and blackened around the edges from crying. Her lips, hands and feet were purple from the cold. She shivered uncontrollably, partly due to the cold and partly because she was in desperate need of a hit.

The reception area was empty aside from a row of plastic chairs, secured to the floor opposite a large blue counter beneath a heavy-duty glass security screen. She scanned the room, before spying an intercom attached to the wall with the words 'PRESS FOR ASSISTANCE' emblazoned across the top. She walked over and pushed the button, then waited. When she got no reply, she tried again.

Eventually a male voice spoke. 'Can I help you, miss?'

Chloe was paranoid that she had been followed, and scanned the empty room again before answering, 'I want to speak to the woman in charge.'

'And who might that be?'

'You know, that one who's in charge out at Failsworth.'

'Do you have a name, love?' the voice asked.

With every fibre of her body aching from the cold and withdrawal, her patience was thin, 'No, I don't know her bloody name. I just know she's the boss at Failsworth.'

There was a delay before the voice spoke again, sounding weary. 'Wait there. I'm coming out.'

Chloe did as instructed. All the time she kept her eyes locked on the door that led back to the street.

A minute later, a door buzzed and a tall uniformed officer stepped out into the empty space behind the counter. He was an older man with salt and pepper hair and a matching beard. He smiled and pointed to his right ear. 'Sorry, love, I can't hear a thing through that intercom. Who is it you're looking for?' He stepped up to the glass and his expression turned grave when he saw her battered bare feet. 'Are you all right, love? This is not the kind of weather to be walking around without shoes on.'

The warmth in his voice took Chloe by surprise. She softened for a moment before remembering where she was and how much she hated the police. Her impatience returned. 'I want to speak to the woman detective from Failsworth.'

'What's this all about?'

'None of your business. I just need to speak to that woman from Failsworth.'

The officer looked confused. 'It's a big place over there, love. Can you be more specific?'

Chloe exhaled in frustration. 'She wears glasses and her hair is tied back.'

The officer offered her a sympathetic smile. 'I'll need a little more than that I'm afraid. Do you know her rank, or maybe which team she works for?'

Chloe was struggling to hold it together. 'I dunno. She's the cocky bitch in charge of a team of blokes. They all dance around her. One of them is a big Italian fella, goes by the name Bovalino.' For some reason, his name, given during her recent interview, had stuck in her head.

'Well, there can't be too many Bovalinos in the staff directory. Let's have a look, shall we?' The officer began typing into a computer screen on the counter, humming 'Jingle Bells' under his breath as he did, His jolly demeanour was a stark contrast to the pain enveloping Chloe's body – a mixture of the cold and lack of heroin. It was almost unbearable.

As he reached the Bs in the internal telephone directory, the officer began reading from the list of names on screen. 'Bailey...Baird...Baldwin...Bannister...here we are...Bovalino. Says here, he's a Detective Constable with the Major Crimes Unit based at Ashton House. Does that sound like him?'

Chloe shrugged. 'I guess so. Do you have a picture of him?'

'I'm afraid not. Just his name rank and direct phone number. But now we know he's in MCU, let me find out who's in charge of it over there.' He began typing again for a few moments, 'Here we are.' A look of recognition flashed across his face. 'Oh wow, it's her you're after; Detective Chief Inspector Phillips. I'm surprised you didn't remember her.'

Chloe didn't recognise the name. 'Why should I?'

The officer took his phone from his pocket and began typing. 'DCI Phillips is a bit of a celebrity across Manchester. She was all over the news last year.' He turned the phone screen to face her and pressed it up against the glass.

Chloe inspected it closely. She was looking at a *Manchester Evening News* report that stated Phillips had been shot in the line of duty. It featured a picture of her standing with arms folded outside Ashton House.

'That's her!' Chloe's relief was palpable. 'Can you put me through to her?'

The officer chuckled. 'It's 2 a.m. love. Somehow I don't think she'll be at her desk, do you?'

His laugh made Chloe even more agitated. 'Can you at least fucking try?'

The officer's expression changed, now grave. 'Hey, there's no need for that kind of language. I'm just trying to help.'

Chloe's frustration brought tears to her eyes and they rolled down her cheeks. '*Please*, you've got to help me. I really need to speak to her.'

His expression softened again. 'Come on now, there's no need to get so upset. I'll see what I can do.' He checked the computer screen for a moment before turning back to Chloe. 'See that phone on the wall over there.' Chloe looked to where he was pointing. 'Pick that up and I'll connect you to DCI Phillips's direct line, ok?'

Chloe nodded and followed his instructions. She walked over and picked up the phone, then turned to face him.

'You'll hear a beep and then it'll ring through to her extension at Ashton House.'

Chloe nodded and, as the phone began to ring, she turned her back on the officer. She held her breath, willing Phillips to answer, but to her dismay it eventually went to voicemail. 'Damn it.'

'She's not there then? I didn't think she would be,' said the officer from behind the screen.

Chloe turned back to face him. 'Can you try again, please?'

'It's no use, love. She's won't be there.'

'*Please*. I really need to talk to her.'

The officer nodded, and reconnected the call to Phillips's desk. The same thing happened, but this time, when Chloe heard the woman's voice stating she had reached the voicemail of DCI Phillips, she plucked up the courage to leave a message.

Covering the mouthpiece with her hand, she whispered as loud as she dared into the receiver, just in case the officer might be eavesdropping. 'This is Chloe Barnes. I need to speak to DCI Phillips urgently. I know who killed Candice because they tried to kill me tonight, too. Please, you have to protect me. I've lost my mobile so you'll need to come to my flat. It's number 12A Princes Gardens, the Belmont estate. Please hurry.'

She put the phone down and prayed she'd done the right thing trusting a cop. Nothing good had ever come from her previous dealings with the police. Turning, she saw the older officer looking at her with a look of sadness in his eyes.

'Are you ok, love? You look sick.'

She hadn't noticed she was shivering violently now.

'Do you have somewhere to go tonight, out of the weather?' he asked.

Chloe nodded. 'I have a flat on the Belmont estate.'

'How will you get home?'

'Probably walk, I guess.'

'That'd be a bloody long walk in the sunshine, never mind this kind of weather.' He fished something out of his pocket and passed it under the gap in the glass. 'I have a grand-daughter about your age. Here, take this.'

Chloe stared at the twenty-pound note in front of her.

A warm smile spread across his face. 'That'll get you home safely. Make sure you get a hot bath and something to eat before you catch your death.'

Chloe snatched it away. 'Thank you.' She smiled at him for a moment before turning around and heading for the door.

'Be safe, love,' he shouted after her, but she pretended not to hear him.

Out on the street, the snow had at last stopped, but lay deep on the ground. The Town Hall clock lit up opposite reminded her it was 2.30 a.m. Her body was begging for heroin.

Staring at the money in her hand, she was tempted to jump

into one of the two black cabs parked up at the taxi rank on St Peters Street, but there was no point going home without any gear to block out the pain. Shoving the cash into her jacket pocket, she decided to take the short walk to Piccadilly Gardens to score the drugs she craved.

She would shoot up as soon as possible, then wait for the first bus home at 5.30 a.m.

32

Phillips unlocked her office and hung up her coat just before 7.00 a.m. On her way to work this morning, she'd bought a fresh coffee along with a copy of last night's *Manchester Evening News* from the garage on the Princess Parkway. She tossed it onto the desk by the phone as she sat down. Taking a long swig from her drink, she reclined in the large leather chair – a legacy from her former boss DCI Brown – spinning it to face the window and the world outside. Her mind fizzed back and forth about whether DC Don Mountfield could be the killer or if it *was* just a coincidence. But, as she never tired of telling her team, she didn't believe in them. Plus, there was just too much evidence – albeit circumstantial at this stage – pointing to the fact he was somehow involved in the girls' deaths.

A knock on her office door made her jump and spin round. Gibson stood in the doorway. 'Morning, Guv. You're in early.'

'Couldn't sleep.'

'Me neither,' said Gibson as she wandered in and took a seat. 'I can't stop thinking about Mountfield.'

Phillips nodded. 'Same here.'

'Do you really think it could be him, Guv?'

'I don't know what to think if I'm honest, Gibbo. Imagining one of our own as a cold-blooded killer makes me feel sick. But I know from experience that not all coppers live by their oath to protect and serve.'

'Are you referring to Blake?'

Indeed she was. Two years before, the head of the GMP, Chief Constable Blake, had been involved in a spate of murders that had rocked Manchester and almost cost Phillips her life. He was now serving a life sentence in Hawk Green maximum security prison. 'Yeah. That bastard has more blood on his hands than a butcher. And if someone that high up can go rogue, then there's no reason to think a DC couldn't.'

Gibson sat forwards in her chair. 'But it doesn't make sense, Guv. He's just a normal bloke, a family man with two daughters. What could drive him to murder four young women?'

Phillips shrugged. 'What drives any killer to do it? In the end, it's not our job to figure out why, but rather how, and when, he killed them.'

'And *prove* it, of course.'

Phillips took another swig of coffee. 'Yeah, that's the hard bit.'

Just then, Entwistle walked into the main office and, seeing Phillips and Gibson together, made his way over. 'Morning. You guys are in early.'

'We could say the same about you,' said Gibson.

'Yeah. I couldn't sleep.'

Phillips smiled. 'It's a problem that appears to be catching.'

Entwistle pointed at the newspaper on Phillips's desk. 'Do you mind if I look at the match report from last night's game, Guv?'

'Be my guest.' Phillips handed it over, uncovering her desk phone. A red light blinked, indicating she had a voicemail.

Gibson nodded towards the phone. 'Looks like you've got a message, Guv.'

Phillips followed her line of sight. 'Well, that's a first. No one ever calls me on the landline. They all use my mobile. It's probably some old fart looking for DCI Brown. This used to be his office.' She leaned forwards and hit play. 'Let's see what they want.'

The girl's voice on the message was hard to hear, just louder than a whisper. She sounded panicked and edgy. '*This is Chloe Barnes. I need to speak to DCI Phillips urgently.*'

'It's Chloe Barnes for me.' Phillips looked surprised as she pressed pause on the tape and turned to Entwistle, who was perched on a low cabinet to the left of her desk, engrossed in the sports pages. 'How do I turn this up, Entwistle? I can hardly hear it.'

Entwistle looked up before putting down the paper and wandered over to the machine. He picked it up and fiddled with a button on the side, causing a loud beep. 'That's up to maximum volume now. Try that.'

Phillips pressed play and the message continued. '*I know the person who killed Candice because they tried to kill me too. Please, you have to protect me. I've lost my mobile so you'll need to come to my flat. It's number 12A Princes Gardens, the Belmont estate. Please hurry*'.

The room fell silent for a moment as they processed what they'd just heard. Phillips was the first to speak. 'Jesus. Gibbo, you know her. Do you think she could be telling the truth?'

'God knows, Guv. She's off her face on drugs most of the time.'

Phillips hit rewind, and they listened to the message again. When it finished, she deferred to Entwistle's expertise once more. 'How can we find out what time this call came in?'

He picked up the receiver. 'Should be easy enough.' Pushing buttons on the keypad, he listened for a moment before nodding. 'The message bank says it was logged at 2.26 a.m. this morning.'

'Can you find out where the call came from?' said Phillips

Entwistle pressed more buttons and began reading a number out. '0161 299 1000.'

Phillips wrote it down on the pad in front of her.

'That number sounds familiar. Where do I know it from?' said Gibson.

'I've heard it before too,' Entwistle agreed.

Phillips took the phone back and dialled the number. Her eyes widened when it was answered. 'This is DCI Phillips from MCU at Ashton House. I was called from this number at around 2.30 this morning. Do you know who connected the caller?'

She waited for a response, then hung up the phone. Entwistle and Gibson stared at her.

'Looks like Chloe Barnes walked into the city-centre station last night and called me from there.'

Gibson looked shocked. 'As in the *police station*?'

'Yep.'

'Jesus, she must have been scared. She'd never set foot in a cop-shop of her own volition,' said Gibson.

Phillips checked her watch. 'It's 7.30 a.m. now, so I'm guessing she'll be back home. Come on, let's pay her a visit. See if there's any truth in what she's saying.'

As Phillips and Gibson made their way towards the main office door, Entwistle walked over to his desk, where he removed his coat before hanging it on the back of his chair.

Opening the door, Phillips stopped and looked over at him. 'You not coming, Entwistle?'

He looked surprised. 'You want me to?'

'Of course.'

'It's just that normally, when you get a breakthrough, you ask me to stay in the office and "dig into something".'

'Well, if you'd prefer to stay here and "dig into something"?' said Phillips.

'No, no. Not at all, Guv.'

'Well then, stop arsing about and let's get going.'

Entwistle jumped to attention and pulled his coat back on. 'Yes Guv!'

33

The door to Chloe Barnes's apartment was locked up tight, but as they stood on the exposed walkway outside, Phillips and the team could hear the cries of a small child emanating from within. Phillips pressed the bell for a long moment in the hope Barnes was asleep inside, but when there was no answer, she feared the worst.

The door to the flat next door opened and a lady, probably in her sixties, peered out, a sneering expression on her face. 'That kid's been crying like that for most of the night. It's kept me awake all night.'

Phillips turned to face the woman. 'Do you know if Miss Barnes is inside?'

'Wouldn't matter if she is,' she scoffed. 'She's off her head most of the time. That kid gets no attention whether she's in the flat or not. She cries day and night. It's a bloody nightmare. I've asked the council to move me to another flat, but they said I'm not a priority. Can you believe that? And me a pensioner 'n' all. Five times I've been up to the council—'

'I don't suppose you have a spare key, do you?' Gibson cut the woman off.

'Me? Why the bloody hell would I want a key to a junkie's flat?'

Gibson persevered. 'Well, do you have any idea what time Miss Barnes left here last night?'

The woman sneered again. 'No I bloody don't. I've got better things to do that keep a track of what that silly bitch is up to.'

Phillips suspected the opposite was actually true. Still, they were getting nowhere. Their priority right now had to be to get inside the flat and ensure the child was safe. Then see if they could locate Chloe.

'Thank you, you've been very helpful,' Phillips lied. The woman finally took the hint and closed her front door.

Luckily, Chloe's door had received a makeshift repair recently. Where there was once a glass panel above the door handle, a fibre-board wooden panel had been crudely attached.

Entwistle was dispatched to the car to retrieve a tyre wrench and, returning a few minutes later, handed it to Phillips. Expertly wedging the heavy piece of metal into a gap between the door and board, she yanked it back in one rapid movement. A loud crack followed as the wooden panel splintered and bulged away from the door. She repeated the process a couple of times before the panel gave way, leaving a hole big enough to fit a hand through. Phillips reached through and unlocked the latch from the inside. The weight of her body caused the door to open inwards as she did so, and the sound of the crying child was amplified.

Stepping inside, she gestured for Gibson and Entwistle to follow her along the narrow hallway towards the source of the crying. Pushing open the door facing her, her heart sank as she came face to face with a toddler standing in a cot and facing the door, her hands grasping the side. The child's eyes were filled with fear, and red and swollen from crying, and her tiny face was filthy. Phillips rushed across the room and instinctively swept the little girl up in her arms, holding her tightly as she turned to face Gibson and Entwistle.

'There, there, sweetheart, it's all right. You're safe now,' soothed Phillips.

'We'll check the rest of the flat for Barnes,' said Gibson, turning quickly and leaving the room, flanked by Entwistle.

Phillips cuddled the little girl and rocked back and forth, trying to stop her crying. The poor child was soaking wet and stank of stale urine and faeces. Scanning the filthy room, anger boiled in the pit of her stomach. How could anyone leave a child alone overnight? Let alone in squalor like this?

Gibson returned. 'There's no sign of her, Guv.'

Phillips was doing her best to soothe the child whilst trying to figure out their next move as Entwistle stepped back into the room. He walked over and placed a pacifier in the little girl's mouth. 'I found this in the lounge. Don't worry, I've given it a thorough clean.' Gently leaning forwards, he began chatting to the little girl. Mercifully she responded, and stopped crying.

'You're a natural, Entwistle,' said Gibson.

'I'm the eldest of five kids, so I've had lots of practice. My youngest sister Clara was an accident, and she's just a little older.'

Phillips stepped towards Entwistle. 'Can you take her?'

'Sure.' Entwistle handled the child like a precious package and grinned as she placed her head on his shoulder and cuddled into him.

Phillips watched him soothe the child and smiled. 'Who'd have thought it, hey? Entwistle, an expert in childcare.'

Entwistle smiled and held the little girl against his chest. 'I'll see if I can find some fresh nappies and dry clothes for her. Then I'll call an ambulance to get her checked over.'

Phillips touched him on the arm. 'Thank you. Whilst you're doing that, we'll see if we can track down Barnes. Gibbo, come with me.'

They moved into the squalid living room, which was filled with dirty clothes strewn across the floor and overflowing ashtrays. A small plastic table covered in drug paraphernalia had been placed in front of the couch.

Phillips put a call in to Jones to update him. She wanted to check CCTV footage outside the city-centre station from last night. She hoped they could pick up Barnes's trail when she left at 2.30. Jones promised that he and Bovalino would get onto it right away, and call back as soon as they had anything worth sharing. As she ended the call, Phillips was aware of the foul stench emanating from the open bin in the corner of the room and began to feel nauseous. 'I need some air.' She moved briskly to the door and stepped outside.

The Belmont estate was like many other council estates across Manchester with high-rise blocks. Built in the sixties to replace the post-war slums, they had promised a new way of life for their wide-eyed tenants, each hopeful of a fresh start filled with opportunity. However, their dreams soon turned to nightmares as poor construction and planning, coupled with unsuitable materials, meant the homes had quickly deteriorated. Sadly, over the decades that followed, they became crime-riddled breeding grounds for drug-dealing gangs, violent crime and sexual assaults. Standing on the exposed walkway that ran in front of Chloe Barnes's tenth-floor flat, looking out at the boarded-up doors and windows of many of the properties – most covered in graffiti – Phillips was reminded why crime had reached epidemic levels across the UK. How could the people living in this kind of environment be expected to abide by the rules of society when, to all intents and purposes, society had all but denied their existence?

'What a shit-hole,' said Gibson, as if reading her thoughts.

'Yeah. It's so sad that, in a world of so-called abundance, people are forced to live in a place like this. I mean, what kind of future does that poor little girl have to look forward to?'

'Seeing this kind of poverty and neglect is the hardest part of the job for me,' said Gibson. 'The only way I stay sane is to remind myself – *every single day* – there's only so much we can actually do.'

Phillips exhaled loudly as she stared at the scene in front of her. She knew Gibson was right, but it didn't make it any easier. The phone vibrating in her pocket came as a welcome distraction. It was Jones. She turned it to speaker phone so Gibson could hear what was being said.

'You're on speaker, Jonesy. What you got?'

'As we thought, it looks like Barnes left the station just after 2.30 a.m. and set off across Albert Square. She crossed over Princes Street. We lost her on Clarence Street as there are no cameras on there. But we picked her up again a few minutes later on Booth Street, before she turned left onto Mosley Street. She then walked all the way up to Piccadilly Gardens, where she used the payphone at 2.44 a.m. She waited there for twenty minutes until a guy on a moped turned up and handed her something.'

'Sounds like a drug deal to me,' said Gibson.

Phillips agreed. 'What happened then?'

'She disappeared into one of the shop fronts that are too dark for any visuals, and stayed there until just before 5.30 a.m.,' Jones continued, *'at which point she emerged again and jumped on the number 33 bus towards Worsley.'*

Gibbo stood to attention and turned west, pointing towards the Patricroft Recreation Ground, 'The 33 runs along Liverpool Road. Her quickest route home would've been through the park.'

Phillips nodded. 'Jonesy, can you see if we have any CCTV footage of Liverpool Road, running along the edge of the Patricroft Recreation Ground?'

'Give me a second.'

Jones went quiet for a moment on the other end of the

phone, as the sound of sirens filled the air from the other side of the building. They appeared to be drawing closer.

'Hopefully that's the ambulance for the girl,' Gibson muttered.

Jones returned. '*I'm afraid not, Guv. There's no cameras on that stretch of Liverpool Road.*'

'Bugger. That's annoying. We're gonna have to do it the old-fashioned way in that case. We can assume, at this stage, she was heading home. If she was telling the truth and she is in danger, then we need to find her before the killer does.'

'*Unless he already has,*' said Jonesy.

'Yeah, that's what I'm afraid of. If you and Bov can get over here ASAP, I'll organise a uniform crew and dog team. We need to find her.'

WITHIN AN HOUR, Patricroft Recreation Ground was teeming with uniformed police and two dog teams. With the aid of a dirty T-shirt lifted from the lounge floor of the flat, the dogs soon picked up Chloe Barnes's scent. Starting at the Liverpool Road bus stop, they followed their noses to a disused public toilet on the far side of the park. The whole area surrounding the building was overgrown with bushes, nettles and tall weeds, and hidden behind a thick privet hedge.

Standing just two hundred meters away when the dogs started barking, Phillips and Gibson raced to the area, followed by Jones and Bovalino. When they pulled back the bushes, none were prepared for the sight that greeted them.

Chloe Barnes's body was laid out on her back, partially covered with thick snow. Her bare feet were exposed, as were most of her legs and torso. Only her bra and knickers remained. Blue from the cold, the right side of her face was caved in.

Dried blood and grey matter had congealed in her matted hair, and her right eyeball hung from the socket.

Gibson turned away and vomited violently onto the snow-covered grass.

Phillips stood motionless, staring down at the body. 'She was trying to tell me who the killer was, and it got her killed. I failed her.'

'What could you have done differently?' said Jones. 'She called you in the middle of the night, Guv?'

Phillips didn't respond, and continued to stare at Barnes's battered body.

Bovalino crouched down to take a closer look at the frozen corpse. 'Whoever our killer is, it looks like he panicked on this one, Guv.'

Jones agreed. 'Yeah. This is totally out of character for him.'

The anger and frustration bubbling inside Phillips felt like a living thing now. Struggling to keep her emotions in check, she turned to face the team. 'If anyone has lost control here, Jonesy, it's us. Chloe is the fifth girl to die in this case and we're still no closer to catching the bastard that's responsible. We've gotta get our shit together guys, *and fast*. We can't let anyone else die. Do you hear me?' She was shouting now.

'Yes, Guv,' said each of the team.

Phillips marched back towards the car, straight past a pale-looking Gibson, who stood upright before wiping her mouth on a tissue.

34

L ater that day, the wider team gathered in the incident room for a full briefing. Since her return from the Patricroft Recreation Grounds, Phillips had holed up in her office. Scowling, she'd made it clear visitors were not welcome. Her frustration at their lack of progress had boiled over in the park this morning, and she berated herself for losing control. She shouldn't have taken it out on the team, but holding Barnes's terrified little girl in her arms that morning, feeling the fear and pain in her tiny, shaking body, had made this case personal.

She finished writing up her notes and closed her leather-bound A4 notepad before sitting back in the chair. She took a few deep breaths to compose herself for the team briefing.

After a couple of minutes, she stood up from her desk and made her way out into the incident room. Since the wider team had been vetted and cleared of any involvement in the deaths, Bovalino, Gibson and Entwistle had returned to working at their usual desks. A host of expectant faces surrounded them, all waiting for an update.

Walking to the centre of the room, Phillips was in no mood

for pleasantries. 'Right, you lot, listen up. I can confirm that the body we found in the Patricroft Recreation Grounds this morning was that of Chloe Barnes. She'd been savagely beaten about the head which, until we get the full post mortem results, we can assume was the cause of death.'

Opening the leather-bound pad in her hands, she removed a printout of one of the CCTV images of Chloe Barnes and held it up. 'This is Barnes, leaving the city-centre police station at 2.30 a.m. this morning, just a few hours before she was found dead.'

She held up another. 'And this is her at 2.44 a.m., talking to a man on a moped in Piccadilly Gardens. I want know who this guy is and what was said between them as a priority.'

Phillips produced a third CCTV picture. 'And this is Chloe at 5.30 a.m. getting on the number 33 bus to Worsley. Her body was found just five hundred metres from her flat, so we can presume she boarded this bus, intending to travel home to the Belmont estate in Salford.'

Phillips pinned up a route map of Barnes's journey from the police station to Piccadilly Gardens. 'DC Entwistle is sourcing CCTV footage from the bus company as we speak.' She tapped the map with force. 'And we already have footage of her walking along Booth Street and Mosely Street, but for about five minutes she went off the grid when she ducked down Clarence, Kennedy and Cooper streets. I want the rest of you to check the CCTV footage from all the shops and businesses along those routes. If she talked to anyone during that part of her journey, I want to know where and when, ok?'

A couple of routine questions followed, and when everyone seemed satisfied they knew what was expected of them, Phillips called the meeting to a close before signalling for her own team to join her in her office.

Jones, Bovalino and Gibson followed her in, with Entwistle last in carrying his laptop, 'Close the door, Entwistle,' said

Phillips as she sat down and faced the team huddled around her desk. 'First up, I want to apologise for my outburst this morning. I allowed my frustrations to boil over onto you, and that wasn't fair.'

Jones shrugged. 'It's understandable, Guv. It was bloody horrific. It affected us all.'

Bovalino chortled, pointing at Gibbo. 'Yeah, but some more than others.'

'Piss off,' replied Gibson, before flashing a sheepish smile. Thankfully it defused the tension.

A wry grin spread across Phillips's face. 'So, how you feeling now?'

Gibson blushed. 'Embarrassed to say the least, Guv. That's never happened to me before. I mean, I've seen some awful things in this job, but nothing as brutal as that.'

Phillips nodded sympathetically. 'I have to admit, the eyeball hanging out of its socket was a first for me too.' She turned to Entwistle. 'How you getting on with the bus CCTV?'

'Still waiting, Guv. The bus company's IT department is archaic to say the least, but they've assured me I'll have it before the end of the day.'

'I want eyes on it as soon as it lands. We may be able to see if anyone was waiting for her when she got off.'

'Of course, Guv. But in the meantime, I've spotted something else that I think is significant.'

Phillips looked intrigued as Entwistle opened his laptop and placed it in front of her.

'Last night's ANPR footage from Liverpool Road by the Patricroft Recreation Grounds. I was looking for a blue Ford Mondeo like that spotted around the other crime scenes. I looked through from midnight last night to 7.00 a.m. this morning but drew a blank. So, I decided to go back through again, this time looking for any cars of a similar style and size.' He tapped the screen. 'This nondescript silver Vauxhall

Insignia was captured at 5.40 a.m. this morning. On any normal day, blink and you'd miss it, but when I ran the plates, it turns out they're actually from a Nissan Micra that has been officially registered as off the road—'

'By Adders Scrap Metal Merchants by any chance?' Gibson cut across him.

Entwistle appeared disappointed now. 'I'm afraid not. No. This car was registered to a place out in Oldham...' He cast an eye over his notes. '...er, a JK Hughes Scrap Ltd.'

'Any connection to Adders?' asked Jones.

'Nothing yet, but I've not had that much time to look into them. That's next on my list.'

'And what about Mountfield? Did you get anything on him, Jonesy?' asked Phillips.

'No, Guv. On paper he's clean.'

Phillips pointed to Entwistle's laptop. 'Do you recognise that silver Vauxhall car, Gibbo? Could it be one of SCT's?'

Gibson asked Entwistle to run the video again, then once more. She shook her head. 'It doesn't ring any bells, Guv. Sorry.'

'Bugger.' The room fell silent for a moment as Phillips contemplated their next move. 'Ok, here's what we'll do. Jonesy and Bov, you get over to JK Hughes in Oldham, see if you can find out how they make their money.'

The two men nodded.

'Entwistle, find out where Don Mountfield spent last night and if SCT have been using a silver Insignia. Maybe it's a recent addition since Gibbo moved over to our team.'

'Will do, Guv.'

'Gibbo, you've got the short straw. You're working late tonight with me. I think it's time you introduce me to some of the girls up in Cheetham Hill. Let's see if there's any truth in the rumours about Mountfield using his warrant card to get free sex. But before we hit the streets, let's go and visit the bus driver. See if he saw anything unusual when Barnes got off'

'Sure thing, boss,' said Gibson.

Phillips dismissed the team, but held Entwistle back for a moment. 'Any update on Zoe Barnes?'

'I spoke to the doctor at Wythenshawe Hospital about an hour ago, Guv. They've admitted her to the children's ward with dehydration, malnutrition and impetigo, which they suspect she'll have picked up from all the bacteria in the flat. The good news is, she'll make a full recovery. Social services have already found her a home with foster parents.'

'Wow, that was quick.'

'Yeah. Thankfully she's going back to a family she lived with last year. *Before* she was given back to Chloe.'

'That's really good news. Really good.' Phillips patted him on the shoulder. 'And well done, Entwistle, you really stepped up to the plate for that little girl today.'

'It's hard to do anything else, Guv. The poor thing didn't choose a junkie for a mother, did she?'

Phillips nodded gently and turned around to face the window as Entwistle left the room. Staring out onto the car park, images of that frightened little child's face played on a loop in her mind, and a mix of emotions enveloped her: pain, sorrow, anger and hope. Hope that little Zoe Barnes would finally receive the love and security every child deserved in life. Swallowing away the lump in her throat, she wiped her eyes and took a deep breath. It was no time for tears. She had a killer to catch.

35

J ones and Bovalino's visit to JK Hughes Scrap Ltd provided nothing that might connect Mountfield – or anyone else, for that matter – to the murders. The owner, Mr Hughes, was an elderly man who ran his small operation in Stockport alone. He couldn't have been a day under seventy-five, and if his physical frailty was anything to go by, it was unlikely he had the strength to overpower a small animal, let alone a young woman. The yard was run down and in disrepair. What little fencing remained was on its last legs, making it easy for anyone to enter the site after dark and remove number plates from the cars littered around. Hardly a slam-dunk for the prosecution, and the Nissan Micra that had provided the plates for the silver Insignia was just a shell; the wheels, engine, doors and windows had long since been removed.

Phillips and Gibson's interview with the bus driver fared no better either. He did remember Barnes getting on and off – mainly due to her lack of footwear on a snowy morning. However – by his own admission as a regular driver through the Belmont estate – he paid no attention to the 'weird and wonderful people' on that part of his route. He recalled she had sat downstairs towards the rear of the vehicle and kept herself to herself for the duration of the journey before finally alighting on Liverpool Road next to the recreation grounds. If anyone *had* been waiting for her there, he hadn't noticed.

Growing more frustrated with every dead end they hit, the next challenge was to speak to some of Chloe's friends on the street. The hope was that one of them would remember the last person or car to pick her up last night – but with pretty much every girl feeding a daily heroin or crack habit, Phillips knew the chances were slim. Still, they had to try.

At least Entwistle had provided a breakthrough, discovering that Don Mountfield had been involved in a number of surveillance operations in the last twelve months focused on Adders Scrap Metal. Although it proved nothing concrete at this stage, it at least connected him to the source of the fake plates and, with nothing else to go on, it was at least *something*.

On the ten-minute return journey from the bus depot to Ashton House, Phillips had suggested that Gibson take the lead when questioning the girls. The fact that she already knew most of them would make it easier and quicker to get a much-needed result.

Later that night, when they arrived in Cheetham Hill, Gibson made a point of parking the unmarked squad car away from the main drag where the girls plied their trade. She believed moving around on foot was less likely to spook them, making it easier to garner information from them.

It was just past 10 p.m. when they got out of the car. It was bitterly cold as they walked up the hill on Pimblet Street. For Phillips, the icy chill brought Chloe Barnes's body to mind, lying in the snow, half naked and frozen. She shuddered and pulled her collar up against the biting wind; how could the girls function in this kind of weather, wearing next to nothing?

They walked for about five minutes, passing a number of

working girls as they did. Rather than making general enquiries, because time was short, Gibson had decided to focus on tracking down a couple of girls she knew who were close to Chloe. Eventually, as they turned onto Empire Street, she signalled that she'd found someone they should talk to. As they moved closer, the girl in question stepped towards them and adopted her best sultry pose in an attempt to get their attention. Evidently she believed Phillips and Gibson were potential customers, but as they moved closer to her, her body language changed. She had recognised Gibson.

'Oh shit, what do you want?' she said.

Gibson offered her a cigarette, which she grabbed and lit in one fluid motion. 'Come on, Trudy, that's no way to speak to an officer of the law.'

Trudy was a tall, wiry girl with blue-dyed hair. She was dressed in a miniskirt that accentuated her long pale legs, which ran into impossibly high heels. As she moved, she resembled a baby giraffe taking its first steps. A cheap-looking fake-fur coat was her only protection against the sub-zero temperatures.

'How's business?' asked Gibson

'I don't know what you're talking about,' Trudy replied sulkily.

'Cut the crap, Trudy. We're not here to nick you. We just want to talk to you about Chloe Barnes.'

Trudy blew out a large plume of smoke. 'Why, what's she done now?'

'She's dead,' said Gibson.

Shock spread across Trudy's face. 'Jesus Christ. When?'

'Early hours of this morning.'

'Did she OD?'

'No. I'm afraid she was beaten to death just a few hundred metres from her flat.'

Trudy's eyes widened. 'Oh my God. That's so fucked up.'

'Yeah. It really is, and we need to find the bastard that did it before it happens to another girl.' Gibson nodded towards Phillips. 'This is Detective Chief Inspector Phillips from the Major Crimes Unit. Just in case you were wondering.'

'I wasn't.' Trudy's eyes darted around them.

'You look nervous. Is everything ok?'

'Vadim won't be happy I'm talking to you. It's bad for business.'

'Her pimp,' Gibson said by way of explanation to Phillips. 'So where is he tonight?'

'Around. Always watching.'

Phillips was keen to press on. 'Did you see Chloe last night?'

Trudy took one final drag from her cigarette and stubbed it out under her shoe. 'For a bit, yeah.'

'When and where?'

'She was working across the street, over there.'

Phillips followed her line of sight. 'What time was that?'

'Not long after we started, so probably about ten.'

'And how long was she there before she was picked up?'

'Dunno. I wasn't really paying that much attention.'

'But she *was* picked up? She didn't just walk away,' asked Phillips.

'No, she was definitely picked up. Some guy drove up and called her over. She spoke to him like she knew him, then she got in.'

'Can you remember the model of the car?'

A cold blast of wind rushed along the street, causing Trudy to hug her arms in an attempt to keep warm. 'No, just that it was a big one. Like a family car.'

Gibson produced her phone from her pocket and opened up the photos app. She presented Trudy with a still image of the silver Insignia they had spotted last night on the ANPR cameras, 'Was this it?'

Trudy scrutinised the image for a moment. 'Could be but, like I said, I wasn't paying much attention.'

It was Phillips's turn to produce her phone this time, presenting Trudy with an image of Don Mountfield. 'Do you recognise this man?'

Trudy scowled. 'All the girls know that creep.'

'Tell me how,' said Phillips.

Trudy gestured to Gibson. 'He's one of *her* lot.'

'Has he ever asked you for sex?'

A look of uncertainty crossed Trudy's face as she shot a look at Gibson.

Phillips spotted her nervousness. 'It's ok. There'll be no recriminations. DS Gibson and I just want to know the truth.'

Trudy took a moment to answer before nodding.

'And did he pay for sex?'

This made Trudy laugh. 'Did he fuck. *He never pays.*'

Phillips pressed on. 'Are you saying you wanted to have sex with him?'

'No chance.'

'Then why?'

'He pays me in kind.'

'What do you mean "he pays me in kind"?' asked Gibson

Trudy glanced around the street once more before answering. 'I give him sex whenever he wants. In return, he makes sure I don't get picked up by *you lot.*'

'So when was the last time you had sex with him?' asked Phillips.

Trudy shrugged. 'Must be a month ago now, which is a long time for him. He usually wants something every week.'

Phillips's heart sank. If Mountfield hadn't been around for a month, it was unlikely he was the killer. 'So you've not seen him for a month, then?'

'I'm not saying that. No, I've *seen* him a few times driving around, but he's passed me by each time, thank God. Sex with him is bloody awful.'

Phillips's spirits rose. Mountfield *could* still be their man. 'Oh. Why's that?'

'Because he likes it rough. *Plus*, he won't wear a rubber; insists on coming inside me too. Every time I ask him to cum on my back or my arse, but he won't have it. So I have to get the morning-after pill on my way home. That means waiting for the chemists to open at 9.00 a.m., which is a massive pain in the arse. Especially when you've been out in the cold all night.'

'Do you know if you're the only girl he has this arrangement with?' asked Gibson.

Trudy scoffed. 'You're kidding, aren't you? He's shagging most of the girls on the strip. I'm surprised he has time to work. He's always down here.'

'Was Chloe giving him sex?'

'Yeah.'

'Could he have been the man who picked her up last night?'

'Not sure. I didn't see the guy's face. If it was him, he was in a different car to normal.'

Phillips cut in. 'I thought you said you didn't know cars?'

'I don't, but *everyone* knows Mountfield's car round here. We all try and get out of the way when we see it cruising around.'

'Can you describe it?' asked Phillips.

'Big and blue. That's all I can tell you, but I'd know it from a mile away.'

Another blast of wind surged up the street, causing Gibson to plunge her hands into her pockets. 'So which of the other girls was Mountfield using?'

'Just ask around. You'll find them.'

'We don't have time for that, Trudy. We need names,' said Gibson.

'Look, I'm not a grass.'

Phillips was in no mood for the 'honour amongst thieves'

bullshit. She leaned in close to Trudy, her voice threatening. 'Stop wasting our time. Either you give us the names now or I'll lock you up for obstruction and soliciting, and I'll guarantee you get a custodial sentence.'

Trudy raised her hands in defence. 'Jesus. All right, all right. No need to get out of your pram.'

'We're waiting,' said Phillips sternly.

Trudy shot a furtive glance around and spoke in a whisper. 'You didn't hear this from me, ok?'

Phillips and Gibson nodded.

'He uses Siobhan and Nat – that *I* know of.'

Phillips looked at Gibson. 'Do you know them?'

'Yes, Guv. They work over on the next couple of streets.'

'Ok. Let's go and pay them a visit. Thanks for your time, Trudy,' said Phillips as she turned to walk away.

Trudy appeared agitated now. 'You won't tell anyone what I said, will you?'

Phillips ignored the question as she moved up the street, with Gibson following closely behind.

36

Despite their initial reluctance to talk to the police, both girls backed up Trudy's account of her experiences with Mountfield, as well as sharing their own stories of his abuse. They too had identified him as driving a large blue car each time he picked them up. Siobhan Ferris had even recalled it having a radio fitted that allowed him to monitor police chatter. The evidence was starting to mount up: three eyewitnesses had identified Mountfield as a constant presence at the locations where the girls were found dead.

ANPR camera footage clearly showed a blue Mondeo – identical to one he used regularly – driving around those same locations within a two-hour window of each murder. His own sickness and leave record demonstrated he easily had the opportunity to commit to the crimes. Plus, he had inner knowledge of the workings of Adders Scrap Metal, meaning he could easily have stolen the plates spotted on the mystery blue Mondeo. Phillips decided it was time to bring him in.

The plan was that they would arrest him at his home in the early hours of the following morning.

Phillips had agreed to Gibson's request to sit out the operation, understanding how difficult it would be to arrest her own partner. The remainder of the team, however, now dressed in stab vests, sat in a squad car, waiting for the Tactical Firearms Unit to take up their positions outside Mountfield's flat in Sale, a large suburb six miles south-west of Manchester city centre.

As the time approached 5 a.m., Phillips turned to brief the team, Bovalino in the driving seat, Jones and Entwistle in the back. 'Ok, guys. When the TFU boys give us the signal, we'll follow them in. Mountfield's car is parked at the rear of the property, so we expect him to be inside. Hopefully he's asleep and we can take him by surprise.'

'How many bodies are we expecting inside the flat, Guv?' asked Jones.

'Four, if everyone's at home; Mountfield, his wife Trisha, and his twin daughters Gracie and Gillian, both aged seven. So, as much as we want this guy, we need to be careful not to scare the kids. Gibbo says he also owns a large Siberian Husky, so we'll wait for the all-clear from the dog unit before we head in, ok?'

The team agreed and waited for the signal from the TFU unit.

A few minutes later, the radio crackled into life. 'This is Alpha-1-3. We're in position and ready to go.'

Phillips replied. 'Standby. We're heading your way.'

Phillips took point. As she and the team reached the entrance to Mountfield's flat, the TFU guys launched into action, smashing open the external door with a large metal battering ram before rushing through.

Inside, shouts of 'armed police' could be heard, alongside the sound of savage dog barking for a moment, before the dog team managed to control and muzzle it.

Once they received the all-clear, Phillips led her team in and made her way through to the main bedroom, where Don

Mountfield and Trisha were sitting up in bed, looking shocked and confused.

Phillips wasted no time. 'Don Mountfield, I'm arresting you on suspicion of the murder of Candice Roberts, Chantelle Webster, Sasha Adams, Estelle Henderson and Chloe Barnes...'

'What the bloody hell are you talking about?' Mountfield sputtered, incredulous.

Phillips continued. '...You do not have to say anything, but it may harm your defence if you do not mention, when questioned, something which you later rely on in court. Anything you do say may be given in evidence.'

Trisha was crying now and looking to her husband, desperate for answers. 'What's happening, Don?'

Mountfield was doing his best to keep her calm. 'I've no idea, love. This must be some sort of mistake. I'm a bloody copper, for God's sake!'

Bovalino stepped forwards and pulled back the duvet. 'Can you step out from the bed please, Mr Mountfield?'

As Mountfield reluctantly got out of bed, Bovalino grabbed his arm. He pulled away violently, pushing Bovalino backwards. 'Get your bloody hands off me. I'm not a criminal.'

The big Italian, reacting with lightning speed, grabbed Mountfield's wrist and twisted him round in one movement. Forcing him forwards onto the bed, Bovalino yanked both arms behind his back and locked them in handcuffs.

Trisha was hysterical, screaming and wanting to know what was happening and why.

Phillips ignored her and left the room in search of a uniformed female officer. She found one talking to the twins in their shared bedroom. Both looked scared and confused. Phillips smiled and spoke softly to them. 'It's ok, girls, there's nothing to worry about. Everything is going to be fine. We just need to ask your dad some questions.' She moved her gaze to the officer. 'Are you the only female in the unit?'

'No Ma'am. PC Sahni is here too.'

'Where is she? I need someone to look after Mrs Mountfield. She's a bit upset.'

The officer pointed towards the front door. 'She's just walked in, Ma'am.'

Phillips turned to see a fresh-faced young officer stepping into the flat. She moved towards her. 'PC Sahni?

'Yes Ma'am.'

'I've got a job for you. Come with me.'

A few minutes later, with Trisha now sat safely in the kitchen flanked by her two daughters, Phillips and the team could focus on gathering the evidence they needed against Mountfield. Having calmed down sufficiently, Bovalino had removed his cuffs and helped him get dressed. He had continued to protest his innocence throughout, and showed no sign of letting up as Bovalino, accompanied by a couple of uniformed officers, escorted him to the waiting police van.

When he was finally out of the way, Jones and Entwistle began a preliminary search of the flat, looking for anything that might connect him to the girls. Entwistle soon found a laptop and mobile phone, which he presented to Phillips. 'I'm hoping there'll be something on these, Guv.'

'Do you have passwords for them?'

Entwistle smiled wryly. 'No, but that's never stopped me before. Once I get back to the station, Digital Forensics can open this lot up pretty quickly.'

As Bovalino returned to the flat, Phillips called the team together. She checked her watch; it was coming up to 6 a.m.

'Right. Mountfield will be processed in the next hour, which means we've got until approximately 7 a.m. tomorrow to find something to charge him with. If we don't, we'll have to let him go. So, we need to work fast.' Phillips passed Bovalino a pair of latex gloves. 'Extra Large for you, Bov.'

Bovalino grinned.

'Right, guys. I need this place taken apart inch by inch. Jonesy, you carry on in the living room, Entwistle take the kids bedroom, Bovalino, you're in the kitchen, so make sure you take it steady around the wife and kids, ok?'

'Of course.'

'I'll take the Mountfield's bedroom. We're on a clock here, guys, so I want it done in double-time, understood?'

'Yes Guv!' the team replied in unison, and set about their search.

37

Sometime later, back at Ashton House, Jones approached the open door to Phillips's office and knocked on the glass. She looked up from her notes. 'You don't usually knock. Is everything ok?'

'You looked fed up, Guv, that's all.'

Phillips reclined in her chair. 'I am, Jonesy. How can the search of Mountfield's flat turn up *nothing* to connect him to the girls? I was convinced it was him. I'm seriously starting to doubt myself now.'

Jones took a seat in the chair opposite her. 'Do you think we have enough to question him, Guv?'

Phillips pursed her lips. 'I think so, but as a copper himself, he'll know it's pretty thin. A blue car captured on ANPR cameras that we suspect could belong to Sex Crimes, a loose connection to a scrap yard dealing in fake plates, and eyewitness accounts from three sex workers with drug problems. Hardly enough to get the CPS excited, is it?'

'Well, when you put it like that...' said Jones

Phillips was suddenly consumed by doubt. 'Shit, Jonesy.

Have I jumped too soon on this one? We're supposed to be one hundred per cent certain when we go after our own.'

'From what the girls told you, he has to be a wrong'un. And if that's the case, he's bound to let something slip in questioning that will incriminate him.'

Phillips said nothing for a moment, deep in thought. 'I guess you're right.'

'Well, the clock's ticking before we have to charge him or let him go. So it's time to shit or get off the pot.'

Phillips nodded.

'He's in Interview Room Three with his police rep when you're ready, Guv.'

'Who's he's got?'

Jones paused. 'Daniel Thiel.'

Phillips dropped her pen on the pad in front of her and let out a frustrated sigh. 'Oh God, that's all we need. He's a right bloody snake.'

'I've only ever met him a couple of times, and that was twice too many. Horrible little man.'

Phillips said nothing for a moment, drumming her fingers on the desk. 'We're gonna have to box clever with Thiel. As I said, our evidence is very thin at this stage. He'll rip it to shreds if we're not careful.'

At that moment, Entwistle walked through the main door to the incident room and headed straight towards Phillips, an excited look on his face. 'I've just got back from Digital Forensics. Wait till you see this, Guv.'

Entwistle handed her a thick Manila folder, which she opened and laid out on the desk. As she ran her eyes down the pages, a wide grin spread across her face. 'Jesus Christ. I think we might just have enough to charge the bastard!'

Jones sat forwards, his eyes dancing. 'What have you got, Guv?'

'Have a look at this lot.' Phillips began passing him the pages, which he took and scanned, one at a time.

'Bloody hell,' he whispered at length. 'This stuff is dynamite.'

Phillips sat back and clapped her hands with glee. Finally, she had some evidence the CPS couldn't ignore. Standing, she gathered the pages back into the file and picked up her notepad. 'Come on, Jonesy. Let's see how Mountfield explains this little lot.'

38

Before they started the interview, Phillips and Jones stepped into the observation suite to check out what was waiting for them in Interview Room Three. On the large monitor attached to the wall, they could see the two men sitting side by side behind the plastic-topped table. Thiel's miniature frame was dwarfed by Mountfield, who had folded arms and was staring straight at the camera.

'Look at the arrogance of the man,' said Phillips.

'Yeah, I doubt he'll be quite so cocky when he sees that file.'

As eager as she was to confront him, Phillips wanted to ensure their strategy for the interview was clear. 'Let's not rush straight to the new info. Thiel is smart, and we have more chance of blind-siding him if he thinks the circumstantial evidence is all we have. If that's the case, he might drop his guard a little.'

'Agreed.'

'So follow my lead. But, as usual, if you see an opportunity, jump in.'

Jones nodded as Entwistle stepped into the room. It was his job to monitor the conversation and, if necessary, find evidence that either backed up or contradicted Mountfield's account of events as the interview progressed. The door opened again. This time, to Phillips's surprise, Gibson stepped inside. 'I wasn't expecting to see you in here, Gibbo.'

Gibson looked a little sheepish. 'No Guv, neither was I. But I'm finding it hard to sit on the sidelines. I can't ignore the fact all the evidence is pointing towards Mountfield. I took an oath, and if he *did* kill those girls, we need to get him for it. I was hoping to sit in with Entwistle if that's all right with you? I know him well enough – or at least I thought I did. Maybe I can help.'

Phillips admired her courage. It was never easy investigating coppers, especially those you've worked alongside for many years. 'I'd be glad to have you, Gibbo.' She patted her on the arm and turned to Jones. 'You ready?'

'As I'll ever be,' he replied, and followed her out.

Once inside, they moved through the formalities with the speed you would expect from a room full of police officers, and as soon as the loud beep of the DIR had faded, Phillips set to work. 'DC Mountfield, can you tell us where you were on the evening of Tuesday 6th of November?'

Mountfield stared impassively at Phillips. 'I don't know offhand. Either at work or at home.'

Phillips passed over the Sex Crimes Squad staffing rota for that week. 'This is a copy of your departmental staff rota. As you can see from the date marked, you were not on shift that night.'

'Like I said, I must have been at home then.'

David Thiel inspected the document and made a note in his pad

Phillips continued. 'Can your wife confirm that?'

Mountfield looked unfazed. 'Of course.'

Phillips held his gaze for longer than necessary. 'And what about Friday 16th of November?'

Mountfield ventured a belligerent grunt. 'I don't have a photographic memory of my rota. Anyway, you obviously know the answer – so why don't *you* tell me where you think I was.'

Phillips passed over the rota for that week. 'Well, you definitely weren't at work that night either.'

'Well, I would have been at home with the wife then, *wouldn't I?*'

Thiel continued making notes in his pad, but had yet to engage. Phillips recalled it was his tried and tested strategy: keep his powder dry until he was ready to use it.

'Can you remember where you were on the night of Sunday 9th of December?'

Mountfield said nothing for a moment before exhaling loudly though his nose. 'Really? Is this what you broke into my home for? Why you dragged me out of bed and upset my wife and kids?'

'Answer the question please, DC Mountfield,' demanded Phillips.

'I don't know without looking at the diary on my phone. And seeing as how you lot took that this morning, you'll know better than me where I was.'

Phillips passed over the staffing roster for that week. 'Well, once again I can tell you, you weren't at work. So where were you?'

'I'll have been at home.'

'And you're sure of that?'

'Yes,' said Mountfield forcefully.

Phillips tilted her head to the side as she looked at him for a moment. 'But I thought you said you couldn't know where you were without looking at your phone?'

Mountfield flinched for the first time, a small eye twitch, but Phillips caught it. Jones scribbled something on his notepad; it looked as if he had spotted it too. 'Er, what I meant was that if I'm not here, then I'm always at home.'

Phillips took a moment before moving on to the night Estelle Henderson was killed. The night Mountfield had pulled out of the Billy Armitage surveillance operation with severe vomiting, 'What do you think caused you to be violently sick the night you joined Gibson on our operation?'

'Like I told her at the time, I had tried a new kebab shack in Rusholme that lunchtime and felt nauseous all afternoon. Must have been food poisoning.'

'So what happened after you removed yourself from the squad car?' asked Phillips.

'I carried on being sick.'

'All night?'

Mountfield shook his head. 'No. It carried on for another fifteen minutes or so, until there was nothing left to bring up.'

'So what did you do when it finally stopped?'

'I went home, of course.'

'Straight home?'

'Yes.'

'And how did you get from Salford to Sale?'

'I took a taxi.'

'What kind?'

Mountfield appeared confused. 'What do you mean, "what kind"?'

'Did you get an Uber, a mini-cab, a black cab?'

'Oh right, a black cab. I flagged one down.'

'In Salford? That's unusual, isn't it?'

'Not really. The driver was on his way back into town from a job in Eccles.'

'Whereabouts did you flag it down?'

'I don't remember. I wasn't paying attention – *because I was very sick,*' sneered Mountfield.

Phillips's eyes narrowed. 'Ok. So, do you remember anything about the cab that might help us track it down.'

'Yeah. It was black,' Mountfield said sarcastically.

Phillips ignored the self-congratulatory grin that spread across his face. 'What time did you get home?'

'I have no idea. Like I said, I was sick, so I wasn't checking the clock. I just wanted to get home and get to bed.'

'I see. Well, we'll need to speak to your wife to verify all this.'

Mountfield shrugged nonchalantly. 'Be my guest.'

Phillips moved on to Chloe Barnes now. 'Have you ever been to the Belmont estate in Salford?'

'Of course.'

'When was there last time you were there?'

'I dunno. I'm SCT. We're up there all the time.'

'How about two nights ago?'

'No,' he said.

'And you're sure of that?' asked Phillips.

'One hundred per cent.'

'So where *were* you two nights ago?'

'You tell me. You're the one with the rotas.'

Phillips produced a thin smile. It was time to change tack. 'Do you drive a Blue Ford Mondeo for work?'

'I drive a lot of cars.'

'One of them being a Blue Ford Mondeo?'

'Probably. I'm colour blind, so it could be blue, could be green.'

Phillips made a note in her pad. 'And have you driven that same blue or green Ford Mondeo around Cheetham Hill, Miles Platting and Ancoats before.'

'That's SCT's patch, so I can assume so.'

'You don't remember?'

'I'm not a bloody Sat Nav, love,' he chuckled.

Phillips stared at Mountfield for a long moment before responding. 'I would remind you that I am the ranking officer here, and you will refer to me as DCI Phillips or Ma'am.'

Embarrassment, then anger, flashed across Mountfield's

face. It was evident he didn't like being reprimanded by a woman.

'How well do you know Adders Scrap Metal Merchants in Ancoats?'

Thiel was at last ready to engage. 'What does this have to do with DC Mountfield's arrest?'

Phillips shot him a look. 'I assure you, it's relevant.'

Thiel nodded before averting his eyes and making a note in his pad.

'As I was saying, how well do you know Adders Scrap Metal Merchants in Ancoats?' Phillips continued.

'It's a front for prostitution and trafficking. We've been watching him for over eighteen months now.'

'And have you ever been involved in a surveillance operation of the Ancoats yard?'

'Of course I have. I'm a Sex Crimes officer,' he said sardonically.

'Have you ever entered the premises of Adders Scrap Metal Merchants?'

'I've interviewed Adders a few times, yeah. But he's a slippery bastard and always has an answer for everything.'

'I see,' said Phillips, making another note. 'And have you ever been out into the yard itself, amongst the vehicles?'

'I've had a look around once or twice.'

Phillips changed tack again. 'DC Mountfield, how well did you know Candice Roberts?'

'She was a prostitute. I knew her from my work on the streets.'

'And how about Chantelle Webster?'

'The same.'

'And is that how you knew Sasha Adams, Estelle Henderson and Chloe Barnes?'

'Yeah. They were all sex workers who we picked up from time to time, trying to clean up the streets. Not that it worked. It didn't matter how many times those girls got arrested, they always went back to the life.'

Phillips nodded before glancing at Jones; it was time to turn the pressure up a notch. 'DC Mountfield, did you ever use prostitutes yourself?'

Mountfield didn't flinch. 'No.'

'So you never had sex with Candice Roberts, Chantelle Webster, Sasha Adams, Estelle Henderson or Chloe Barnes?'

'No. I did not.'

'What about any of the other girls working in Cheetham Hill?'

'I don't need to pay for sex,' Mountfield said, very sure of himself.

Phillips affected an expression of surprise. 'Really? I'm glad you said that, as that's what three other working girls have told us. That you had sex with them, but rather than pay them, you forced them into the sex in exchange for not arresting them.'

Mountfield swallowed hard. 'They're lying.'

'Really, all three?'

Thiel decided to re-enter the fray. 'DCI Phillips, do you have written statements from these women?'

Phillips kept her eyes fixed on Mountfield. 'Not written, no—'

Thiel didn't let her finish. 'Well, in that case, given that DC Mountfield is a decorated officer with an unblemished record, could I respectfully ask that you keep the questions related to evidence you *do* actually have in your possession?'

Phillips locked her gaze on Thiel. 'They may only be verbal statements at this stage, but if need be, I'm quite happy to send a uniformed team down to Cheetham Hill right now and have each of the girls picked up and brought back here to make their statements official. I'd rather not go through the rigmarole of all that, but unless DC Mountfield starts telling the truth, I'll have no other option.'

'I told you, they're lying. All of them.'

Phillips sighed. 'Very well. In that case, I have no choice but to pause the interview and instruct one of my officers to organise the arrest and detention of Trudy Tench, Siobhan Ferris and Nat Barker, who all claimed you forced them to have sex or face arrest.' She stared intently at Mountfield. His left eye appeared to twitch and his lip curled a fraction at hearing the girls' names. The cockiness ebbed away and he leaned into a whispered exchange with Thiel, who eventually nodded.

Mountfield sat upright again and cleared his throat. 'Ok. I'll admit, I have had sex with those girls, but they consented. There was never any quid pro quo.'

Jones decided to step in now. 'I'm a little confused to be honest, DC Mountfield. Why would three women who *charge* for sex, give it to *you* for free?'

'They liked me.'

'Really?' Phillips cut back in. 'Because I spoke to all three girls, and each of them told me they hated having sex with you. *Hated it.* That you made their skin crawl. In fact, whenever they saw your car pull up, they'd all try and get out of the way.'

Hatred sparked in Mountfield's black eyes and his face flushed red as he stared back at Phillips. 'They're lying, and in the end it's their word against mine. And who do you think a jury is going to believe – a bunch of junkie whores or a decorated officer like me?'

Phillips didn't respond and instead took her time, intently scribbling notes on her notepad for a moment before looking up at Mountfield and Thiel and feigning surprise. 'Sorry, I was just jotting down your exact words there, "junkie whores". Like you say, I'm sure a jury would be very interested to know how a decorated officer like yourself describes these women.'

Mountfield opened his mouth to speak, but Phillips removed a printed image from her file and placed it in front of him. 'Do you recognise this information?'

Mountfield looked down at the page for a moment and returned to his gaze to Phillips. 'Never seen it before.'

'Really? It's a number of Google searches on how cold water shock can lead to death through drowning.' She tapped one of the images. 'This one here even describes how it can be accelerated.'

'What's that got to do with me?'

She handed him another printout. 'And how about this? It's another Google search that suggests how to drown a person as quickly and quietly as possible.'

Mountfield gave the pages a cursory look. 'And?'

Phillips passed across a document that was a quarter-inch thick, bound together down one side. 'Maybe this lot will jog your memory. It's over two thousand search results for violent porn, with some of the girls' heads being held under water in the bath whilst being penetrated from behind.' She watched his eyes bulge as he stared at the images on display in front of him. She pressed on. 'All of this data was retrieved from *your* phone by the Digital Forensics team, after your arrest.'

Mountfield's eyes shot up to meet hers. 'This stuff isn't mine.'

'Well, if it's not yours, then whose is it?'

Mountfield pointed at Phillips and Jones. 'You lot must've planted it. I'm being set up.'

'Digital Forensics don't lie, DC Mountfield.'

Mountfield looked desperate now. 'I don't know where you got that stuff from, but I'm telling you, it's not mine!'

Phillips had one last ace up her sleeve. She produced copies of ANPR printouts and placed them in front of him. 'As you'll see here, these are copies of images taken from ANPR cameras located in and around the Cheetham Hill, Miles Platting and Ancoats areas on the nights Candice Roberts, Chantelle Webster, Sasha Adams, Estelle Henderson and Chloe Barnes were killed. Note the make, model and colour of the car: a blue

Ford Mondeo.' She passed him a registration document from the police vehicle records. 'Just like the one used daily by Sex Crimes and Trafficking. A car that a number of eyewitnesses claim to have seen in and around those same areas in the hours leading up to each of the girls going missing.'

Mountfield remained defiant. 'This is bullshit. Anyone could have driven that car. There's ten of us in SCT.'

'That's true, but one of the girls you had sex with, Siobhan Ferris, specifically remembers the make and model of the car as a blue Ford Mondeo. She also recalls you having a police radio in the car at the time you were together physically. She said you seemed to be getting off listening to the chatter, laughing because you could do what you wanted to her and stay one step ahead of the police.'

Mountfield began to flounder as Phillips summed up the evidence against him. 'Three different women claim to have been forced to have sex with you against their will. That's rape, DC Mountfield and carries a long prison term. Those same women independently state they saw you driving a large blue car through Cheetham Hill at the times of the murders. A car identical to one captured on ANPR cameras driving close to the murder scenes when the girls were killed. That same car carried plates stolen from cars bought and decommissioned by Adders Scrap Metal Merchant, an organisation you admit you had access to on a number of occasions, meaning it would have been easy for you to pick up the fake plates without anyone noticing.'

Phillips placed her hand flat on the printouts of the internet searches. 'Added to that, your mobile phone is filled with pornography focused on violence against women and, in particular, women who it appears are being drowned during sexual assaults by men. Plus, you have multiple searches on how cold water shock kills – and can be accelerated – as well as a guide on how to drown people quickly and quietly. And finally, you say your alibi for each of the murders is your wife, but so far you cannot recall the specific details of what you were doing on any of the nights each of the girls died. In fact, I'm pretty confident that when we dig into your actual whereabouts, we'll find you weren't home with your wife at all.'

Mountfield appeared lost for words.

Phillips went in for the kill. 'DC Mountfield, did you kill Candice Roberts, Chantelle Webster, Sasha Adams, Estelle Henderson and Chloe Barnes?'

Thiel touched Mountfield's wrist and drew him into another whispered exchange for a long moment. Eventually Mountfield nodded and turned his attention back to Phillips. He glared at her, hatred brimming from every pore. 'No comment.'

39

Phillips arrived for her five o'clock briefing and took a seat in Fox's office as instructed by the chief super's PA. Apparently she was on her way back from a meeting with the mayor of Manchester, and only a few moments away.

Looking around the space, she noted the self-congratulatory 'wall of achievement' behind Fox's enormous smoked-glass desk and tan leather power chair, where a host of framed photographs depicted the chief super shaking hands with a wide range of dignitaries and celebrities, most likely taken at various charity events. The largest and most prominent space, in the middle of the wall, was dedicated to an image of her clutching her Manchester Hero award outside the Town Hall, her Cheshire Cat grin fixed across her face. Phillips marvelled at the contrast of her smile to the blackness of her eyes, and was reminded of the adage, 'The eyes are the window to the soul.' She nodded to herself as she considered what that meant in Fox's case; a dark soul to match her black eyes. Phillips was also struck by the way in which Fox presented herself to the outside world versus the reality; in public, a wholesome, honest copper dedicated to catching villains. Behind closed doors, widely regarded as a narcissistic sociopath, obsessed with her own progression and power within the GMP. It was no secret that she and the chief constable did not get on. *He* believed she wanted his job, and *she* was convinced she could do it better.

The door behind her opened and Fox strode in. 'DCI Phillips.' Fox sounded agitated as she stomped across the room before dropping into the seat behind her desk. It was obvious she was in no mood for pleasantries. 'So what have you got on Mountfield?'

Phillips opened the case file on the desk and over the next ten minutes walked Fox through everything she had presented to Mountfield and Thiel earlier that morning. When she was finished, Fox remained silent, staring at the images and documents before her. When she eventually spoke, her agitation appeared to have increased. 'So it's just bloody circumstantial then?'

'Regarding Mountfield's whereabouts at the time of the murders, yes, but Jones and Bovalino have spoken to his wife, who admitted that even when he's home, he usually takes their dog for a walk. It's a Siberian Husky, so he can be gone for up to two hours. That's more than enough time to drive to Cheetham Hill and commit the murders.'

'True. But what does he do with the dog if that's the case? It's not what you'd call a discreet breed, is it?'

'Maybe he leaves it tied up somewhere or gets a mate to walk it?'

Fox appeared unimpressed, so Phillips drew her attention to the documents they'd found on Mountfield's phone. 'This stuff will paint a pretty grim picture in court, Ma'am; how to drown people quickly and quietly; how to accelerate cold water shock. Violent pornography depicting women being drowned.'

'A grim picture of what, though? A guy who gets off watching women being screwed in the bath?'

'It's a lot more than that, Ma'am.'

'Is it, though? In today's world, I don't agree. This stuff is all over the internet, and downloading it is *not* illegal.'

'Well, it certainly puts him in the frame for the girls' deaths. Why else would he be looking at how to drown women?'

'Because, as the pornography attests to, he likes to see women with their heads in the bath, being screwed roughly from behind. Nothing more than that.'

'Ok. Even if that is the case, we still have him for abusing his position as an officer of the law to solicit sex by force. That alone means jail time, Ma'am.'

'Inspector, the last thing the force needs right now is our reputation being sullied by a randy copper who couldn't keep his dick in his pants. Whether we like it or not, the harsh truth of the matter is, the public don't care about his victims. Sex workers being forced to have sex is considered, by many, an occupational hazard. Plus, it'll be his word against theirs in court. And we all know what juries think of prostitutes. We'll never get a conviction.'

'With respect, Ma'am, we can't just let him go.'

Fox was angry now. 'I'm well aware of that, Inspector. In fact, I've just spent the last *two hours* with the mayor droning on at me about how disappointed he is that we're yet to make a breakthrough on the canal death cases. He's particularly upset that Don Townsend has now made the whole thing public in his disgusting rag of a newspaper. When I sanctioned this investigation, *you* promised me you'd make rapid progress. So far, you've delivered nothing.'

Phillips bit her tongue. She wanted nothing more than to remind Fox that it was *she* who'd pushed for the investigation in the first place, and if she hadn't, then the press coverage would have been a whole lot worse. However, it was pointless arguing; Fox was infamous for re-writing history to suit her own needs.

'We still have fourteen hours to hold him on the murders,'

said Phillips, 'and if we need to, we can buy ourselves a further twenty-four hours by arresting him tomorrow morning on the sex charges.'

'Agreed.' Fox's eyes glazed over. She appeared to be deep in thought for a moment, before turning her attention back to Phillips. 'That said, though, ultimately – and for all the reasons we've already discussed – I'm reluctant to arrest him for the sex stuff. Which means, Inspector, the grim reality for you is, you have thirty-eight hours to solicit a conviction from Mountfield *or let him go.*'

Phillips pushed her feet into the floor and clenched her toes inside her shoes in a desperate attempt to ground herself, to fend off the raw anger and frustration rising in her gut. She wanted to scream but, remembering her therapist's advice, breathed deeply and managed to remain in control; just. Sure, she wanted Mountfield for the murders, but if there was no conclusive way to prove he was responsible for the girls' deaths, then they at least had him on the hook for abusing his position as an officer. And, with a bit more work from Phillips and her team, the CPS could potentially push for rape charges. However, it appeared Fox was more interested in preserving the reputation of the force than protecting a whole community of women based solely on how they earned their living. Mountfield was a predator. If he was allowed back on the streets, Phillips knew, without a doubt, he would abuse again.

Fox handed the case file back to Phillips. 'So it appears there's no time to waste, Inspector. You'd better hurry back down to interrogation and get that confession, hadn't you?'

Phillips took the file and stood. 'Yes Ma'am.'

'You understand how important this case is to the reputation of the GMP, don't you, Inspector?'

Phillips nodded. 'Of course, Ma'am.' The words stuck in her throat.

Fox's fake smile returned, but her eyes remained menacing. 'Good. I'm glad we understand each other, Jane.'

'Yes Ma'am.'

Fox waved her away. 'Right. I have a function to prepare for this evening. Dismissed.'

40

Phillips headed to the rear exit of Ashton House in need of some air; the colder the better, or she feared she would explode with rage. Once again she had found herself on the end of an unwarranted bollocking for not delivering a result to Fox's timeline; a result that less than a week ago was of zero importance to the chief superintendent. The duplicity of the woman was incredible and, not for the first time, Phillips wondered why she put herself through so much shit each and every day, working for yet another political animal. It was almost as if she attracted them. Or – she was forced to consider – was it that her own methods and values were hopelessly out of touch with modern policing? Had her goals of bringing criminals to justice and protecting the innocent been usurped by selfish career-focused coppers hell-bent on their own advancement?

Stepping out into the dark rear car park, she took a deep breath, closed her eyes and tried to clear her head. Standing alone under the night sky, she could hear the faint sound of Dean Martin singing 'Baby, It's Cold Outside' floating out from one of the open windows above her. She listened for a moment, taking in the lyrics. The words brought Chantelle Webster's mother and father to mind, and their devastation at losing their daughter so unexpectedly. She then thought of Chantelle's little boy Ajay, growing up without his mum. Her stomach churned at the pain that had descended on that household just a few weeks before Christmas, at a time when family was at the centre of everything. Feeling their pain in her gut as if it were her own, the guilt weighed heavy knowing Chantelle's killer could potentially be set free. In that moment, she was reminded of why she became a copper in the first place, why staying true to her values was so important. Innocent people needed Phillips and her team to protect them, to care about their loved ones. To go the extra mile, to resist the urge to let people off just because it might make the police look bad.

Re-energised, and with renewed determination, she headed back inside. Somehow, she needed to get Mountfield to admit to his crimes.

Striding into the incident room, she spied Gibson sitting at her desk. She looked troubled, a thousand-yard stare locked across her face. Phillips walked over to her. 'Penny for your thoughts, Gibbo?'

Gibson appeared startled, blinking back into focus. 'Sorry, Guv. I was miles away.'

Phillips took a seat at one of the empty desks. 'Where are the lads?'

'In the canteen getting some food. Ahead of a long night, I guess.'

'You didn't fancy joining them?'

Gibson's eyes were filled with sadness. 'I've got no appetite.'

'It's tough when you find out someone you trusted isn't what you thought they were. I know that better than most.'

Gibson sighed. 'Look, I always knew Mountfield had a bit of a roving eye and fancied some of the girls, but I would never have imagined he was forcing them to have sex with him. I mean, he has two daughters of his own. I never believed a father could act like that. And he's such a normal bloke. There's nothing exceptional about him at all.'

'They're often the ones you have to watch. People with low self-esteem, and in many cases emasculated. What's his wife like?'

Gibson smiled. 'Actually, she's quite sweet. Very down to earth and really caring. She would often make cakes and pastries that Mountfield would share around the office. She's involved in the local church and dotes on the twins.'

'Maybe she's too nice in that case?'

'How do you mean?'

'Well, you know, some men like a bit of danger. Judging by Mountfield's pornography of choice, your description of Mrs Mountfield doesn't seem to match his taste in violent sex, does it?'

Gibson shook her head as Phillips fixed her with a steely glare. 'I really need you to help me get Mountfield's confession.'

Gibson stared back for a long moment. 'I can't, Guv.'

'Tell me why. What's stopping you, now you know what he's capable of?'

'I know he's abused his position to have unlawful sex, but I'm really struggling to see him as a killer. What if he's right and he is being set up? You know what that's like; it happened to you, after all.'

Phillips had to admit, what Gibson was saying was true; she herself had been set up during the Michaels investigation by a chief constable looking to discredit her after she uncovered his corruption. It almost cost her her career, *and* nearly killed her. However, the circumstances here seemed very different, especially given Trudy, Siobhan and Nat's recollections of the abuse they had suffered at his hands.

'Guv, I want to help the team, I really do. I'm happy to work with the girls to get him on the sex charges. But murder? If we're wrong and he didn't kill those girls, I couldn't live with myself.'

'Fox isn't looking to prosecute the sex charges.'

Gibson was incredulous. 'What? Why on earth not?'

'Because we don't have any physical evidence, and it's Mountfield's word against that of three sex workers. She believes a jury will never convict him and it'd drag the GMP through the mud unnecessarily. So, we either get him on the murders or he walks.'

'That's crazy.'

'That's politics, I'm afraid.'

It was obvious Mountfield knew how to play the game, but Gibson knew him better than most. Phillips believed she was probably their best chance of pulling out a confession, so kept on pushing her. 'In these situations, when you're conflicted, I believe there are two things you can do to get clarity.'

Gibson appeared hopeful. 'And what are they, Guv?'

'Well, firstly, you look at all the evidence. In Mountfield's case, we have three women claiming that he was, to all intents and purposes, raping them on a weekly basis, using his privileged position as a police officer to remove their ability to say no. Then there's the fact that, even though he claims to have been at home at the time of the attacks, his wife says he was out walking the dog for hours when each girl was killed – giving him plenty of opportunity. We also believe that whoever murdered Estelle Henderson likely had inside knowledge of the police, and in particular of our operation to follow Billy Armitage. An operation he conveniently removed himself from moments before it was about to start.'

'Yeah, I know that. To be fair, though, I was sat next to him and he *was* projectile vomiting. He couldn't have faked that.'

Phillips raised an eyebrow. 'Really? I've seen it done before. It happened to one of the victims in the Cheadle Murder cases.

All it takes are a few eyedrops in a drink and you can induce violent vomiting.'

'Jesus. Is that right?'

'Yeah. Just ask Chakrabortty. In that case, the victim had ingested the eyedrops in chocolates sent by the killer. You can read the details in the post mortem report for Ricky Murray. And let's not forget, when you started the pursuit of Armitage, you left him vomiting in the car park. But when a uniformed team went looking for him half an hour later, he'd miraculously disappeared, conveniently flagging down a black cab – a vehicle we've been unable to find any trace of on the ANPR cameras in that area at that time.'

Phillips's words appeared to be landing with Gibson, so she pressed on. 'And on top of that, his mobile phone is packed with images of women being violated, effectively being drowned during violent sex acts. Plus, he made a large quantity of Google searches on how to drown women quickly and quietly, and the best way to accelerate cold water shock. I mean, you just have to look at the post mortem results for each of the girls; *death from drowning, likely brought on by cold water shock.*'

Gibson leaned forwards and placed her face in her hands for a moment.

'Let's not forget, Siobhan Ferris identified Mountfield as driving a blue Ford Mondeo when he had sex with her – one fitted with a police radio. Not to mention, Mountfield had access to the scrap yard where the rogue plates were stolen from. Do you really believe that's all a matter of coincidence?'

Gibson dropped her hands. 'You don't believe in coincidences do you, Guv?'

'No, I bloody don't. I believe in evidence – and all the evidence, even though it may be circumstantial at this stage, points to Mountfield as the killer.'

'So why kill Roberts, Webster and the rest, but then leave the Trudy and the others alone?'

'Maybe he wasn't finished. Maybe they're next.'

Gibson digested Phillips's words. 'You said there were two things to look at in a case like this, Guv. What's the other?'

Phillips sat back and placed both hands on her stomach. 'This, Gibbo. Listen to your gut. It's never wrong.'

Gibson nodded.

'So, what is *your* gut telling you?'

Gibson sat in silence for a moment before responding. 'That he's a bad man and we need to stop him from hurting any more girls.'

'In that case, Gibbo, please help me get a confession.'

Gibson took a long time to answer. 'Ok Guv. I will. If he did kill those girls, I can't sit back and let him walk. I have to do everything I can to prove he's the killer.'

Phillips let out a relieved sigh. 'Thank God for that. It won't be easy, but it'd be a damn sight more difficult without you, Gibbo.' She glanced at her watch. 'Let's round up the troops and get back in front of him. Every second counts on this one.'

41

With Entwistle, Jones and Bovalino watching from the observation suite, Phillips entered Interview Room Three alone and took a seat opposite Mountfield, who once again sat next to Thiel. Mountfield's hair was flat and messy on one side from where he had slept on it, and he was in need of a shave. He fixed his gaze on Phillips, who noted an involuntary snarl of agitation flicker under his nose. She said nothing for a long moment, instead placing her case file on the table and making notes on her pad. It was all part of their carefully planned interrogation strategy. Right on cue, Gibson knocked on the door and entered. Mountfield appeared shocked. Gibson flashed him a warm smile and asked if he was ok as she passed him a hot mug of tea. 'Two sugars, as usual.'

Mountfield smiled and took a noisy slurp.

'This is all a bit of mess isn't it, mate?' said Gibson.

'It's bullshit is what it is, Gibbo. Total bullshit.'

Phillips took a moment to go through the formalities of using the DIR, and a few minutes later they restarted the interview. 'DC Mountfield, I'd like to go back to the night you were due to take part in the surveillance of Billy Armitage. You claimed you pulled out of the operation due to severe sickness—'

'I don't claim, it's a fact. I was chucking my guts up. Gibbo will back me up, won't you?'

Gibson looked at Phillips. 'He's correct, Ma'am. I saw it for myself – he was very, very poorly.'

'See. I told you,' said Mountfield, grinning as he folded his arms in triumph.

Phillips ignored him and continued. 'Ok. So, after you left the car driven by DS Gibson, what happened?'

Thiel cut in now. 'DC Mountfield has explained all of this, Inspector.'

'Yes, and I'd like him to explain it again. So, if you don't mind, please tell us again what happened after you left the car?'

'I continued to throw up for about fifteen minutes, then got a cab home.'

'And where did you pick up the cab?'

'Like I said before, I flagged one down from the street.'

'Which street was that?'

'I dunno. The nearest main road to Armitage's place.'

Phillips flicked through her notes until she found what she was looking for. 'That would be Langworthy Terrace?'

Mountfield shrugged. 'If you say so.'

'And the cab took you straight home?'

'Yes.'

'What time did you get to your house?'

'I can't recall.'

Phillips looked down at the notes Jones had made during his interview with Mrs Mountfield. 'I understand your wife wasn't at home that night?'

'No, she was up at her mother's with the kids.'

'And where does her mother live?'

'Darlington.'

'Does she spend a lot of time away from home?'

'She goes up once a month; wants the girls to be as close to their North East family as they are to their Manchester grandparents and cousins.'

'So when they go to Darlington, they leave you at home alone?'

'I have the dog.'

Phillips checked her notes again. 'A Siberian Husky?'

Mountfield nodded.

'What's its name?'

'*He's* called Zeus.'

Phillips looked taken aback. 'Father of the gods. Are you a fan of Greek mythology?'

'Not really. There was a character called Higgins in the TV show *Magnum P.I.* years ago. He had a Doberman called Zeus. I've always liked it.'

Phillips smiled and made a note in her pad. 'How much was the cab ride?'

'What?'

'How much did you pay for the taxi ride home?'

Mountfield looked confused. 'What the hell has that got to do with anything?'

'I'm just wondering how much you paid for the taxi that night. It's a twenty-minute drive from Langworthy Terrace to your house in Sale. In a black cab, that wouldn't have been cheap.'

He puffed out, rattling his lips. 'It was about thirty quid, I think.'

'You don't remember?'

Mountfield's frustration was evident. 'No I don't. I was sick and I just wanted to get to bed. To be honest, the way I was feeling, I'd've paid whatever was necessary to get home that night.'

'And did you pay cash or card?'

'Cash.'

Phillips forced a thin smile. 'That's a shame. We could have at least traced a card payment.'

'I don't trust those machines; especially not in taxis.'

'In that case, can you tell us anything else about the cab that might help us track it down? After all, it'd really help backup your story of what happened that night.'

'No. Like I said, I was sick.'

Phillips decided to switch focus. 'We've spoken to your wife about the nights Candice Roberts, Chantelle Webster, Sasha Adams and Chloe Barnes were all killed. She confirms you were at home on each of those evenings.'

'Which means you have no case, Inspector,' Thiel jumped in.

Mountfield's triumphant grin returned and he reclined in his chair.

Phillips turned to look at Thiel. 'I'm afraid you're wrong. You see, Mrs Mountfield *did* confirm DC Mountfield was at home on the dates in question. However, she also admitted that her husband was out of the house on each of those nights, sometimes for up to two hours at a time, walking the dog.' Phillips produced a printout of a Google map with a route marked in blue from Mountfield's address in Sale through to Cheetham Hill. 'As you can see from this map, it's a twenty-seven-minute drive from your house to where the girls were killed, which would mean you would have enough time to get there, pick up the girls, drown them in the canal and get home.'

Thiel snorted. 'Really, Inspector. You're reaching now.'

'Am I? We'll just have to see what a jury has to say, won't we? With DC Mountfield's cast-iron alibi now looking distinctly unstable, plus what we took from his phone, the ANPR cameras and eyewitness statements, it doesn't look good.'

'Your confidence is unwarranted,' Thiel volleyed back, 'and if I'm honest, an obvious charade, Chief Inspector. Everyone in this room knows the CPS will never sanction charges on the evidence you have presented up to now.'

Phillips held his gaze and adopted her best poker face. He was right, of course, but they had planned for this. Now it was time for Gibson to take the lead. Phillips gave her the signal.

Gibson appeared nervous at first. Her neck had flushed under her collar, and when she spoke, her tongue clicked against her dry palate. 'Don, what's been going on with these girls? Have you really been sleeping with them?'

Mountfield seemed surprised and a little embarrassed by the question. 'God, not you 'n' all. I thought you'd be on *my* side.'

'Come on, Don. We've been working together for over five years. I'm entitled to ask.'

'So I slept with a few hookers. Big deal.'

'The report says you offered leniency in exchange for sex with Trudy, Siobhan and Nat.'

'So what?'

All nerves seemed to vanish now. Gibson recoiled in her seat, her mouth falling open. '*So what?* Jesus, Don, we've worked those streets together for years. We were supposed to help them get out of the life, not push them further into it.'

'Oh, piss off with your holier-than-thou routine. You're no angel.'

'And what's that supposed to mean?'

'You know what I'm talking about.'

Gibson stared at him unflinching. 'No, I'm afraid I don't.'

Mountfield unfolded his arms and appeared uncertain of what he was going to say next.

'Come on, Don. Explain to me why I'm no angel,' demanded Gibson.

'It doesn't matter, just leave it.'

'No, Don, I won't leave it. What did you mean? I'd like to know.'

Mountfield scoffed. 'Well you can't deny you're a regular in those dodgy clubs, can you?'

Gibson looked confused. 'What dodgy clubs?'

'Those sex clubs in the village. I've seen you going into them when you think no one is watching.'

'You mean gay clubs?'

'Call 'em what you like. They're nothing more than brothels. You're no different to me.'

Gibson let out an ironic chuckle. 'I'm *nothing* like you, Don. Yes I go to gay clubs...because I'm gay. And there's nothing sordid about them at all. They're just nightclubs, and visiting them is completely legal.'

'How can you say that when we've arrested people outside them for having sex on the streets.'

'Yes. *Outside.* That didn't happen inside the clubs. And if I'm off duty, unless someone is being attacked or in danger, I'll leave people to do whatever makes them happy. That's what life in the village is all about.'

Mountfield had the look of a petulant child. 'Whatever.'

Phillips refocused the interview. 'Can we get back to the matter in hand please?'

Gibson took her cue. 'So did you sleep with Candice?'

'No.'

'What about Chantelle and Sasha?'

'Nope.'

'And Estelle and Chloe? Do you deny having sex with them too?'

'I do.'

'So why did Trudy, Siobhan and Nat all say you did?'

'Because they're liars and don't like the fact I've arrested them before for hooking. They'll say anything to get back at me.'

Gibson looked down at her notes for a moment, then back at Mountfield. 'But in your earlier interview with DCI Phillips and DS Jones, you said they liked you Don. That's why they gave you sex for *free*.'

Mountfield stuttered. 'E-e-er, yeah. They did.'

'They liked you?'

'Yes.'

'So, if they liked you enough to give you free sex, why would they say you had been sleeping with Candice and the other girls – as a way to get back at you?'

Mountfield was caught in his own lie.

Gibson looked him dead in the eye. 'Tell me the truth, Don. You did have sex with Candice, Sasha and the others, didn't you?'

Thiel touched Mountfield's wrist, signalling for him not to answer. His scrawny face was matched by his thin, nasal tones. 'I feel like we're going over old ground here, Sergeant. DC Mountfield has been very clear on the matter. He did not have sex with either Candice Roberts, Chantelle Webster, Sasha Adams or Chloe Barnes, and without their testimony – which for obvious reasons is no longer available – you can't prove whether he did or didn't. The truth is that the claims of three drug-addicted sex workers is unlikely to satisfy the CPS enough to bring charges against DC Mountfield. So, unless you have anything new to discuss regarding your case, it would seem like we've exhausted all avenues connecting him with the canal deaths. Wouldn't you agree?'

Phillips remained poker-faced. 'We still have nine hours to hold DC Mountfield for questioning. So I'll be the one to decide when all avenues have been exhausted.'

Thiel produced a crooked smile. 'Ok. So what else would you like to ask DC Mountfield, Chief Inspector?'

The truth was, she had nothing left. Their whole strategy had been based on Gibson luring Mountfield into an exchange, hoping he would make a mistake and trip himself up. She had almost done it, too, when she caught him in a lie, but Thiel had spotted it and closed down that line of questioning. They had played their hand and failed. The opportunity had been missed.

Phillips did her best to appear confident and in control, when inside she was reeling. Mountfield and Thiel had beaten them. Unless something miraculous happened before 7 a.m. tomorrow, Mountfield would not only be a free man – unless Fox was willing to sanction action on the sex-abuse claims – he'd be back on the force as if nothing had happened. Sure, he would likely be transferred out of Sex Crimes, but he would still be a copper, and that killed Phillips.

It was time to take a break and regroup. Maybe one of the watching team had spotted something she and Gibson had missed. Something; *anything* that would prove Mountfield was the killer.

After closing the interview and making their excuses, Phillips and Gibson joined Entwistle, Jones and Bovalino back in the observation suite.

'You almost had him there, Gibbo,' said Jones.

'I know. I could feel him losing track of his story, but Thiel was too bloody quick.'

Phillips dropped the case file on the desk next to the wall and took a seat. 'Mountfield has an answer for everything.'

'And Thiel has enough for both of them,' Jones agreed.

Phillips let out a frustrated sigh. 'I told you we'd have to box clever with him. The reality is, we've got tons of evidence to implicate Mountfield in these murders, but nothing whatsoever that can *prove* he was actually involved in anything.'

'I'm sorry, Guv. I wasn't much use to you in the end,' said Gibson.

Phillips waved her off. 'Don't be daft, Gibbo. It was always going to be a long shot. Any police rep with Thiel's experience could have seen what we were trying to do.'

Gibson dropped into a chair and spun round to look at the

big screen, on which they could see Mountfield standing next to the custody sergeant, ready for the short walk back to his cell. 'I'm not sure what's worse; knowing that I've been working with a sex predator all this time, or the fact I didn't see it.'

'They're predators for a reason, Gibbo: they know how to hide,' Bovalino observed.

'Thanks, Bov, but it doesn't make me feel any better. It's like I said to the Guv before, I knew he liked the girls and was a bit of a misogynist, but I never thought he was dangerous. I mean, he used to grow his own tomatoes, for God's sake, just like my grandad. He'd bring them in by the bucket-load for the team to take home.'

'First rule of being a murder detective, Gibbo,' Jones joked, pretending to dig a hole, 'Always look for the guy with the shovel.'

The team laughed loudly. At times like this, when the pressure was almost crippling and results weren't going your way, black humour was the only antidote.

Gibson watched the monitor as Mountfield left Interview Room Three under escort, before standing. 'I could do with stretching my legs. Anyone want a coffee?'

A chorus of 'yes's filled the small room, but Phillips remained silent, her gaze fixed in front of her.

'Guv, do you want a coffee?' asked Gibson again.

'What?'

'I'm gonna sort some coffees. Do you want one?'

Phillips shook her head. 'Where did he grow the tomatoes?'

A wall of confused faces stared back at her. 'You feeling all right, Guv?' asked Jones.

Phillips stood now. 'Never mind how I feel, *where did he grow the tomatoes?*'

'In his garden, I'd guess,' said Bovalino.

'That's just it. He lives in a flat. He doesn't have a garden, or a yard, or a balcony.'

Gibson's face seemed to light up. 'Jesus, Guv. He's got an allotment.'

'Where?'

'I don't know. He told me once but I can't remember. Maybe somewhere in Sale?'

'That's where he's been going at night. And that's where we'll find our evidence.'

42

W ith limited time before Mountfield was due to be released, Phillips decided to split up the team. It made sense for Entwistle, Jones and Bovalino to remain at Ashton House to take a second look at the digital forensic data for anything that would link Mountfield to the murders. Jones and Bovalino concentrated on ANPR and CCTV footage whilst Entwistle once again reviewed all the evidence collected from the laptop and mobile phone.

Whilst they were doing that, Phillips and Gibson had made the thirty-minute journey to Sale, where they woke Mrs Mountfield for the second night in a row. This time it was to secure the location of her husband's allotment. As expected, she wasn't happy about the intrusion, and at first had refused to help, but thanks to their shared history, Gibson managed to convince Mrs Mountfield it was in her husband's interests to help. Still reluctant, she had eventually given up his plot number and its location. During the conversation, she let it slip that Mountfield had a shed up there too.

Back in the car, with Phillips driving to the Riddings Hall Allotments in Timperley, they discussed the evidence so far.

'In the interview, Guv, you mentioned the fact he could have killed the girls when he was allegedly walking the dog. Do you believe that?'

'When I was presenting it to him, I really thought so. But as time has gone on, I hate to say it, I'm starting to think Thiel might have a point. It does feel like a stretch for him to drive thirty minutes into town, find a girl, drive her to the canal, kill her, then drive home.'

'So if everything else we have is circumstantial, do the timings then rule him out as a viable suspect then?'

Phillips was reluctant to consider that an option. It had to be Mountfield. All the evidence suggested he was the killer, even if they couldn't prove it. 'Let's see what the allotment has to offer. Hopefully we'll find some answers there.'

They drove in silence for a long moment, passing house after house covered in the neon glow of Christmas lights left on overnight by their proud owners. Phillips imagined the families tucked up in bed inside, the children dreaming of Santa's arrival in just over a week's time. It was an image of Christmas she had never really experienced, growing up in Hong Kong, especially as her mother and father had seemed to view the whole festive period as a massive inconvenience.

As the car slowed and she pulled left off Washway Road onto Eastway, they discovered an incredible front garden display of lights depicting a life-size laughing Santa driving his sleigh with a full complement of reindeers up front. A neon sign flashed the words, 'Santa's little helpers.' Gibson had noticed it too, and repeated the words out loud with a half chuckle. 'Santa's little helpers. Some people just love Christmas, don't they?'

Phillips didn't answer, her mind suddenly awash with a new possibility. She came to a sudden stop and turned to Gibson. 'That's it. That's how he did it.'

Gibson appeared confused. 'What is?'

'What if Mountfield wasn't working alone? What if he had someone *helping* him?'

'Do you think that's possible, Guv?'

'It would certainly explain how he managed to keep them in the water, wouldn't it? I've always wondered why the girls didn't just swim to the other side. Well, if he had an accomplice stood on the opposite bank blocking their escape, there's no way the girls would be able to climb out. They'd be forced to stay in the ice-cold water until the shock took hold and they drowned.'

Gibson nodded. 'But what about the dog, Guv? What did he do with the dog during that time?'

'He locks it up somewhere out of the way with no lights, passers-by or surrounding homes. Sound familiar?'

Gibson's eyes widened. 'His allotment.'

'Exactly.' Phillips searched for Entwistle's number on the in-car display and hit dial.

'*Guv. Is everything ok?*'

'All good. The Sat Nav says we're a couple of minutes away from Mountfield's allotment.'

'*Shall we head over and help you with the search?*'

'No, I think we've got this one covered. It's a pretty small space. But I *do* need you to do something else for me, urgently.'

'*How can I help, Guv?*'

'I want you to check the ANPR cameras again on the night of each murder. Specifically, around the streets where the girls' bodies were found in Ancoats and Miles Platting.'

'*What am I looking for?*'

'Any vehicles that were seen driving to the locations of the bodies before and after the time of death.'

'*But didn't we already do that, Guv?*'

'Yes, but we were looking for vehicles driving from Cheetham Hill to Ancoats and Miles Platting. I want you to look specifically for any car or van that drove *directly* to and from the locations only.'

'*Ok, Guv. What you thinking with this?*'

'That Mountfield might have had an accomplice. Someone who helped him drown the girls in the canal.'

'*God. I never thought of that.*'

'None of us did. Serial killers generally work alone, and with so much evidence pointing to Mountfield, why would we think he had a partner?'

'*So what made you think of it now?*'

'Santa.'

'*Hey?*'

'I'll explain when we have more time. Let me know as soon as you have anything, ok?'

'*Sure thing.*'

Phillips ended the call. She then checked Google Maps on her phone to get an aerial view of the terrain. 'It says the allotments should be just down here. This road only goes so far, then it's a dirt track through to the plots.'

Slipping the car in gear, she moved the car forwards, filled with a mixture of adrenaline and anticipation at what they would find in Mountfield's shed, just moments away.

43

Driving under full-beam headlights, the squad car pitched and rolled along the dirt track as Phillips navigated her way through a maze of large ice-covered potholes. As they moved closer to the allotment entrance, the car hit a big patch of ice. Instinctively Phillips applied the brakes. It was the wrong thing to do, and they skidded towards the heavy wooden fence running around the perimeter of the allotments. By yanking on the handbrake and pulling the steering wheel into the skid, Phillips was able to regain control, bringing the car to a stop a split second before it crunched into the fence. 'Jesus. That was close,' she said.

Gibson pulled up the collar of her coat. 'Probably best to walk from here, Guv.'

Phillips agreed, and killed the engine before opening the driver's door. She swung her legs out and took care placing her feet on the icy ground, holding on to the frame of the door as she lifted herself up. To her left, Gibson mirrored her movements, and a moment later they regrouped at the rear of the car, where they opened the boot. Phillips reached inside and pulled out two flashlights, handing one to Gibson. Then, pulling up the panel that covered the spare wheel, she removed a large plastic pouch. Opening it at one end, she pulled out a crowbar. 'We're probably gonna need this.'

'Good idea.'

Closing the boot, they switched on their flashlights and moved slowly across the iced dirt track towards the allotment entrance.

Once they were through the rickety old gate, Gibson swept her heavy torch beam across the ground in front of her. 'Trisha said it was in the far right-hand corner, next to the fence that runs parallel with the canal.'

Gibson nodded, and both women took a moment to orientate themselves before the beam of Phillips's flashlight landed on a large shed in the general location of where Mountfield's plot should be. 'Over there. Let's check it out.'

Phillips took the lead, taking careful steps over the slippery ground. 'I wish I'd thought to put my walking boots on,' she shouted back towards Gibson, who was tucked in behind her.

It took a couple of minutes to reach the shed. Inspecting it under the glare of their flashlights, it appeared much larger than its closest neighbours. As they circled its perimeter, they noted there were no windows to speak of, and it appeared that a wide, padlocked door was the only way in or out.

Gibson trained her flashlight on the heavy-duty padlock. 'It's a good job you brought that crowbar, Guv.'

Phillips slid the metal between the wooden panel and the lock. Using all her strength to pull the bar towards her, it began to yield. After repeating the process a number of times, the screws that held the lock in place were soon exposed. Sweating and breathing heavily from the exertion, Phillips wiped her brow and took a moment to catch her breath.

'Shall I have a go, Guv?' Gibson asked.

Phillips nodded, and swapped the crowbar for her own

flashlight. A moment later, Gibson used all her weight to finally release the lock.

'Gotcha!' cried Phillips as the door flung open.

As she moved forwards and stepped inside, the stench of stale blood was instant and overwhelming, causing her to cover her mouth and nose with her hand.

Gibson followed her in, with much the same reaction. 'Jesus, it smells like death. What the hell's he got in here?'

Phillips pulled on her latex gloves and handed a pair to her partner. 'Let's find out, Gibbo. You take that side, I'll take this.'

Examining the walls, Phillips found an array of gardening tools hanging from long nails sticking out from the wooden panels. She began checking for any isolated nails or gaps on the wall that might indicate a missing tool – maybe the murder weapon used on Chloe Barnes. However, on first inspection everything seemed to be in order.

In the corner in front of her, a heavy-duty plastic bag had been covered by an unopened sack of fertiliser. She moved the fertiliser to one side just enough to allow her to look inside. Holding the flashlight in her right hand, she leaned forwards and pulled the bag apart with her left hand, her heart racing as she expected the worst. Peering inside, though, she found it was filled with nothing more sinister than loose fertiliser. *Shit.*

She continued her search. Scanning the floor around her feet, she noted a large metal trunk fitted with another heavy-duty padlock. 'Pass me the crowbar will you, Gibbo?'

Gibson handed it over and Phillips made light work of the lock, ripping it off with one pull before dropping the crowbar, which clattered on the floor. Kneeling, she reached inside and pulled out what looked like a woman's bomber jacket. Inspecting it under the flashlight for a moment, she then handed it Gibson. 'All of the victims were found without coats or jackets. Do you know if this belonged to any of the girls?'

Gibson examined it at close quarters, noting the label. 'I

don't recognise the label, but it seems pretty cheap. I couldn't say for sure, but it certainly looks like something the girls would wear.'

'Shine your light over here, will you?' said Phillips, as she lay her own flashlight on the floor. Rummaging in the box with both hands now, she removed four more jackets, similar in style and size. 'One for each of the girls.'

'Jesus,' whispered Gibson.

'Do you have an evidence bag handy?'

Gibson thrust her left hand deep into her coat pocket, pulled one out and handed it over.

'If we find the girls' DNA on these, we've got him.'

'Fuck. He really did kill them didn't he, Guv?'

'Let's not get ahead of ourselves, but it's looking promising.' Phillips picked up her flashlight once more and stood up. 'Right, let's see what else is in here, shall we?'

Gibson turned and lifted a blanket behind her. She pulled out a large pole.

'What's that?' asked Phillips.

'Looks like a fishing rod, but without the net.'

'Let me have a look.'

Gibson passed it over and Phillips held it under the light. She found herself holding a long metal pole, around two metres in length, with a rubber loop on the end. There were two buttons on the handle; one appeared to release more of the rubber loop, while the other contracted it.

'I'm sure I've seen one of those before, Guv, but I can't recall where,' said Gibson.

'I recognise it now. It's an animal control pole. The dog units use them to subdue a suspect's dog and keep them at a safe distance. Ironically, we used one the other night on Mount-field's own Husky.' Phillips moved the end of the pole just inches from Gibson's face. 'Take a closer look at that. Does it remind you of anything?'

Gibson appeared confused. 'Should it?'

'Look closely.'

'I'm still not seeing anything, Guv.'

Phillips tapped her finger on the end of the pole, where the rubber loop connected. 'The end of that pole is the *exact* shape and size of the bruises we found on backs of the girls' necks.'

A look of realisation spread across Gibson's face. 'Bloody hell. So that's how he held them in the water.'

Phillips nodded. 'Clever bugger.'

Gibson let out a heavy breath. 'All this time, how could I not see what he was up to?'

Phillips placed a reassuring hand on Gibson's arm. 'Killers hiding in plain sight are the hardest catch. He's fooled everyone, not just you.'

Gibson nodded sagely, and they both stood in silence for a moment. 'Do you mind if I step outside, Guv? I could so with some air.'

'Of course. I'll carry on and see if we can find whatever he used to kill Chloe.'

With Gibson outside, Phillips scanned the space with her flashlight, looking for anything else unusual, but found nothing. Her frustration building, she began muttering to herself. 'What are you not seeing, Jane? What are you not seeing?' Her own words brought to mind her old mentor when she was a young detective, DCI Campbell. At times like this, he would repeat the same words, followed by the mantra: 'Often, when we're stuck, it's because the eyes and ears will only see and hear what we want them to, whereas the nose – the nose can never hide what it smells.'

Standing in the same position, she closed her eyes and took a deep breath in through her nose before exhaling loudly, allowing her senses to focus on the foul smell itself. Struggling against nausea, she continued taking deep breaths, trying to locate the source. It was strongest in the centre of the space, but there was nothing near her feet on the concrete floor. Then it dawned on her. Opening her eyes, she arched her head back and scanned the ceiling above. Something resembled a rolled-up towel. It looked like it had been lodged in the apex of the A-frame rafter running across the middle of the shed. Reaching up, she dislodged it and lifted it down. It felt heavy in her hands. Unwrapping the fabric, she revealed a large metal base-ball bat caked in dried blood and small lumps that looked like congealed cottage cheese, but which she suspected were bits of Chloe Barnes's brain. Her pulse quickened as she carefully placed the blanket on the side and carried the bat out to where Gibson stood staring back towards the car, her breath visible in the cold air.

'Gibbo, check this out.'

Gibson turned. 'What it is, Guv?'

'A baseball bat. Looks like the weapon that was used to kill Barnes,' said Phillips.

Gibson stared at it. 'Jesus. Poor Chloe.'

Phillips cradled the bat in her gloved hands. 'This could be the final nail in Mountfield's coffin.'

Gibson nodded before turning away.

'You ok, Gibbo?'

'Sorry, Guv, I'm just feeling a bit overwhelmed.'

Phillips placed a reassuring hand on her shoulder. 'It's understandable. It's a lot to take in.'

'Mountfield is a stone-cold-murderer. Seriously, what kind of a detective am I? How could I not see it?'

'He's very clever. He fooled everyone in the team, including DCI Atkins.'

Gibson scoffed. 'Well he can't be that clever, can he? I mean, what kind of an idiot wraps the murder weapon in a blanket and sticks it in the roof of his allotment shed?'

Phillips took a moment to process what she'd just heard. 'How did you know it was hidden in a blanket in the roof?

Gibson looked taken aback. 'Er, that's where you said you found it.'

'No, I didn't. I didn't tell you any of that. I just showed you the bat.'

Gibson let out an awkward laugh, but said nothing.

'How did you know it was hidden in a blanket in the roof, Gibbo?'

Gibson's whole demeanour seemed to change in an instant. She hunched her body and scanned her surroundings. Holding the heavy flashlight by her side, she took a step closer to Phillips. 'A lucky guess, I suppose,' she said, her voice cold and measured, menacing.

In that moment, an icy chill ran down Phillips's spine and she stepped backwards. 'I think I'd better call this lot in.'

Gibson thrust the flashlight upwards and pointed it directly at Phillips's face, blinding her for a moment. Acting on instinct, Phillips raised her hands to protect herself. Then she heard the unmistakable sound of a gun being cocked at close quarters.

'I wouldn't do that if I were you, DCI Phillips,' Gibson said, lowering the light so Phillips could see her again. Standing just a few feet away, Gibson held what appeared to be a Glock automatic pistol in her extended right hand. 'Now, give me your phone and turn around.'

'Jesus Christ. *You're* Mountfield's accomplice.'

'Give me your phone. Now!'

Phillips did as she was instructed.

'Turn around.'

'You can't possibly think you'll get away with this.'

Gibson laughed as Phillips turned her back. 'That's where you're wrong. Thanks to you, DCI Phillips, *I can*.'

A split second later, a heavy thud turned Phillips's world black.

44

The overwhelming pain at the base of Phillips's skull was the first thing she noticed as she regained consciousness. Opening her eyes to blackness, she became aware that she was moving and could hear the rumble of tyres on asphalt. She sensed she was in the boot of a car, with her back to the driver. The small space smelt stale and metallic, and as she reached upwards to touch the smooth plastic lining of the boot's interior, she realised her hands were locked together in handcuffs. Her legs were bent almost double in front of her and there was little room to move. Something rigid and hard stuck in her back. Fumbling around in the darkness, she located the spot in front of her where the boot locked shut, and began to pull and prod at it in the vain hope she could somehow find a way to leverage it open. But it remained shut.

Fighting her mounting claustrophobia, she lay still for a moment and closed her eyes as she attempted to calm her rapid pulse and consider her next move. With the car swaying around her, she refused to panic. She knew her best chance of survival relied on her maintaining a clear head and thinking smart. Easier said than done.

The car turned a corner and picked up speed, the accelera-
tion forcing her forwards as the volume of noise from the tyres
increased around her. The road surface was mercifully smooth
now, limiting the pain she felt with each bump and dip. She
assumed they must be travelling on a motorway or dual
carriageway. In her head, she began to pull together the potential escape routes Gibson could have taken from the allotment
in Timperley, but without knowing which direction she had
taken in the first place, *and* how long she had been unconscious, she really had no idea where they were.

Gibson had also removed Phillip's Apple watch, so she had
no idea what time it was, adding to her sense of disorientation.
As the car rolled on, she couldn't be sure how far they had
travelled.

After what felt like an hour, but was likely less, the car
slowed and took a series of left and right turns in close succession before once again maintaining a steady course, but at a
much slower speed.

The cabin of the car behind her was suddenly filled with
the sound of loud music booming through the built-in
surround-sound speakers. The car came to a stop, but the
engine continued to idle. Phillips guessed they may have
reached a set of traffic lights or a pedestrian crossing, and
began banging as loud as she could muster. It was no use,
though. No-one came to her rescue, and as soon as the car
began to move again, the noise of the stereo vanished too. The
same process happened a number of times in close succession,
and Phillips soon came to realise that the onset of loud music
meant the car was coming to a stop; Gibson was using it to
drown out her cries for help. *Jesus, that's smart.*

Eventually the terrain changed to what Phillips suspected
was either gravel or a dirt track, and they continued at a slow
pace for a few minutes before coming to a complete stop. This
time, though, there was no music, and the engine was soon

switched off. A moment later, Phillips heard the driver's door open and then close with a loud thud. Waiting in the silent darkness, she readied herself for whatever lay ahead, attempting to stave off the overwhelming panic that began to creep through her body.

As the boot released upwards in front of her, she prepared to fight, but to her surprise she found herself staring up at the clear night sky, the world around her deadly silent. Cautious, she lifted herself up on her aching limbs and peered out of the boot. The glare of Gibson's powerful flashlight blinded her.

'Climb out of the car slowly and keep your hands where I can see them.' Gibson's voice was measured.

Phillips did as ordered and lifted herself up and over the rim of the boot, throwing her stiff legs out and placing her feet onto the rough ground below.

'Stand up,' shouted Gibson, and Phillips obeyed. The flashlight still blinded her. 'Now step forwards and get on your knees.'

Phillips hesitated.

'On your knees, now,' growled Gibson.

The car was parked on a dirt track near to some trees. As Phillips knelt, the sharp edges of the frozen ground dug painfully into her kneecaps.

Gibson stepped carefully past Phillips and pulled the now-retracted animal control pole from the boot – that must be what had stuck in her back. Slinging the carrying strap over her shoulder, she moved back in front of Phillips.

Up close now, without the flashlight blinding her vision, Phillips could see Gibson's face. She appeared possessed by rage and hatred, and Phillips was shocked; her features were hard and sharp, her eyes as black as the night.

'Stand up,' said Gibson, waving the gun upwards.

Phillips did as directed. She knew that to have any chance

of survival, she had to try and humanise herself and get inside Gibson's head. 'Where are we Gibbo?'

'Not far from Lymm Golf Club.'

'*Lymm*? Why did you bring me all the way out here?'

Gibson laughed. 'Because it's quiet. There's isn't another human being for miles.' The flashlight returned to Phillips's face. 'Now, turn around and follow the track towards the water. My torch will guide you. And don't try anything funny or I *will* shoot you. Unlike Frank Fairchild, *I* won't miss.'

45

Phillips's mind raced as she walked with some difficulty across the rough terrain, down the dark track towards the Manchester Ship Canal running parallel to the perimeter of Lymm Golf Club. Unlike the city-centre canals, this stretch of water was wide and deep enough to carry frigates. Opened in 1894, its primary purpose had been to carry cargo from Eastham in Merseyside, all the way into Salford Quays in Manchester. If Gibson forced her into the water here, the strong currents would make her chances of survival almost zero. She had to try and stop that happening.

As they approached the water, Phillips could hear the waves, kicked up by the winter wind, lapping against the bank. A moment later, she caught a glimpse of the moonlight dancing across the surface of the canal through the trees, and as they stepped out of the thick line of trees, she came face to face with the vast expanse of water.

Gibson jabbed Phillips in the back with the gun. 'That way.' She nudged the gun towards a patch of ground at least four feet up from the water's edge.

Phillips reluctantly moved over to it as Gibson dropped something to the ground nearby.

'Turn around.'

As she followed the instructions, she was again blinded by the flashlight.

Gibson lowered the torch, but the afterglow clouded Phillips's vision. A moment later, she felt her handcuffs being unlocked. Then Gibson moved to a safe distance before Phillips could react, flashlight in hand.

Phillips raised her hands in surrender. 'Please, Gibbo, drop the flashlight, will you? I can't see a thing. I promise I won't try anything stupid.'

Gibson agreed and released Phillips from the grip of the light.

'Thank you.' She waited for her eyes to adjust. 'So I'm guessing you've brought me here for a reason, Gibbo.'

'I'm afraid so. But I mean it when I say, this was never part of my plan.'

'So why are you doing this to me?'

'Because I fucked up, that's why; back at the shed, I got ahead of myself and made a school-boy error with the bat and blanket. I knew you'd rumbled me as soon as the words left my mouth.'

'But this is madness. You know as well as I do that you can't get away with it. I've already sent Entwistle off looking for Mountfield's accomplice. It's only a matter of time before the team pressure him into giving you up. And he *will* cave.'

Gibson let out an ironic cackle. 'He won't cave. He has *no idea* what's going on.'

'What are you talking about?'

'Jesus, Phillips. I thought you were smart, but you really don't get it, do you?'

'Get what?'

'Mountfield is a prehistoric, old-school copper with all the sophistication of a house-brick. He couldn't be trusted with something as important as this.'

Phillips frowned. 'Are you saying he's *not* involved in all this?'

A broad grin spread across Gibson's face. 'Bingo.'

'So then *who* are you working with?'

Gibson raised her eyes to the sky for a moment before dropping her gaze back to Phillips. 'God, Phillips. I'm working with God.'

Phillips couldn't hide her contempt. 'God? How the hell does God come into this? Have you gone fucking mad?'

Gibson didn't appreciate Phillips's reaction. Her eyes narrowed as she began maniacally gripping and un-gripping the handle of the gun in her right hand. 'How dare you. I'm doing *His* work, you contemptuous bitch!'

Phillips's plan to humanise herself with Gibson had veered badly off-point and she knew she had to change tack. If not, she was going to die. She immediately softened her tone and attempted to get her back on-side. 'Hey, look, I'm sorry, Gibbo. I didn't mean to upset you. It just wasn't what I was expecting to hear. I wouldn't have put God in the middle of a case like this, that's all.'

Gibson remained silent.

Phillips figured playing to Gibson's ego might also help her stay alive. 'I'm intrigued Gibbo, and it's obviously your doing. How *is* Mountfield involved in all this?'

Gibson's chest appeared to puff with pride. 'Doing this work, I knew at some point I'd need a fall-guy. And if anyone deserves to rot in Hawk Green, it's Detective Constable Don Mountfield.'

'Because of what he was doing to the girls, you mean?'

'Exactly! I've known all along that that creep has been abusing his position and power to rape and brutalise women on the street.

He's been at it for years. I've worked with him for five of them, and he was doing it long before I joined the team. Once I figured out what he was up to, I tried to talk to Atkins about him, but they're both part of the old-boys network; they trained together. So I was fobbed off and told to leave it alone. But why should he get away with forcing girls to have sex with him just because he's a copper?'

'So you set him up for *murder*?'

'Call it what you like and judge me how you will, but I've made sure he'll spend the rest of his life in prison.'

To buy herself precious time, Phillips continued to massage Gibson's ego to keep the conversation going. 'That was really clever, you know. Killing the girls on Mountfield's days off, or when he was sick. You made sure he was squarely in the frame for their murders.'

'He's a creature of habit, so it wasn't difficult.'

'And I bet you're the reason he vomited on the Armitage surveillance op too, aren't you?'

Gibson flashed a wicked grin. 'Guilty as charged. I have to admit, I enjoyed that bit.'

'Wow. You screwed him good and proper.'

'I did more than that. I got *justice*.'

Phillips was confused and couldn't hide her feelings. 'But how can you say *you* want justice when *you've* been killing innocent women?'

'Because he's nothing but a predator, whereas *I've* been doing God's work,' Gibson said, proud of herself.

'You've been drowning women in the name of God?'

'No, Phillips. I've been *baptising* them.'

Phillips bit her tongue in an attempt to stifle her incredulity. 'I don't understand. What do you mean, you've been "baptising" them?'

'Exactly what it sounds like, Phillips. I put each of those women into the water in order to baptise them. To ensure they were ready to face God. It was my job to send them to be judged in the next life.'

'But why?'

'Because they were junkie whores who had neglected their God-given duty to protect their children. It couldn't be allowed to carry on. Those children had to be saved, whatever the cost.'

Phillips struggled to understand the logic in Gibson's words. 'But how does killing their parents protect the kids?'

Gibson said nothing for a moment. Her grip tightened on the handle of the gun, which seemed to quiver in her hand, increasing Phillips's anxiety as she flashed back to the last time she was on the business end of a gun.

Gibson steadied herself and swallowed hard before answering, 'Killing those whores was the only way to ensure their innocent children were taken away from them *for good*. I mean, look at Estelle Henderson. Her daughter has been in and out of care for years, and Social Services keep giving Henderson chances. That poor kid could never know security and stability, living like that. But with Henderson dead, and no grandparents to look after her, she can finally find a foster family to give her the life she deserves.'

'But what about Chantelle's little boy, Ajay? He *has* grand-parents. Why did she have to die?'

Gibson's voice trembled now, brimming with raw emotion. 'Precisely because he has grandparents. With Chantelle gone, they'll be able to give him a stable home. And he won't have to watch his mother slowly kill herself on that junk. Day after day, turning into a zombie. Showing no love, no attention, no kind of care at all. It's no way for any child to have to grow up. It would destroy Ajay.'

Phillips had seen enough historical victims of abuse in her time to recognise that Gibson could well be describing her own childhood, or that of someone very close to her.

'Is that what happened to you, Gibbo?' Her voice was soft and gentle.

Tears began streaking down Gibson's face, glistening in the moonlight. Her words appeared caught in her throat. 'Enough talking,' she said coldly as she wiped her cheeks. 'Turn around and face the water.' Gibson moved the gun closer to Phillips, which caused her heart to quicken and her breath to shorten.

'Please, Gibbo, don't do this. I'm not your enemy.'

Gibson remained unmoving. 'Turn around and link your hands together over the back of your head.'

Phillips reluctantly obeyed as Gibson prodded her in the back with the barrel of the gun, 'Move!'

As they edged towards the water, Phillips continued her attempts to connect with Gibson, talking over her shoulder. 'Who hurt you, Gibbo?'

'Shut it. I don't want to talk about it.'

'Please, Gibbo, tell me what happened. If I'm going to die, I at least deserve to know what drove my killer to do it?'

'I said I don't want to talk about it.'

Phillips had reached the water's edge now, and time was running out. She had to keep pushing. It was the only way to stay alive. 'Was it your mother, Gibbo? Was she the one who caused you so much pain?'

Gibson remained silent for a long moment, but Phillips could hear her breathing heavily. Desperate to keep her talking, she tried another avenue.

'So how are you planning to get away with murdering a copper, Gibbo? You know the guys won't rest until they find my killer.'

Gibson chuckled now. 'I'm sure they won't, but thanks to you, they'll be looking in all the wrong places. Your call to Entwistle ensured they'll be looking for Mountfield's accomplice.'

'Which helps *you* how?'

'Because it gives me an oh-so-easy way out. All I have to do is drive back to the allotment and make it look like you and I were attacked whilst searching the shed for evidence. The scene and my physical injuries – which will be self-inflicted, of course – will point to the fact we disturbed our attacker, who then left me for dead. I'll sound panicked and confused when I call it in. Naturally, all hell will break loose as the hunt for DCI Phillips ensues. A hunt I'll insist on being at the centre of, and ensure leads as far away from me as possible. The current in this stretch of water will send your body towards Liverpool. It could be weeks before they find out you drowned. And all the time, hidden in the shadows, I'll continue doing God's work, baptising more and more of those wretched mothers, giving their kids a chance at life. Their deaths will only add fuel to the fire that Mountfield had an accomplice; someone still at large. And as Mountfield continues to protest his innocence, the identity of his accomplice will remain a mystery. It's perfect.'

'And what about when they start looking into Mountfield's former colleagues, which they will. What then? If they figure out what happened to you as a child, they'll make the link.'

'There's no way that can happen. I made sure of that a long time ago. And besides, you know what male coppers are like. They always look for men when it comes to dead prostitutes. They seem blind to the fact a woman might be the killer.'

'Got it all figured out, haven't you?'

'More good luck than planning, to be honest. Your call to Entwistle was a real stroke of genius, and I thank God for giving me the chance to continue His good work.'

Phillips finally lost control. 'It's not good work, or God's work. It's murder!'

Gibson pressed the gun hard against Phillips's spine. 'I don't expect you to understand. Now, shut up and get in the water!'

Before Phillips could respond, Gibson shoved her hard in the back, causing her to tumble forwards, headfirst, into the icy ship canal. The shock was instantaneous as crippling pain consumed her entire body. It felt like she was being jabbed by a million ice-cold needles.

Instinctively, she kicked her legs, and a second later she surfaced, gasping for air. Her arms flailed wildly as her water-filled boots began dragging her back under. Her lungs were working overtime now, contracting and expanding at a rapid rate in their desperate pursuit of oxygen, and her heart felt like it would explode.

Struggling to stay above the surface of the choppy water, she felt something loop around her neck. Initially it felt loose, but a second later it was pulled so tightly around her throat, she was lifted upwards. Overwhelmed by the cold and disorientated by the lack of oxygen in her lungs, Phillips began to hyperventilate. She attempted to cry for help, but no words would come out.

In the melee, she could just make out the fact Gibson was talking to her from the bank now. 'What you're experiencing, Jane, is cold water shock. I'm sure you're familiar with the concept by now.'

Phillips could feel her limbs growing heavier as her body began diverting blood to her vital organs in an attempt to keep her alive. Grabbing at the rubber around her neck, she tried in vain to release herself from its grip.

'It's no use, Phillips. It won't come off unless I release it at this end,' said Gibson as she pushed the pole down under water, forcing Phillips's head beneath the surface. She held her down for a long moment before allowing her to resurface. Instinctively, Phillips continued grabbing at the rubber loop around her throat, desperate.

'Don't worry. It won't take long for your body to completely shut down.' Gibson forced her under again. Longer this time.

Panic now took hold of Phillips.

Acting on pure instinct, when Gibson finally allowed her to

resurface, Phillips reached out and grabbed at the handle of the pole behind her head, but Gibson coolly yanked it from her grip and pushed her under again, forcing Phillips deeper into the water. As her arms flailed in the freezing darkness, her hand struck something solid sticking out of the mud; a metal tube of some kind. Pulling at it, she managed to dislodge it a split-second before she was pulled back up to the surface.

Gasping for air and kicking her heavy legs, she raised the metal tube above her head and swung it as best she could against the pole behind her. Despite being unable to see Gibson, she smashed the tube into the pole over and over. Then she felt it jerk against her neck as though pushing her forwards.

She dropped the tube and grabbed the pole. There was more give, so she yanked down hard again. A split-second later, there came a splash and Phillips realised Gibson no longer held the pole.

For a long moment there was no sign of her, until eventually she broke the surface of the water, gasping for air. Gibson's mouth was opening and closing but as the cold water shock set in, no words would come out. She struggled to keep her head above the choppy waters, and it was clear to Phillips something was wrong. Gibson appeared to be sinking rapidly as she splashed and flailed in the water like a terrified child. Grabbing one of her arms, Phillips attempted to pull her towards her, but she was like a dead weight.

'I can't...s-s-swim...' Gibson managed to say before going under again.

Phillips was struggling to stay afloat herself, and could feel her body shutting down. Despite everything that had happened, though, she couldn't stand by and let someone drown.

Reaching around in the water, she found Gibson's arm and tried to pull her back to the surface, but with her own weakening body, it was no use. She tried again, but Gibson was getting heavier and heavier with every passing second. With one last-ditch effort, she wrapped her fingers around Gibson's thick hair and tried to pull her upwards. Her fingers could not maintain their grip, however, and simply slipped through it. In that moment, Phillips realised she herself was sinking. Her only chance of survival was to get out whilst she still could.

With the pole still wrapped around her neck, Phillips kicked and lurched her way through the water, inch by inch, hoping and praying for land beneath her feet. To her dismay, the water remained impossibly deep, and her limbs grew ever heavier. Feeling her body shutting down, she reached hopelessly for the shore, which seemed a mile away.

To her surprise, her hand slapped down onto something hard. Lifting her head as much as she could muster, she realised she had swum to a fallen tree lodged in the thick ice at the edge of the canal. Frantic, she grabbed at it with her right hand before pulling her left hand round and onto a branch sticking out of the ice.

Using every ounce of strength she could muster, she managed to lift her shoulders up and out of the water in one arduous movement. She rested a moment. The frigid wind rushing over her soaking wet body was unbearable. Gripping onto the branches for dear life, she pulled herself out a little farther before being forced to rest again. She repeated the process for the next few minutes, until her shins and ankles were all that remained in the water. In that moment, soaking wet, frozen to the bone and exhausted, all she wanted to do was close her eyes and go to sleep, but she knew hypothermia would kill her if she did.

Gritting her teeth, she somehow lifted her leaden arms, one at a time, up to the next set of branches, and with one last Herculean effort hauled herself free from the water to collapse heavily on the fallen tree.

Resisting the urge to stay where she was and let sleep take

her, Phillips continued to drag herself over the tree and onto the bank, where she dropped to the ground, overwhelmed by exhaustion. Lying on the frozen surface, her body shook violently and she could feel her life ebbing away. She knew she had to stay awake, she had to keep moving. Forcing herself onto her feet, she stumbled forwards into the darkness, hoping and praying she could find the squad car and radio for help.

EPILOGUE

TWO MONTHS LATER.

Manchester Crematorium, Chorlton-cum-Hardy.

Phillips finished her call and wandered back towards Jones.

'How's Don?'

'I think it's fair to say he's not a happy bunny, Jonesy. I promised him an exclusive and I didn't deliver.'

'He'll live, Guv.'

Phillips put her phone in her coat pocket. 'Yeah. More's the pity,' she said as he pulled her collar up against the bitter wind that blew across the crematorium car park.

Jones grinned. 'Shall we go inside?'

Phillips nodded and led the way.

They stood against the back wall as Rachel Gibson's coffin was carried into the Chapel of Rest. The benches in front of them were packed with mourners, many of whom were serving police officers.

Each had come to pay their respects to the fallen Sex

Crimes officer killed accidentally in line of duty. That was the coroner's official verdict, of course, but Phillips and Jones knew different. Thanks to the wonders of the law, whatever crimes Gibson had committed when she was alive had died with her. The case against her had been officially discontinued due to her death. And with that, the deaths of Candice Roberts, Chantelle Webster, Sasha Adams and Estelle Henderson had all been filed under their original classification: accidental drowning. Meaning Richard Webster would never really know what had happened to his daughter Chantelle.

In a way, Phillips was glad about that. Chloe Barnes's murder would also officially remain unsolved, now that Gibson was no longer around to speak in her own defence. Phillips had pushed for a Trial of the Facts, where a court would hear the facts and decide whether there was a case to answer on the available evidence. Her request was denied. Trials of the Facts were rare and very expensive, so not deemed a good use of public money. It was the worst possible outcome for Phillips and her team, but one they had to reluctantly accept.

Ironically, Gibson's prediction of what would happen to a body left in the Manchester Ship Canal had been scarily accurate; she was found almost two weeks later near Liverpool, the exact amount of time it had taken Phillips to recover from hypothermia and exposure.

In the weeks that followed, Phillips had quietly set about finding out the truth of who Rachel Gibson, born Rachel Fletcher, really was. Based on the nature of her crimes and her justification for committing them, it came as no surprise that Rachel's birth mother had been a prostitute and a drug addict.

Like the children she claimed to be saving, the young Rachel had been in and out of care homes for a number of years, many of which were later closed down after investigations found evidence of systemic and wide-scale child abuse. It was only when she was twelve years old, and her mother had drowned in her own bathtub, that Rachel had been fostered, and later adopted, by Frances and Michael Gibson. The Gibsons had given Rachel a stable home for the first time in her life, which had seen her graduate from university and enter the GMP ten years ago.

In nearly twenty years of policing, Phillips had seen first-hand just how deep the wounds of neglect and childhood abuse can run. From their conversation on the banks of the canal in Lymm, Phillips knew Gibson's desire to work in SCT had been driven by hope. Hope that she could somehow get the girls off the street, away from pimps and heroin. The driving factor was her desire to give their kids a normal, stable life – the complete opposite of her own childhood. However, as she had been at pains to explain, the system didn't work and the problem was only getting worse.

Phillips wondered if the brutality she had seen in her job had become too much to bear, and caused her to move outside the law in her efforts to protect the kids. Sadly, she would never know.

As the service came to a close and the thick purple and gold-lined curtain closed, Gibson's favourite song began to seep from the speakers on the wall of the chapel. A moving piece by Eva Cassidy. That was their cue to leave.

Avoiding the line of family members waiting to greet the mourners, Phillips and Jones stepped outside into the winter sun shining down on the crematorium car park. They made a point of taking up a position opposite the main exit, deliberately out of earshot. As the mourners began to file out, Phillips mused over the death of Gibson's birth mother. 'It does make me wonder if the mother was Gibbo's first victim, Jonesy.'

'I was thinking that myself, Guv, but that's a helluva thing for a twelve-year-old to feel compelled to do.'

'Yeah, but it certainly could explain her obsession with drowning, don't you think?'

'Well, if she got away with it once, then she probably thought she could get away with it again.'

Phillips nodded. 'And again, and again, and again.'

At that moment, a mournful-looking DC Mountfield finished shaking hands with Gibson's parents and stepped out into the sunshine. Spotting Phillips and Jones, he smiled and walked towards them.

'Look at that arrogant prick,' mumbled Jones under his breath just before he joined them.

Mountfield had a smug look on his face. 'DCI Phillips and DS Jones, fancy seeing you here. You guys ready to apologise for wrongly accusing me of murder?'

Jones couldn't hide his disdain. 'Piss off, you sanctimonious piece of shit.'

Mountfield feigned feeling hurt. 'Now now, DS Jones. Please remember, I'm a free man and deserve your respect as a fellow officer.'

'You're a fucking predator who got away with raping women in the line of duty,' Jones sneered, doing his best to keep his voice down.

Mountfield scoffed. 'They *weren't* women, Jonesy, no, no, no. They were low-life hookers. There's a difference, and it seems our bosses agree with me.'

Phillips remained silent as she glared at Mountfield. As their eyes met, he suddenly appeared unnerved. 'Cat got your tongue, Phillips?'

'I'm just wondering how cocky you'll be when you start your sentence in Hawk Green.'

'You must have missed the memo, *love*, but I'm getting off scot-free with a full pension. Just for keeping my gob shut. No doubt that will eat you up inside, which makes it all the more satisfying. But rest assured, I'll never see the inside of a prison cell.'

'Really? Is that so? There's something I'd like you to see if you have a minute.' Phillips reached into her coat pocket and retrieved her phone. Opening it, she found what she was looking for, clicked on the photo and turning the screen to face Mountfield. 'Do you recognise this girl, DC Mountfield?'

Mountfield glanced at it casually. 'I've seen her around.'

'Her name's Lucy Green, and you're very well acquainted with her, as well you know. You see, according to Lucy, you repeatedly forced her to have sex with you for most of last year.'

Mountfield shrugged his shoulders. 'So what? Like I said, all historical charges have been dropped against me. Makes no difference now.'

Phillips nodded. 'Yes, that's true, all the *historical* charges listed have been dropped as part of your deal. However, thanks to Lucy Green, I'll be bringing *fresh* charges against you in the coming days.'

Mountfield brushed aside the threat. 'For what exactly?'

Phillips smiled. 'I'm curious, DC Mountfield. Do you know how old Lucy is?'

'Eighteen, nineteen, I dunno.'

'No, I didn't think you did. She's actually just turned sixteen years old *this* month. Which means that when you repeatedly had sex with her last year, she was fifteen, and *underage*.'

Mountfield's face dropped.

'You never were much of a detective, were you, Don? That said, even a dumb shit like you knows that's statutory rape, and carries a mandatory prison term of three to five years. So it looks like you may be spending some time at Her Majesty's Pleasure after all. And you can kiss good-bye to that pension of yours.'

Mountfield opened his mouth to speak, but Phillips had no intention of listening to anything else he had to say. 'Goodbye, DC Mountfield,' she said with a broad smile.

Jones stepped in close to Mountfield, so their noses were almost touching. 'Helluva place for bent coppers, Hawk Green,

Don,' he said in a menacing whisper. 'You're gonna love it,' he added, tapping Mountfield on the cheek.

All the cockiness seemed to drain from Mountfield as Jones held his terrified gaze.

'Come on, Jonesy,' said Phillips, 'let's get back to the station. We need time to prepare cell number eight and Interview Room Three for our distinguished guest.'

'Right you are, Guv,' said Jones, winking at Mountfield, who had turned a funny shade of green. 'We'll be seeing you, Don, we'll be seeing you.'

ACKNOWLEDGEMENTS

This book is dedicated to the memory of Michael Ryan and Les Pickering. Two men who had a profound influence on my life. You are missed every day, but always in my heart.

Deadly Waters would not have been possible without the help and support of my amazing wife Kim, who is my biggest fan, and my rock. Thank you for your patience, trust and faith in me.

My gorgeous boy Vaughan. Every day you inspire me to be the best I can be.

A huge thanks to Mum for all your support, love and prayers.

Doreen, you are the first line of defence against my penchant for missing out words when I'm in full flow.

James Eve and Carole Lawford, ex CPS Prosecutor, who helped me accurately reflect the minefield that is British Law.

My publishers, Brian and Garret, and my editor, Laurel, who continually push me to raise my standards.

And finally, thank you for reading *Deadly Waters*. If you could spend a moment to write an honest review on Amazon, no matter how short, I would be extremely grateful. They really do help readers discover my books.

Best wishes,

Owen

www.omjryan.com

ALSO BY OMJ RYAN

DEADLY SECRETS

(A crime thriller introducing DCI Jane Phillips)

DEADLY SILENCE

(Book 1 in the DCI Jane Phillips series)

DEADLY WATERS

(Book 2 in the DCI Jane Phillips series)

DEADLY VENGEANCE

(Book 3 in the DCI Jane Phillips series)

DEADLY BETRAYAL

(Book 4 in the DCI Jane Phillips series)

DEADLY OBSESSION

(Book 5 in the DCI Jane Phillips series)

DEADLY CALLER

(Book 6 in the DCI Jane Phillips series)

DEADLY NIGHT

(Book 7 in the DCI Jane Phillips series)

DEADLY CRAVING

(Book 8 in the DCI Jane Phillips series)

Published by Inkubator Books
www.inkubatorbooks.com

Printed in Great Britain
by Amazon